spirit of the
NORTH

Pemmican Publications gratefully acknowledges the assistance accorded to its publishing program by the Manitoba Arts Council, the Province of Manitoba – Department of Culture, Heritage and Tourism, Canada Council for the Arts and Canadian Heritage – Book Publishing Industry Development Program.

Map of Manitoba courtesy of Clear-View Maps, Calgary, Alberta

Printed and Bound in Canada.
First printing: 2011

Library and Archives Canada Cataloguing in Publication

Ducharme, Linda, 1946-
    Spirit of the north / Linda Ducharme.

ISBN 978-1-894717-63-2

    I. Title.

PS8607.U233S65 2011   C813'.6   C2011-904838-8

**PEMMICAN
PUBLICATIONS
INC.**
Committed to the promotion of Metis culture and heritage

150 Henry Ave., Winnipeg, Manitoba,
R3B 0J7 Canada
www.pemmican.mb.ca

 Canadian   Patrimoine
Heritage   canadien

 Canada Council   Conseil des Arts
for the Arts   du Canada

spirit of the
NORTH

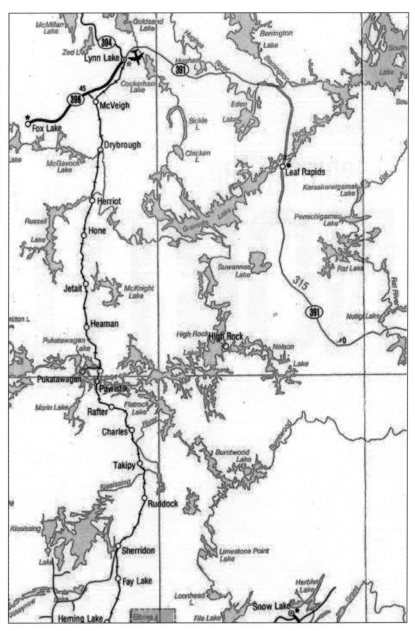

Map of west-central Manitoba – Sherridon is seen in lower left-hand corner

I dedicate this book, *Spirit of the North*,
to the memory of my mother,
Pearl Sklapsky-Holben.

Who trusted God was love indeed
And love Creation's final law
Tho' Nature, red in tooth and claw
With ravine, shriek'd against his creed

—*Alfred, Lord Tennyson, In Memoriam A.H.H., Canto 56*

1
Unsettled Beginnings

May 17, 1946 promised to be a usual morning. There was no indication this day would be any different from the preceding 200 and some that they'd been married. The westerly wind carried the usual biting chill from the Rockies, picking up barnyard odours from the Calgary stockyards, swirling it around outside the small apartment. Early morning sunshine brightened the kitchen where a young couple sat nursing steaming cups of coffee and listening to Clarence Mack, the morning host of *Toast & Marmalade Show* on the radio.

The sun highlighted the red and green apple motif of the white oil-cloth table cover, but cast a shadow across 28-year-old Wilson Daniels's face. The man's usually good-natured expression was strained; frown lines furrowed his broad forehead where a wayward lock of black hair curled.

His wife reached across and covered his calloused hand with her soft manicured one. "You'll find something better soon, Wil. I'll bet many returning servicemen have the same problem. Is there anything I can do to help? Maybe talk to Dad?"

"Working in the stockyards is OK for now, Judith, but there's not much future in it and it doesn't pay well either. I prefer to work at the production end, with cattle on a ranch, rather than near the slaughtering end." Wilson attempted a smile, but it fell flat. "Your father has enough to deal with right now. I appreciated their help paying for the wedding. My serviceman's pay didn't go far, and I hated for you to use so much of your savings. Hopefully some day we'll be able to pay them back."

"We're managing, though, aren't we? We have a roof over our heads and food to eat." A frown flitted across Judith's round face.

"Yes, that we are, darlin', and don't think I'm not thankful. I am. But how long is it going to be until we can get a house of our own and quit throwing away our earnings on rent? I looked into the price of a new vehicle today. We'd need more than $1,000, and that wouldn't be a luxury model. It'll take years to save that kind of money. And a new house is five times that. I want to get a house because, as much as I do appreciate this roof, it's not our own. But even an old one we could fix up would be expensive, and let's face it: there aren't many available anyway. I have to find something that pays better."

"Have you talked to your uncle?" It bothered Judith that Wilson was unsettled and obviously unhappy.

"There's not much use, darlin'. Uncle Mac has five boys of his own to consider, and some of them are going to want to continue ranching in his footsteps." His uncle Mac, born Andrew MacDougal, had welcomed his nephew every summer. Wilson had loved the fresh clean scent of the outdoor air, albeit laced with the pungent odour of manure. His summers at the ranch had been the highlight of his youth – riding the open range on horseback, helping with chores and acting like a real cowboy; that was every young boy's dream. It was during this time Judith had first met the boy her neighbours called Wil. "And don't forget Mickey is not able to do much anymore since he got back from overseas. A man with one leg isn't much good on a horse."

"It certainly is a test of faith, isn't it? The Victory Gardens are helping, but there isn't enough soil here in the space we have to grow much. The children and I have planted one outside of the school, but someone who is needier that us seems to be taking most of the produce." Judith gazed into his worried blue eyes.

"I'm trying to have faith. I'm trying, but I sure wish things would hurry and show some improvement."

"Do you want more coffee? I have to finish marking my students' work." Judith saw him shake his head. "Once I finish, let's get the mail and check out what there is in the want ads." She pressed her cheek to the top of his head and moved into the next room, returning with a load of Grade 5 and 6 papers.

Wilson carried the cups to the sink, and watched his wife for a short time as she worked. Every employment opportunity had far more applicants than positions, he thought as he admired the red highlights in her golden brown hair. Judith wore it in the current style, with a smooth crown and a soft curl circling her plump face. "I think I'll go for the mail, then," he said. He didn't notice her green eyes following his wiry, near six-foot frame as he left.

As Wilson made his way to get the mail, he thought of working in the hospital. He'd been trained in the services as a medic, and his honourable discharge listed him as a qualified nurse. He shuddered to think of becoming involved with patients after what he'd gone through in Europe, and refused to contemplate working with medical equipment surrounded by the scent of disinfectants to echo his wartime experiences. No, even the stockyards were preferable to hospital work.

Just as she was finished marking the last assignment, Wilson returned with the *Calgary Herald*. The front page carried news of the Nuremberg Trials. Wilson also had a letter. He dropped the newspaper on the table and Judith turned it over, not wanting to read about the atrocities of the war. She eyed the sale page. Eggs for 46 cents a dozen, apples 12 cents a pound, tomatoes 29 cents a pound, and doughnuts 15 cents a dozen. She sighed. With groceries costing that much, it was hard to plan nutritious meals for the two of them. Then she noticed Wilson studying the envelope and holding it gingerly.

"What is it, Wilson? Is it from the war department? Is something wrong?" Judith watched his expression.

"It's from the legal offices of Sherman, Ottensky, Sweeney and Rutherford," he replied, turning the letter over again and inspecting it with a frown before he opened it. He scanned it, and his increasing puzzlement spurred Judith to rise and try to look over his arm. She was too short for that.

"It says I'm requested to contact the firm at my earliest convenience to discuss the Last Will and Testament of Joseph Wilson Daniels."

Judith didn't know what to say. She knew that Wilson had heard nothing from his father since he'd been abandoned as a boy. They hadn't even known how to contact the man when they'd gotten married. "I guess you should get in touch with them. There's no use speculating about things until we know more." Neither of them remarked on the fact his father was deceased.

The following week, Wilson and Judith made arrangements to visit his grandfather and mother in Airdale, a small town outside the city, where his grandfather still practised medicine. Wilson was determined to find out more about his father. "Judith, could you keep Mother busy while I talk with Granddad? I'm sure I can find out what I need to know if Mother isn't around."

"I think I can manage that. But what do you hope to find out?"

"I want to know why he vanished. I want to know how he could have left us like that. If I can get my grandfather's take on things, I'll be better prepared to meet with the lawyers and see what they have to say."

Once Judith had her mother-in-law busy with the Eaton's catalogue in the living room, Wilson and his grandfather went into the old man's den to have a discussion.

"Now, son, tell me what's so all-fired important. Something has your kilt all out of kilter. Sit down and let's have it." Doc Angus MacDougal, never a man to avoid an issue, packed his pipe with redolent tobacco as he kept one eye on his grandson.

Wilson took the envelope from his pocket and passed it to his grandfather.

Doc MacDougal clamped his unlit pipe in his teeth, pushed his snow-white hair back off his forehead, placed his round, wire-rimmed glasses on his nose and peered at the missive. His expression was blank.

Once he finished reading it, he handed it back to Wilson. "Have you made the appointment?"

"Not yet. I need to know more about the man my father was. What can you tell me? Mother hasn't told me much of anything."

The older man didn't hesitate. "Well, Grandma and I spoiled Marjorie, and her brother Andrew helped. We had money in those days. Back then, doctors were paid with real money, not the produce and meat we get these days. Marjorie was such a pretty little thing, our only daughter and late to arrive as she was. She flirted with many lads, but when the cowboy Joe Daniels came into the picture, she fell hard. Oh, he was a looker all right – tall, well built and sure of himself. He was a pretty straight lad, and he couldn't help but love Marjorie. Well, they married and she tried to get him to fit her mould as a husband, one that held a steady job in an office or bank or some such, and he tried, I'll grant him that, but he was not a happy man. Joe only seemed happy when he was outside, preferably seated on a horse and doing cowboy work. Once you came on the scene things got real tense around here. Marjorie wanted a home of her own, and a fine home at that. She felt she deserved a better one than she'd been raised in. A better life for her son was how she put it. Now, I don't think she intended to put us down, or anything like that; it was just her way.

"One day Joe never came home. We never heard from him again. Anyway, anger and frustration seemed to keep Marjorie going. She held herself together with stubborn pride. She never looked for him, and told us not to bother. The way she said it led me to believe she knew more than she was letting on, but your mother has always had a mind of her own and she has kept her own counsel all these years."

"Was that before Grandma died?"

"No, son. Your grandmother died a few years after. You don't remember her, as you were just a little lad then."

Wilson looked up at the old man. "I guess I'd better let Mother know he's dead. I wonder how she'll take it. Granddad, thanks. Thanks for telling me all this. I wish I'd asked years ago. Sometimes I actually thought he was dead and that's why I never had a Dad. Other times I used to make up stories in my mind of him being a hero and suddenly coming back to us, with a wonderful tale of how he'd wanted to be with us all that time but someone had taken him to another country or something and he wasn't able to get home, or that he was on some secret assignment for the government or something." Wilson shook his head, bemused by his youthful imagination.

"I suppose most kids in your shoes do much the same, son. Kids that are adopted weave fairytales about their wonderful parents that aren't with them, too. It's one way to survive, I suppose. But you're right, Marjorie needs to be told."

Together the two lanky men, one old and one young, made their way back to where the women were looking through clothing magazines and discussing fashion and hairstyles.

The old doctor moved to the large easy chair and folded his brittle bones into its contours. Wilson chose a seat across the room. "Mother, I got a letter this week from a legal firm in Calgary. I think you need to read it."

Marjorie Daniels showed no expression as she accepted the envelope, turned it over and opened it. She unfolded the letter that was inside, and as she read the contents her face paled, but she remained expressionless as she refolded and replaced the letter in the envelope and returned it to her son. Without saying a word, she rose and slowly made her way from the room.

"Mother, are you all right?" Wilson rose to follow her.

Marjorie stopped, turned, looked him straight in the eye and said, "I'm fine. Leave me." She left the room, her back straight as a broom handle, and just as stiff.

Judith rose to her feet. "Should I go to her?"

"Leave her be," Doc MacDougal told them. "She'll handle this in her own way and won't thank anyone for interfering. I'll be here if she needs me."

As Wilson and Judith linked hands he turned to his grandfather. "What did my father look like?"

"He looked just like you, son. You're the image of your father. He was filled out more, a strong, husky lad, but your features are the same."

Judith grinned, and leaned into her husband's shoulder. "He was a very handsome man, then."

Doc MacDougal walked the young couple to the door and bid them a goodnight. "You two keep in touch. Let us know what the lawyers tell you, son."

The next week, following the secretary's directive, Wilson ushered Judith into a book-lined office that was redolent with the scent of furniture polish. He extended his right hand to Mr. Edsel Sweeney, the lawyer handling the legalities of his late father, Joe Daniels.

Sweeney was a heavy-set man, balding and wearing spectacles, over which he peered. He indicated chairs pulled up in front of a massive oak desk. On one side were two neat stacks of folders. The desktop gleamed, reflecting the glow from a lamp suspended by a chain overhead. As soon as everyone was seated, the lawyer opened a thick folder and began to read, first asking that any questions be held in reserve until he was finished.

Once the basic will was read, Sweeney looked up. "You're confused," he said. "I assume you have questions, but let me first just basically set out the terms in layman's language. You have a choice to make at this time, Mr. Daniels. You may choose to take the $5,000 settlement now, sign the receipt and our business is finished. Or you could accept the alternate terms of the will and realize more than twice that amount, plus property and other unspecified holdings.

"The log cabin is situated approximately 550 miles north of Winnipeg. It is on the shores of a stream 120 miles northeast of Sherridon, a mining town operated by Sherritt Gordon Mines in northern Manitoba. I realize the property may not seem much, and it is quite isolated, but once it's yours, the additional funding will be forwarded to you."

Judith stifled the urge to jump to her feet. So much information was coming at them, and the fulsome bouquet of furniture polish was going straight to her head, making it hard for her to think. She was becoming very agitated. Without time to sort out all they were hearing, she began to squirm on her chair, which caused the lawyer to glance up at her.

"Are you all right, Mrs. Daniels? Would you like a coffee or a drink of water?"

"I would appreciate a glass of water. Thanks."

"What about you, Mr. Daniels?"

"Actually I would love a cup of coffee. Cream and sugar, please." Wilson, too, seemed a bit overwhelmed.

The lawyer rose, went to the door and addressed his secretary. "Mary, could you bring in some water and coffee with cream and sugar, please?"

As soon as his clients were sipping the beverages, Sweeney continued. "I must caution you to remember the stipulation, that in order for you to claim the said property, plus the additional funds, you need to reside on that property for a period of not less than three consecutive years. Once you have fulfilled that requirement, the cabin and the land it's on, as well as more than $10,000 and other unspecified properties will belong to you."

Wilson was calculating in his head. If both of them were working it would take more than 20 years to earn that much money. They were being offered a fortune.

"The funds are to be prorated. That is to say, for each month you reside on the property in question, you will be eligible for one-thirty-sixth of the balance of the inheritance funds. If you are unable or unwilling to fulfill these requirements, the land, the remaining monies and the unspecified properties will be given to the band of Indians that lives in the vicinity. You would still inherit $5,000. Those are the terms of your father's will. Now, do either of you have any questions?"

A long silence ensued, finally broken by Wilson. "Could we use some of the money to buy supplies?"

"Your father meant for that to be your responsibility. He intended for you to inherit the property only if you could prove that you have the fortitude to survive there."

The lawyer continued with the details. Wilson and Judith were expected to raise the $1,000 for their initial supplies – a list had been made according to his father's directions – but if they endured through the first 18 months then $1,000 would be made available to them for additional necessities. Once they reached Sherridon they would sign a form to confirm their arrival. At the end of their three years, a lawyer from the firm would travel to the mining town to verify their endurance, at which time the deed would be transferred. In Sherridon there were services and reliable third parties to ensure the young couple served the term as required. The costs for these services had been paid in advance by Wilson's father. As for locating the cabin, an Indian named in the documents could be hired as their guide.

"You will find all necessary documentation and instructions in this folder," Sweeney said.

As Wilson accepted the long list of supplies, he asked, "At the end of all this, once the property is in our names, will we be able to sell it if that's what we wish to do, without penalty?" Wilson tried to think of every eventuality.

"No. If you do not wish to keep the property, it is to go to another beneficiary, but you will be paid the fair market value of it, which will depend upon the improvements you have made, if any." The lawyer peered at Wilson and Judith over his glasses.

"Who is this other beneficiary?"

"We are not at liberty at this time to divulge that information."

Wilson was perturbed. "Why not?"

Unruffled, Sweeney merely replied, "That was the request of the late Mr. Daniels. We are bound to follow his wishes to the letter of the law."

"The $5,000 I'll inherit at any rate, I don't understand why we can't use it for our needs up front." Wilson's features reflected his frustration.

"Once you accept the $5,000, the terms of the will state, in a roundabout way perhaps, that your decision has been to take that amount of money and forfeit the balance." Edsel Sweeney twisted in his huge chair, his fingers steepled atop his shining desk, peering at them over his wire-rimmed spectacles.

Judith frowned. "I still can't understand why Wilson's father would want him to live in northern Manitoba, and why for three years? Can you tell us that?" she asked, wondering about a man she'd never met and now, would never meet.

"I'm sorry, young lady, but the late Mr. Daniels was quite specific about what your husband was to be told. I have given you all the information I am at liberty to disclose at the present time."

"What about these 'unspecified properties' you mentioned? What are they and how does that figure into all this?" Wilson asked.

"I am sorry, Mr. Daniels, but you have the information your father wanted you to have at this time. He left several letters, one for each of your options."

"What does that mean?"

"There is one letter for you, should you decide to take the first option of accepting the $5,000 now and concluding the business, another should you not remain the entire three years, and the third if you do remain for the three years and thereby inherit the entire amount. At the end of the three-year period, you will be informed as to the balance of your legacy. If you are in residency at the aforementioned property, the additional unspecified properties will be turned over to you at that time. That is all we have been instructed to inform you at present. You do realize you have the option to take $5,000 now and conclude this matter?"

"Would it be possible for us to get an advance or make a loan and repay it once the inheritance becomes mine?" Wilson had no intention of asking his grandfather for anything, and hated the thought of starting out with a substantial debt, but bringing Judith to wilderness country without proper provisions was something else again.

"If you are unable to show that you have purchased the provisions you will need through your own efforts, the terms of the will state very clearly that you will be entitled to only the $5,000 and the first letter concluding the terms."

Wilson drew in a deep, unsteady breath. "This list you gave us – that would be to cover just one person, am I right?"

"I believe so. At the time your father prepared his will, he would not have taken into consideration that you may have dependents at the time of his demise."

Wilson looked to his wife before he returned to the lawyer. "How soon would we have to let you know our decision? I think we need to talk this over."

"I was directed to allow you exactly one week."

Wilson saw the confused look on Judith's face. "Judith?" he asked.

"I agree," she said. "We have a lot to think about. One week. I guess that'll give us enough time to weigh the consequences."

Wilson nodded, his thoughts complicated. He would not coerce her into such a situation, however much the idea intrigued him. With $5,000 right now, they could build a small house here, but then they would still be in nearly the same circumstances they were in now. Whereas if they accepted the challenge of living in northern Manitoba for three years, they would have enough to build a substantial house, furnish it, purchase a vehicle and in those three years, perhaps he would find employment that would be fulfilling and provide enough income to support a family.

Later, back home in their cramped apartment, they discussed various scenarios. Taking the $5,000 right now was tempting, but by waiting three years, they would get more than twice that amount. They were young; there were no dependents, and no obligations to prevent them from leaving for three years. "Let's make a list of the pros and cons of a move," Judith suggested. "That will help us decide."

The negative list included missing their families and friends and being isolated from familiar surroundings, people, and customs. A rather important negative was the fact that she had no experience at living far from civilization, except for the camping trips that she, like Wilson, enjoyed frequently as a youngster. With his wartime experience he had an advantage as far as living far from all that was familiar.

"Won't that count against it though, honey?" Judith asked. "You just came back to civilization. Won't it be hard for you to leave so soon?"

"To be completely honest, darlin', the only good thing about being back is you, really. I feel like I don't fit in here anymore. This world is not the one I left. I'm not the same guy I was when I left. If it hadn't been for your letters that kept me sane, I'm not sure I'd have come back. I did my four years for God and country, I was lucky enough to have never been wounded, but oh, the wounded I helped to treat, the injured I tended and the dying I saw. It seems to me people even talk differently now than before I left. I love you. I came to love you through your letters, or maybe it took being away for me to realize the feelings I had. I wanted more than life to marry you when I returned home, but it's so hard to feel that I fit anywhere now. Can you understand that?"

"Wilson, I don't think honestly that I do. You have been places, seen things, and done things I can't even imagine. But I know you're feeling unsettled. I know you're not happy. I've known that for some time, though you've kept it to yourself, not complaining and trying to get by day by day. I want you to have the time and space it's going to take to come to grips with what you've gone through. That alone is reason enough for us to try this adventure."

Wilson sat quietly contemplating, a frown of concentration etched onto his forehead. Judith knelt in front of him and grasped his clenched hands. "Let's do it, Wil. I'm ready to do this if you are. Perhaps this is the answer to my prayers." Judith's eyes were beaming with anticipation.

He remembered his determination to ask for her hand as soon as he returned from the war, and how hard it was to wait until he was back in Canada. They had each declared their love in writing, but he didn't want to ask her to marry him until he could look into her beautiful green eyes. Now, he knew he couldn't bear to be away from her for three days, never mind three years, but he had to offer. "I could go alone," he suggested hesitantly. "Stay there three years and come back to you."

"Absolutely not, Wilson Andrew Daniels. How dare you even suggest such a thing? We're going together."

"I think we should talk this over with your family and I guess mine as well, first."

"Well I agree they need to be told. I've already decided, though. We'll tell them and ask for their blessing. We're going though, Wilson. You need to find yourself, and I think we need to be away from here, away by ourselves for a while until you work things out. I feel sure God's hand is in this, leading us and preparing the way for our future."

"I don't have as strong a faith as you, darlin', but I'm not going to argue. You could very well be right. So we talk to our families and then we go back to the lawyer and give him our decision."

Predictably, Wilson's mother was upset and against the idea, while his grandfather was hesitant but supportive. Judith's family was crestfallen, but with Judith being their first born of 11, and six years older than her eldest sibling, they were accustomed to their daughter deciding things for herself; they agreed, reluctantly, to give their blessing.

Before the allotted week was up they were back at the attorney's office. "We're going north to that cabin in Manitoba," Wilson said. "You have our answer, Mr. Sweeney." Wilson grasped Judith's hand as his eyes caressed her.

"I do wish you both the best of luck." The lawyer rose from behind his massive oak desk, hand extended. "If, before you leave, I am able to give any more information or answer any questions I am allowed to answer, please feel free to call and make an appointment to see me." He concluded the session by giving Wilson a folder containing a copy of the will and all necessary documents. "I await your further communications."

Later Wilson wondered aloud about the unspecified properties. "What else could my father have to leave us? Could it be a mine or mineral rights to some land there?"

Judith raised her hand and brushed back the lock of curly black hair that refused to stay off his forehead. "There is really only one way to find out, my love. I have another month of teaching. Does that give you the time we need to collect our supplies? If we pool our resources, we should have close to $750 with my savings and your pay from the army. And we can save more."

"I think it'll take longer than a month. It's too late in the season for us to go this year. I think if we move to Winnipeg and keep working as we collect the supplies, we should start off really early next spring. I can't help but wonder, though, how the man managed to save over $10,000 during the war years when money was so scarce."

2
Preparations

Judith completed the school year, alternately dreading and eagerly anticipating the move they would soon be making. Her parents were busy with harvesting and gardening – all the work of which farming consists. Beyond agreeing to store belongings Wilson and Judith would not be taking north with them, they were unable to offer much assistance.

Wilson continued to battle demons with which his war experience had burdened him, and their sleep was often disrupted by his screams of horror. Judith tried to get him to talk, but he kept his anguish to himself during his waking hours, saying only he was filled with hatred, anxiety and anger that he'd never experienced before. All he could do for her was promise he would come to terms with it in time. "I know most of the guys that served have the same turmoil going on inside. I've talked with a couple of men at the stockyards who served as well. One older man was discharged a couple of years ago because of injury, and he said the only way is to take each day one at a time and pay no attention to what people say, just work things out for yourself. And that's what I'm trying to do. Just be patient with me, darlin'."

Judith wrapped her arms around him. "One thing you can count on is my love."

Wil's mother didn't attempt to curb her fury with her son. "You are chasing a wild goose, Wilson. I brought you up to be a better man than your father. Why don't you work with your grandfather, get your medical training completed and stay where I can enjoy my last years in peace? I don't know how much longer I'll be alive, and you go traipsing off to God knows where to do God knows what. Oh my gracious, Judith, can't you try to reason with him?"

Judith informed her mother-in-law that she was in complete agreement with Wil, and the lines were clearly drawn. Mrs. Daniels's fainting and crying accomplished nothing more than encouraging the young couple to leave as soon as possible. Wilson's anger exploded once, and he'd stormed from the house where he'd grown up. Before long, Marjorie Daniels assumed her stiff manner of endurance and they were left with the knowledge that she was greatly offended by their disregard for her feelings and would not forgive them.

✻

In July they bid farewell to family and friends, packed up their wedding gifts to be left with Judith's parents and took the train to Winnipeg. Judith got a job working in a hotel, where, to her amazement, she earned as much as she had as a teacher back in Calgary. Wilson was forced to work as an orderly at the general hospital, as it paid the most of the jobs he looked at. His years in the armed services as a medic qualified him as a male nurse, and though his mother's dearest wish had been that he become a surgeon like Angus MacDougal, her father, Wilson wanted nothing more to do with blood, death and suffering. This job as an orderly was temporary and necessary, much like his work in the stockyards had been. At least here the injuries were seldom as severe as wartime wounds had been – the young men and boys burned beyond recognition; the bodies blown apart or embedded with shrapnel; the missing limbs. He remembered incoherent men crying in pain. There were the prisoners of war, some of them seemingly decent people, others steeped still in Nazi venom. All the horrors of war hounded his dreams, but the very worst, the terror of his life, was the flamethrower. The sparks that lit that terrible war machine never left his mind, and he wondered if they ever would.

Gradually, Wilson and Judith spent more than $2,000 to buy food provisions, most of which were dried, as well as army surplus clothing for them both, a .22 and a .303 high-powered rifle plus ammunition for each, various household items and tools, a tent, ground sheet and down-filled sleeping bags. They eagerly checked off on the list the items they accumulated once they had the funds to make the purchases.

The first part of February was stormy, and a 10-day blizzard buried rails and towns from Winnipeg to Calgary, but by the middle of March they were ready to head north with the supplies they had amassed. They had saved an extra $850 in case there were other expenses once they arrived at Sherridon. The balance of their savings went to pay their tickets and freight on the supplies.

Judith watched from a dirty window of a coach as CNR Steam Engine 6043 puffed and chugged its way toward their destination, the clanging bell and raspy whistle punctuating its progress. Clouds of dirty, cinderladen steam sailed past, at times obscuring her view as she noticed the scenery changing from flat, open grain fields, still blanketed by snow, to rocky Precambrian shield with mixed pine and leafless forests that grew thinner and more weathered the farther north they travelled. Finally all she could see was a pattern of marshy land through which countless rivers and creeks laid a maze of interwoven bare spaces. Occasionally rocky expanses poked icy ridges skyward. There was no sign of any human population, just marsh, rocks and miles of stunted spruce trees. How will we ever survive in this godforsaken land?, she wondered.

❋

The trip by train from Winnipeg to Sherridon took several days, and Judith and Wil used the time to get acquainted with some of their fellow passengers. The train carried a few families from The Pas. Since there was no direct rail line between Winnipeg and Sherridon, the CNR took them west to Portage la Prairie before turning northwest to Dauphin and on to Swan River. Northward, ever northward, but with Lake Winnipegosis in the way, the track spiralled west to circumvent it. There were some rough-looking men hungry for employment, and families returning to Sherridon to resume work in the mine. As the women admired her fashionable clothes and hairstyle, Judith asked about their destination.

"There are Indians everywhere you look," one passenger told her. "You watch yourself. Don't trust them."

"Just keep your distance and they'll leave you alone," advised an elderly lady from The Pas, patting Judith's arm.

Judith worried about living among the Indian people, as she hadn't had contact with any before. She knew there were tribes in Alberta, but they did not frequent the cities, and none were enrolled in schools where she taught.

The trip seemed interminable. They caught the Hudson Bay line, turned northeast and stopped at The Pas, where some people disembarked and others came on board. Then, with a mighty whooshing, steam swirling and bells clanging, the train headed almost directly north toward Sherridon.

Judith encouraged Wilson's chatting with other passengers, and learned he had been cautioned by a few men to watch his belongings around the "redskins." One older man, Oscar, reminded him of his uncle Mac, with a similar massive build, twinkling eyes and jolly laugh. Wilson was drawn to Oscar, who said he never had a problem with the Indians. "They are not a bad lot all in all, same as any other group of people, I think. They work during the winter hauling cordwood for SGM."

SGM, Wilson learned, stood for Sherritt Gordon Mines, the principal employer in Sherridon. Oscar explained that the mine was the sole reason for the town's existence. The war had necessitated the mining of minerals to build and sustain the war machinery and now it had come into its own as a vital employer – one helping to rebuild the nation after the hardships of war.

Wilson seemed unconcerned about the local tribes, and when Judith voiced her doubts, he tried to ease her mind. "Let's just take things one day at a time, darlin'. Oscar said the Indians would be useful, and we may need their services. I don't exactly know where my father's cabin is, and I sure don't know how to get there unless we get an Indian guide. I met a few Indians in the services and they seemed no different from any other people, and better than some."

Judith sighed and attempted to smile. "I guess I'll just have to trust in the Lord to see us through whatever we have to face."

3
Sherridon, Manitoba

On March 21, 1947 the train pulled into Sherridon, giving them their first impression of the bleak mining town. Clouds skulked overhead while a brisk northerly wind yanked at their hair and clothing. Judith clung to Wilson, eyeing this northern settlement, so different from Winnipeg or Calgary and even from Airdale, the neat little Alberta town where Wilson had grown up. The drifted and rutted snow did not improve their first impression.

The town consisted of about 200 green-roofed white cottages, a bank, several churches and two business blocks composed mostly of general shops. From the train, the tall box-like building with a sharply sloped roof could be seen in the near distance. Oscar, coming up behind them, informed Wilson that it was the mine, SGM.

All passengers left the now familiar but dubious comforts of the CN train, to be met by a crowd of curious people gathered to see the arrivals and to collect provisions they'd ordered from the south. Wil assembled the supplies they'd bought in Winnipeg, and Oscar caught up to Wil again, clasping him on the shoulder. "Come along, young fella. I want you to meet my friends."

Oscar's beefy hand steered Wilson, with Judith clinging to her husband, over to where a young couple stood smiling. "Hey there Clarence, Annie, meet my new friend Wilson Daniels. He and his pretty wife here are planning to stay for a spell with us. I wonder if you'd have room to put them up for a while? Wilson, this is Clarence and Annie Mills, my friends I told you about on the trip up here." Both wore welcoming smiles and seemed genuinely happy to meet Wil and Judith.

Clarence was short and heavy, not fat, but muscular. Annie had a round, flat, pleasant face, with long pale eyelashes that gave her a dreamy appearance.

"Annie will enjoy having another woman close for a while, won't you Annie? We're expecting a baby and she misses her family." Clarence had his muscular arm firmly around Annie's sturdy waist.

Judith noticed the colour flush Annie's cheeks as she looked down momentarily, then up at her husband. Judith smiled at the love she saw as they gazed into each other's eyes. Their generosity surprised her, nonetheless. "No, no. We can't impose on you like that. You are so kind to offer, but surely there is a hotel or an inn or something of the like where we could stay for a while."

Wil was more at ease as, having talked a fair deal with Oscar on the way up from Winnipeg, he realized the friendliness and generosity of the people in the mining town. Oscar had said there were no strangers in Sherridon; everyone was a friend or one of the family. On the train, Oscar mentioned the young couple was likely to offer a place to stay for a month or so.

"The Hotel Cambrian is downtown, but I won't hear of you going anywhere but to our place. We have the room and will love the company. It's nothing fine and fancy, mind, but you are more than welcome to share our lodging." This time it was Annie, the young wife, who insisted.

"This is so kind of you. If you are really sure we won't be imposing." Judith glanced at Wilson, who smiled and nodded.

"Yep, we surely appreciate the offer. Will our stuff be safe here by the station, or should we move it to your place?" Wilson asked Clarence.

"You sure brought along a lot, all right. It'll be just fine right where it is. No one will disturb it."

As they walked with Clarence and Annie, Wilson explained the reason they had made the journey and the time they were committed to staying in order to gain the inheritance left by his father. "At the end of three years, we'll be rich. We'll be able to move wherever we want and build a really great house for this wonderful girl I married. I figure three years isn't much compared to the time I was in the services overseas, and I'll be able to help Judith cope."

Annie looked at Judith, a worried expression on her kindly face. "Are you really OK with this? It'll be hard and lonely. I get lonesome, even though there are lots of other people living close. Where you are going sounds so isolated."

"I'll have my husband, and a promise of a bright future to sustain me, Annie. We've thought this through and worked almost a year to get our supplies together and get here. Since we managed so far, I'm sure we'll be just fine. I've spent many summers camping, and canoeing and earning my own way through Normal School to become a teacher."

"You're a teacher? You could probably get work here at the school. Being alone in the bush isn't at all like teaching, you know," Annie cautioned.

"I grew up on a farm, and helped raise my 10 brothers and sisters, so I'm no stranger to hard work," Judith replied with a laugh. "We're ready for this."

As they walked, the ladies chatted. "You look so glamorous, your hair and your clothes. It won't be like that where you're going. How will you manage?"

Judith laughed. "Oh, Annie. I learned to dress up when I moved to the city. On the farm, we dressed in serviceable clothes. I only brought a couple of stylish outfits with me, and I know I won't be needing them where we're going. I'm a lot taller than you, but you're welcome to them when we leave. Maybe you can remake them for yourself."

"Oh, dear me. I'll be the belle of the ball at our next dance if I do that. Can you show me how the women are wearing their hair? Yours looks so nice. I'd like mine like that."

Judith promised her new friend that they would do hair and talk fashion until it was time for the Daniels to leave.

Once they were settled into Clarence and Annie's cottage, Wilson accompanied his host to the headquarters about a mile distant, where Clarence worked in the mine. Clarence informed Wil that he earned $25 a month working there. SGM owned the house, but charged little for rent. "We are well paid and the work isn't bad once you get used to it," he said.

When Wil asked what life was like so far from larger centers, Clarence replied, "We love it here. This is beautiful country, and the people are wonderful. You should stay and work here. It's a good life."

"The money's tempting, so I'll keep that in mind," Wilson said. "First, though, I need to find the Indian guide the lawyer said my father suggested, a Tommy Lightfoot. Do you know him?"

"I don't, but if he works for SGM hauling lumber for the fires, the boss'll know who he is. Come. I'll introduce you and you can take it from there."

The burly mine foreman pointed out to him an elderly Indian man who was supervising the stacking of logs that added to the immense amount of cordwood covering a huge section of land. Wilson had never before seen so much timber cut and piled in neat rows in his life.

As he approached the Indian, Wilson regarded the straight-backed old man, seeing a nose that resembled a squashed rotten potato hooked over a toothless mouth. His chin jutted out under sucked-in lips to complete a dark, pockmarked and wrinkled face. His grey-streaked hair was pulled back in a long, loose braid hanging down over his ill-fitting brown jacket that topped dark twill pants and brown, badly worn work boots. His eyes, almost hidden within a nest of wrinkles, were so dark they were almost black.

Wilson greeted the old man, introduced himself, explained his quest, and waited for an answer. It seemed at first he was being ignored, but once the last log was placed, Tommy looked him over. For a long time the older man said nothing. "You want to go to the cabin, huh?"

The younger man nodded. "My wife, Judith and I intend to stay there for three years. We were told by my father's lawyer you would be the best one to ask for help getting there."

The elder man drew a long breath and looked away into the distance. Finally he turned back toward Wil. Without looking at him directly, the man said, "You give me any trouble, you're on your own."

Wilson raised his eyebrows, but knew he had no choice, as they needed this old man's knowledge. "I agree. You won't get any trouble from me. You know a heck of a lot more about this country than I ever will. I hope to learn a lot from you. You knew my father, Joe Daniels?"

Tommy glanced at Wilson. "I knew him."

The curt reply took him aback, and he decided not to press the matter. He would rather not speak at all, but he needed to know what other supplies were needed, so he inquired. His father must have left a poor impression on the old man, he reckoned, and clearly it was one to last, if not one to be shared. He waited to see what additional equipment Tommy would suggest.

"What do you have?" Tommy asked.

Wilson rattled off most of what he could remember buying, adding that his supplies were by the tracks in town where the train dropped off passengers.

Tommy looked away again, but suggested a canoe, paddles, warm clothing, mosquito block netting, rubber boots and felt-lined winter boots, plus a horse to help them travel, along with a sturdy section of canvas or well-cured moose hide.

Wilson was relieved they had extra cash. It would be a tragedy if he had to stay to work at the mine, delaying their departure until he had accumulated enough to get all they needed before setting off; he saw a year lost if that happened. He could purchase most of what they needed from the store in Sherridon, but he'd have to look elsewhere for the horse.

"Where are we going to get a horse, Tommy?" Wilson asked.

"My grandson, Jimmy has a few. Maybe I can get him to sell you one." He turned and shouted, "Jimmy! Ashtum. Come," he said, motioning with his head. As a well-built, rugged-looking young man disengaged himself from the working crew and came within speaking distance, Tommy added, "Come meet Wilson Daniels. Joe Daniels' son."

The grandson was in his teens, but he was almost as tall as Wilson's six feet. He ambled over, scowled at Wilson a little too long, spat on the ground and said a few words in a strange language to his grandfather. He wore his black hair in a style similar to the old man. Wilson was surprised to see deep blue eyes in the young man's grim countenance, but looked away from the anger plainly visible there. Jimmy kicked the stony sand at his rubber boot-covered feet, frowning as Tommy spoke sharply to him. The younger man spat on the ground again, uttered more undecipherable words brushing his hands against his pant legs, and turned away. Wilson remembered seeing the same venom in the eyes of Nazi soldiers captured in Holland, and wondered at the reason for the unwarranted hostility. As Tommy continued to chastise the youth, Jimmy whipped out one arm in a dismissing manner and nodded briefly, a fierce scowl marring his features.

In discomfort, Wilson gazed off into the distance at the spruce woods and rocks. He heard Tommy say, "OK. Jimmy will part with a young mare."

"Thanks," he said to Tommy. Turning toward Jimmy, he asked, "How much?"

"A rifle, ammo, the best hunting knife in the store and a parka. Winter boots with felt liners, too." Jimmy did not look directly at Wilson.

Tommy uttered a few more angry-sounding words in his native tongue, but Jimmy simply made another dismissive gesture, and Wilson hastened to say he agreed to the amount. He figured it would cost him roughly $65, which was quite a lot for one horse, unless it was a really good one, but he needed it and there were no others from which to choose. "All right. I'll give you $65. That should about cover it."

"No. You buy," Jimmy stated unequivocally.

"Wouldn't it be easier if I just gave you cash then you can buy whatever you want?" Wilson asked.

"No, you buy," Jimmy insisted, hostile and a bit too loud.

Wilson turned to Tommy, with a question etched across his face.

"It cost us more. You will pay less." Tommy replied, refusing to make eye contact with Wilson.

"That doesn't seem fair. The prices should be the same, no matter who's paying."

Tommy merely shrugged, so Wilson agreed to the terms of the sale. "I'll go with you to the store to get the stuff you want."

He followed Tommy Lightfoot and Jimmy to the sled used to haul wood, and endured a jolting ride to the town. He hopped off cautiously in front of the general merchandise store. Tommy, Jimmy and the rest of them waited outside. The supplies to pay for the mare ended up costing slightly more than $65. He spent another $75 for bags of oats, a canoe and two paddles, a canvas tarpaulin, a couple of pillows, a small plough and harness as well as extra flour, oatmeal, lard, baking powder, bacon and canned Spam and ham. He asked Jimmy to come in and help haul the load, though the younger man took only the things that were payment for the horse. Wilson asked the store manager if he could leave his purchases there until they left, in about a week's time. "I may end up needing more as well," he said, which clinched the deal.

Tommy entered the store and looked at all the supplies Wilson had bought. After having seen the pile the couple had brought on the train, he asked, "How do you plan getting all that stuff to the cabin?"

Jimmy snorted derisively as though Wilson were a complete idiot. He spoke briefly to his grandfather and stalked out to the other men, who were busy with the horses and sleighs. Wilson looked at the immense collection as well and replied, "I don't rightly know. What do you suggest? We need all those supplies."

"You need two more canoes," Tommy said.

"But who's going to paddle them?"

"I got some strong young fellows, and you can pay them for the hauling by giving them the extra canoes and paddles."

Wilson nodded.

"You need an extra tarp for land travel, too," Tommy advised, glancing again at the pile Wil had amassed.

"I don't get it. How are we going to travel on land with a tarp?" Wilson was really baffled, as he had no idea what the trip to the cabin would entail.

"We travel Indian-style. You will see, young Wilson."

"OK, Tommy. When do we leave, and what's it going to cost us for your services?"

"We leave right after breakup. It's not much out of our way. The two canoes and some more ammo for my rifle. That'll be enough."

"You got it, man, and thanks."

Wilson learned Tommy owned an old Winchester 94/.30-.30, and added two boxes of shells to his growing shopping list. When he found the old man also owned a shotgun, he bought shotgun shells to give Tommy once they reached their destination. He wished he'd bought a shotgun as well, and since there were a couple in stock at the general store, he decided to buy one and more shells, though it cost him more than it would have in Winnipeg. When the shopkeeper heard his young customer was travelling with Tommy's band he suggested a gift of tobacco wouldn't be amiss, so Wilson added a can to his purchases.

"Does Tommy smoke then?" Wil asked.

"Tobacco is sacred to these people. It isn't usually smoked for enjoyment or as a habit the way we whites use it. I think it'll be a good gesture for you to make. Tommy, there, he's a good Injun. I don't keep my eyes off some of them when they come in. They don't think anything's wrong with taking what they want and leaving without paying for it. Not old Tommy, though."

Wilson wasn't sure how to take these comments, so he said nothing beyond thanking the man for his advice.

Not knowing what to expect from the cabin that would become their home, Wilson asked Tommy what he knew about it. The guide kept him waiting, and then finally said, "It was a good cabin at one time. I think it might need repairs now."

"So what else will I need?"

"You have a hammer, nails, wire, a handsaw? You can get logs in the bush, with the axe you got there. We gotta haul all that stuff, you know. Don't buy what you can make."

"I don't rightly know how much I'm going to be able to make. I wasn't brought up to be very self-sufficient. We always bought whatever we needed. Looks like I got a lot to learn. When are we leaving, Tommy? My wife and I would like to get out there soon, 'cause it sounds to me like we have a lot of work ahead of us. How long is this trip going to take?

"If the weather holds out, we can leave sometime next week. I gotta make sure Ni'Ithinimuk are ready."

"Knee what?" Wil asked.

"Ni'Ithinimuk. My people," Tommy replied. "It might take us more than a week, with all that stuff you got."

After thanking Tommy, Wilson went to the store to complete his shopping. He counted out the little remaining of their extra cash, and then left for the cottage. Judith was waiting with Annie. When she learned of the rapidly approaching departure, Judith was excited but panicky to learn they would be leaving civilization within days.

"Do we have to camp with Indians?" she asked.

"Well, darlin', it sure beats camping on our own when we don't know much about the country out here." Wilson went on to explain the agreement he'd reached with their guide, and watched the concern and fear he saw on Judith's face. "It won't be so bad. Where is your faith in the Lord?"

"I know Wil, but I can't help being scared. I'll try though, to keep my concerns under control. I do trust your judgment."

4
The Trek Begins

As Judith accompanied Wilson to meet Tommy Lightfoot and his grandson Jimmy, she grumbled, "I guess if we have to travel with these people, the sooner we get introductions over, the better." It didn't take long to meet the men standing around outside the general store.

Wilson performed the introductions, trying to ease Judith into the meeting. "Jimmy sold us the little mare," he explained.

Judith extended her hand to each, and both men briefly touched hers with one of theirs; there was no eye contact and their hands were swiftly withdrawn. "Thank you for agreeing to take us to the cabin," she spoke hesitantly, looking from Jimmy to Tommy. A short nod was their only concession, making Judith feel uncomfortable. She found them rude and ignorant, treatment she was not used to, especially in dealing with men who usually went out of their way to make her feel like a lady deserving respect.

Judith studied the sturdy brown mare to try to relieve her awkward feelings. It was a shaggy beast in need of a currycomb. She moved over closer to it and the horse allowed her to pat its neck, turning to watch her, tossing its head up and down, snorting softly. Judith held her hand under the mare's nose and laughed as it moved thick rubbery lips against her palm. She was unaware of Jimmy's speculative gaze.

Wilson grinned at Judith and the mare before turning to his guide. "When can we get acquainted with the rest of your group, Tommy? I think my wife would like to meet a few of your women and children."

"When we leave. Two days. Daybreak."

Wilson and Judith exchanged glances. He nodded thoughtfully. She bit her bottom lip.

As they trudged towards the Mills' house, Judith had nothing to say, but Wilson noticed her crestfallen expression. "I think they're uncomfortable around white women, darlin', that's all. It'll get better. You'll enjoy the children."

Judith nodded glumly. "Two days. I can't believe I have only two days left. I'm going to miss Annie." She looked at Wilson, a frown marring her forehead. "That young man, Jimmy. He seemed almost hostile. What's his problem?"

"I have no idea. Maybe he had a bad run-in with some white guys – maybe the storekeeper. Did you know they charge Tommy's people more for supplies than we pay?"

With her thoughts on their trip, Judith did not respond.

Those two days seemed to fly by. The next day they spent a lot of time packing and rearranging supplies to be ready for loading in whatever manner their native guides suggested, and as they finished covering the assortment with the two tarpaulins Tommy strode toward them. "You need to go to the bush. Get four straight spruce poles. About as high as two of you. Cut off the branches. Bring the poles here." Tommy then walked on.

Wilson retrieved his axe and handsaw from under the tarp before accompanying Judith back to the Mills' cottage. As he trudged into the bush, Wilson eyed the scattered collection of buildings outside the town. He walked a fair distance farther until eventually he found and cut down four trees, limbed them and then wondered how on earth he was going to get them back into town.

"Maybe I can ask Clarence for advice." Now I'm talking to myself, he thought and walked back to the Mills' place in time to meet Clarence returning from his shift.

"I've got a problem, and I was wondering if I could get your advice. Our guide said I needed to get four long straight poles from the bush. Well, I found some fairly straight and tall, cut them and limbed them, but darned if I know how to get them back here."

Clarence scratched his head. "What do you need poles for?"

"Darned if I know," Wilson answered.

"You got some rope?"

"Yeah, but even one is pretty heavy. Roping them together will make them impossible to haul. I could manage one by one, but it'll be dark soon." Wilson looked worriedly toward the reddening western sky, noting the lengthening shadows on the stone-strewn ground.

"You got yourself a horse, right?" Clarence asked, scratching his head again.

"Yeah, that's right! I can figure out a way to tie them to the mare and get her to drag them. Thanks, Clarence." Wilson was amazed he hadn't thought of that himself.

"Get your rope and your horse and meet me back here. I'll go along and help you, but I have to check in with Annie first."

With a nod, a grin and a wave of his hand Wilson set out to get a coil of rope and the little brown mare that was tethered close to his piles of tarp-covered supplies. It didn't take the two men long to reach the poles, tie them to the mare and return to the supplies. They relieved the little mare of her load, tethered her again and, just as it was getting too dark to see, returned to the meal awaiting them at Clarence and Annie's house.

✳

At dawn the next morning, Wilson and Judith enjoyed an early breakfast with Clarence and Annie, thanked them for their hospitality and offered to pay for their stay. Clarence shook his head. "Just stop in to see us whenever you're back this way."

Judith wrapped her arms around the younger woman. "I'm going to miss you. Good luck with your pregnancy, Annie. I'll be praying for you both and for the little one." She rubbed Annie's belly. "I'll see you next time we're in town, Baby."

Wilson and Judith strode to where Tommy and Jimmy were waiting with a thin black horse beside their supplies and the brown mare. Wilson called as they approached. "Sorry we're late. I see you've already got the horses hitched up. Now I can see what the poles and tarps are for." The poles stretched out on either side of the horses, the thicker end on the ground behind them. The tarp was tied between the poles like a stretcher and the supplies were being loaded onto the tarps and anchored with more of the rope. Tommy gave a name for the device, then added, "White people call it a travois."

Wilson nodded. "What do we do with the three canoes?"

"Carry 'em." Tommy hoisted one with ease over his head, steadying it on his shoulders with his hands.

Jimmy positioned himself to lead the horses. Judith looked at Wilson and then at the remaining two canoes. She raised her eyebrows. "I guess I can carry one if it's not too heavy," she said. "It won't be the first time, but before, we hauled one together."

Wilson frowned at the two Indian guides. He glanced toward the canoes and hefted one of the craft, then helped Judith get under it. The canoe was light, but it wasn't what he'd had in mind for his wife. He hoisted the remaining boat onto his own head and shoulders and, keeping Judith ahead of him, followed the other two men out of the mining town.

Before the sun was above the trees they'd reached a camp where people were finishing loading supplies. The women led five horses that, like the two mares, had two poles strapped to their sides, covered with supply-laden hides. Wilson and Judith surveyed the people. Although some of the women appeared to be too young to be mothers they had infants strapped onto their backs in some type of carrying device. Most of the women wore shapeless long skirts, big rubber boots over soft leather inner boots, and ill-fitting winter parkas with either hoods or toques on their heads. Some wore their straight black hair loose, but a few had plaited their hair, some with a braid hanging in front of each ear, and a few with a single braid down the middle of the back. There were several heavy-set older women hard at work.

Wilson set his canoe down and relieved Judith of her load until everyone was ready to leave. They watched the camp. None of the adults looked at the couple, but the little children stared – some trying to hide behind their mothers, many with a finger or a hand in the mouth. The children were dressed warmly, if not fashionably. Some wore rubber boots, while others had moccasins. Each had a toque or a parka with a hood to cover their heads. The little boys wore various types of pants, while the little girls had long, loose skirts and leggings. With round, dark eyes they watched the strangers suspiciously, their hair straggling around little brown faces, most of which were none too clean. Men carried canoes and led horses. The women carried small children, or packs tied onto their backs and fastened with wide bands across their foreheads. A few scruffy dogs skulked around, sniffing at the people and horses. Two skinny brown-and-white mutts barked at Wilson and Judith and received a kick from the Indian people for their efforts. One little boy carried a squirming puppy.

Tommy called to one woman. "Sue. Ashtum. Come meet these people."

A slender woman of about 50, with silver streaks in her shiny black hair, moved gracefully toward Tommy and smiled shyly at Judith and Wilson. Her oval face was brown, her nose straight and narrow over a generous mouth. "Hello," she said, glancing briefly at each.

"My daughter, Sue. This is Wilson Daniels and his wife, Judith."

Judith smiled happily at the older woman, noticing her turning swiftly to appraise Wilson. "Hello Sue. I'm pleased to meet you. Is Jimmy your son?" Judith offered her hand.

Sue nodded, smiling as she glanced back toward Judith, but she didn't take the proffered hand.

Wilson grinned and nodded his head, offering his hand. "Hi, Sue. Jimmy sold us his mare. We've made good use of her all ready. We had no idea what we needed when we came out here. Your father has been most helpful."

Sue held his hand, inspected his face and smiled. "Hello, Wilson." She turned to look at Tommy. There was a question in her eyes that Tommy appeared to ignore.

"I expect we have a lot to learn. Judith and I'll be glad of your knowledge as we go. It's been a while since my wife and I have been camping, and I'm a greenhorn in this country."

"Green horn?"

"It means a newcomer, someone not sure of what to do."

"You will learn." Again, Sue scrutinized Wilson's face and smiled. She turned toward Judith. "You too, my girl. Are you OK with carrying that canoe?"

"It's not heavy. I'll be fine as long as we don't have too far to go."

"If it gets to be too much, you tell me. We can strap it onto one of the horses." Sue at least seemed concerned about Judith's well-being.

"I will, but the poor horses have heavy loads as it is."

"They are strong and used to the work," the other woman assured Judith.

"It's late," Tommy grunted.

"Ready when you are." Wilson looked to Judith. "You ready, darlin'?"

She flashed a wide grin. "Ready when you are." Wil helped her with the canoe, making sure it was within her control before raising his own onto his shoulders.

Judith was glad of her summer experience with Wilson's cousins, who often included her in their canoeing adventures. The group set off in a southeasterly direction. Wilson had expected them to head northeast, as that was his understanding of the direction in which the cabin lay, but wisely said nothing. He remembered Tommy's terse warning: *You give me any trouble, you're on your own.*

They hiked single file, Judith behind Tommy's skinny figure, trying to match his footsteps. The light canoe was becoming increasingly heavy on her shoulders, but she was determined to hold her own. Wilson brought up the rear, where he could keep an eye on Judith and watch for any sign of fatigue.

During the seemingly unending trek, young children scampered in and out of the straggling line of travellers, followed by excitedly barking dogs, sniffing at everything, but before too long the children began to lag and finally each walked beside an adult, some begging to be carried. Judith tried to keep up with Tommy, who seemed never to slow down or hesitate. She began to wonder if she had the strength to continue. Wilson called out to her several times asking if she were OK, and though she told him she was fine, she knew he was doubtful.

Shortly after the sun reached its zenith they arrived at a wet, sandy beach where a lake stretched its vast, restless water into the distance. Ice shards rustled along the edge of the lake, moving gently up and down as though the lake were breathing. In some places huge piles of dirty ice could be seen stretching along the shore. No one was happier than Judith and Wil to note the leaders of the party stopping and unloading their packs. The people in the lead already had boats in the water, the loaded travois dismantled, their contents stowed inside the canoes. The horses, still towing the now-empty poles, balked in protest at the coldness of the lake water. Tommy assisted Wilson and Judith to load two canoes, while Jimmy and a stocky man, who appeared a bit older, loaded the remaining canoe with the couple's supplies. He and Jimmy exchanged glances and shook their heads as if amazed at how much these people were transporting. Jimmy left the poles attached to the two horses. The older man got into the front of one canoe, and Jimmy pushed it out into the lake, holding the reins of the two horses and urging them into the water. Both horses resisted, but Jimmy kept speaking calmly and encouragingly to them, and they finally bolted into the icy water, the poles floating behind.

Tommy and a short, strong, younger man handled one of the other canoes Wilson had bought. "You OK to paddle?" Tommy asked Wilson.

"Yeah, we both can handle a canoe. Thanks for asking." Wilson put Judith in one end of the last canoe, pushed it into the water and waded alongside it until he climbed aboard at the opposite end. With his paddle he swung the canoe end for end so that he was in the front.

The group of canoes sped through the water as sunlight danced off the gentle waves. The almost constant winds had stilled, and the spring sun plus the effort of paddling warmed the travellers. Gulls mewed overhead, circling, some landing on the surface, to rise, screeching skyward as the canoes approached. The horses swam behind the canoes, each one towed by the rear paddle-wielding rower.

Wilson and Judith watched, envious and famished, as their companions ate on the move. There was nothing ready to eat unless they dug through their supplies, and that would cause them to lag behind. "I'm sorry," she said. "I never thought to bring along food to eat on the way."

"It's as much my fault as yours," he said. "Wait, I have a bit of meat in my pocket. We can pick off the lint and eat it."

He handed her a dried strip of smoked moose jerky. Judith had never cared for such food, but she was hungry enough to risk a small bite. After removing the lint she bit off a piece of the jerky, chewed it slowly and found it surprisingly edible. It had a smoky taste, reminiscent of bacon. She could hardly believe she was eating raw, dried moose meat; she couldn't remember eating anything more nourishing or delicious.

Seeing the people in the leading canoes dipping cupped hands into the lake and drinking the cold clear water, she did likewise. Wilson followed suit, and when they were done they wiped their hands on the sides of their coats.

They travelled a long way as the sun crept across the sky. As it inched toward the distant treetops, Wilson noticed they were now heading northeast.

As nighttime wrapped its arms around the world, the people pulled canoes up onto another cold sandy beach, and began a swift and efficient erection of tepees using the travois poles, sharing so that each tent used four poles. The horses rolled around on the sand, drying their hides and attempting to warm themselves.

Wilson and Judith set up their tent using the two tarps as additional flooring under the built-in floor of their tent in an attempt to insulate their bodies from the cold ground. They collected wood and borrowed a flame from Tommy's fire by lighting a dry branch.

Judith was exhausted. "I don't know what to cook, Wil. What do you want?"

"It doesn't matter. Let's just open a can of ham. You look exhausted."

Sue looked over at them, got up and brought over a bowl of dough. "If you wrap some of this over a green branch, and hold it over your fire, it cooks. We call it bannock. I made too much for our family."

Judith nearly cried with relief and gratitude. "Can we share our canned ham with your family then?"

Sue looked at Wilson, and when he grinned his agreement she nodded and smiled. She accepted half of the ham and then returned to her campfire.

Judith managed to hold the green branch over the coals, knowing the flames would scorch the bread. Wilson took over for her as her arms played out. "You've gotten more exercise today than you have for a long time. It's no wonder you're tired. I can do this." After he'd held the stick for a while he asked, "How do we know when it's done?"

"I guess when we can't wait any longer, like about now."

Wilson handed the smoking branch to Judith and she broke off the glob of what was no longer dough. She split it and handed half with some ham to her husband. She watched as he bit into it. "What's it taste like?"

"Oh darlin', this is fine. Oh, man, this is good. Leave yours; I'll eat it for you."

"I don't think you will, husband," she retorted before biting off a large chunk. "It is good. Yum! I have to get Sue to tell me how to make this."

Finally, replete with warm, smoky bannock and canned ham, chased with scalding coffee, Judith and Wil relaxed by the fire. They watched sparks spiral upwards, brighten, and then die, falling as grey ash. Before long, he noticed Tommy's people had all vanished into their tents and closed the openings. He stirred. "Well, I see our neighbours have all turned in for the night. I suppose that means we'll have an early start tomorrow."

Judith stretched reluctantly and sighed. "I could sleep right where I am."

"It's going to get cold, and I don't intend to feed the fire all night. Are you going to fight off bears and other wild animals?" Wil reached out his hand and raised his sleepy wife to her feet. "The sleeping bags look mighty comfortable right now."

The next morning, Tommy woke everyone with a shout. "Let's eat and be on our way." Judith felt as though she just lay down, but she heaved a deep sigh and got up, dressed and stepped out of the tent. Wilson had a fire going and the coffee pot of water heating.

Soon canoes were back on the lake, and before long the couple worked the incredible stiffness from their muscles. They watched as their companions ate on the move. "Do you have any more jerky, Wil?"

"Sorry, darlin', we ate all I was carrying yesterday. I thought you didn't like jerky."

"I thought I didn't too." Judith laughed along with him.

Their journey progressed day after day. They navigated by water where possible, and hiked when they had to. Wilson and Judith came slowly to know more of their travelling companions, learning names and relationships. It turned out that Tommy had two sons, Nelson and Bruce. Both had served overseas, and soon they struck up a friendship with Wilson as the three shared some of their wartime experiences. He discovered that another brother, Tom, had been killed in the Battle of the Bulge. The memories were vivid. "We treated many wounded from that battle, most of them American soldiers, with a few Germans and Canadians as well," Wilson said. He and the brothers managed to share a little of the horrors that were locked inside. It seemed no one without the experience of battle could comprehend the things they'd seen and experienced.

That night, Tommy advised Wilson that they had to travel on land again until the river became navigable once more. Wilson informed Tommy he didn't want Judith toting a canoe. "It's enough she has to paddle. Most of your women don't, I notice. I think she would rather carry a pack on her back like your women. I hope that will be OK. Not that I want to give you any trouble," he hastened to add.

This time Tommy laughed and slapped Wilson on the back. "You're OK, young Wilson. We'll take Judith off the canoe for the time being. She's been a tough young woman. She's OK, too."

Each night they camped, Wilson spent time with Tommy's two sons reviewing life after wartime. They talked about how difficult it was to adjust to normal life after they returned from the front. "It was like we were coming home from residential school," Nelson said. "Everything is different, or maybe it was us that changed."

"I think, me, it is both," Bruce said. "We are different, and the people at home, they changed too."

"I have a hard time to talk about it, and little things get me so mad," Wilson said. "Sometimes it's like there's a bomb inside of me that's going to blow." Wilson spoke quietly but intensely.

The other two men nodded. Nelson was first to speak. "It helps to work hard. Cutting wood helped, and this trip up the river is giving me time to think. It is hard, though," Nelson said, chucking a stick into the fire and making sparks fly upward.

"At least my girl is not married yet." Bruce said. "That one you had your eye on up and married Charlie Bighawk."

"Who? Libby? Ah, we weren't serious. It's OK."

As the men talked quietly around a fire, Judith took the time to get better acquainted with Sue. She found the woman to be wise, patient and possessing a quiet sense of humour. Sue guided by example, and answered Judith's many questions to the best of her ability, not once making Judith feel intrusive. Judith came to know Libby, but found the young woman very shy and reserved. At first she had thought the young native to be snobbish, but the first impression soon proved false.

"You and Libby are both newly married. How are you finding married life?" Sue asked.

Judith, noting Libby's confusion and embarrassment, decided to speak first. "It has been wonderful and frightening," she admitted frankly. "I love Wilson so much. We kept in touch when he was overseas. In fact, I fell in love with him through his letters. I knew him when we were kids. My Dad farms close to his Uncle Mac's ranch, and Wil used to spend most of every summer there. I thought he was just a smart-alec city boy, though. He asked me to write when he signed up, so I did. Since he's come back, I'm getting to know the man he's become. He holds so much inside, though. He often has nightmares about the war and he won't share these with me. I just hold him and talk to him whenever he has a bad night."

Sue nodded. "Yes, my brothers, too, have nightmares. It must have been very hard for them. They don't have a lovely young wife to comfort them either. We lost my youngest brother in the war. That was very hard. Especially hard for our father."

"I'm so sorry, Sue. Wil's cousin came back without one leg, and his other is so damaged, he'll never walk again. I'm so glad Wilson wasn't wounded as some of the medics in the field hospitals were. God watched over him for me." She turned to the other young woman. "Was Charlie a soldier too, Libby?"

"No, he was turned down."

"Ah, but you didn't turn him down, did you?" Sue teased her young friend.

"No. He's a good man, Charlie. He treats me very good." Libby volunteered that much but no more.

Just then, Wilson came to claim his wife. With a smile for the other two women, Judith carried some freshly fried whitefish from Sue over to their own campfire for their supper.

The horses, connected to travois once more, appeared happier to travel on land, though they had to drag heavy loads behind them. The people who led them chose the best route through the muskeg and rock, often following trails of jumbled, rock-strewn paths called eskers.

Sue and Tommy shared their knowledge of the land, the animals and the plants that were found in the area. Judith tried to remember as much as possible, knowing it would be useful in the three years she and Wil had to live in the north. With their knowledge, the Indian people were able to nearly live off the land, and not carry all the paraphernalia Wilson and Judith needed. "We buy baking powder, salt, flour and sugar," Sue told Judith. "Tea and coffee, guns and ammunition also need to be bought, but there is much to use and eat here the Great Spirit provides for His people if you know where to look and what to use."

"I'm beginning to realize that," Judith said. "You know a lot. I never knew how much food could be gathered from the wild."

She had expected to see school-aged children with the family groups, and asked Sue why there were only very young children and youths with them.

"Our children are taken to school far away. We only have them a short time in the summer. It is very hard, especially for the little ones."

"It must be hard for the parents, too. Education is important though. I was a teacher in Calgary."

"Did your students live at school?"

"No. They went home every afternoon. Why do you send your children away?"

"We have no choice unless we stay far away from settlements and keep them out of school. We want our children to learn, but it is so hard to lose them."

"It must be. At what age are they taken?"

"They go when they are five until they are 15. By then, many have forgotten our ways and they don't fit anywhere. They do not fit in the white world and they don't fit our world anymore. Most of them have a hard time adjusting. They forget their language and they are angry and confused. It is hard."

Judith thought about it in silence. It didn't seem right, but she had no idea how else the Indian children would be able to get an education. She looked at Sue for a moment. "I'm a schoolteacher, but I've learned a lot from you – useful information that you can't find in books. Your way of life is so different from what I'm used to."

Sue merely nodded.

One day, Tommy announced they were close to the cabin. "Most of my people will continue on. Jimmy and I will bring your supplies as far as the end of the creek that takes you to the cabin. You will be able to walk from there, young Wilson. It is not far. We will catch up with the rest of my people."

Jimmy passed control of his black horse, Midnight, to a rather surly young man named Ben, and he and his uncle Nelson with the brown mare, followed Tommy and Charlie Bighawk along a river that flowed swiftly northeast. The water had warmed considerably from the temperature at first, but it was still cold in the deeper lakes. Wilson and Judith plied their paddles, battling against the current, struggling to keep up. As the river widened, the current slowed and when Tommy turned toward a deep creek, the others welcomed the change. Tall brown rushes created a tunnel through which they rowed. Blackbirds clicked their displeasure at the intruders, and muskrats splashed as they slid from the banks where white interiors of roots indicated their gnawing.

Before long, Tommy pulled up to the edge of the creek, finding it too narrow and shallow to continue in the canoe. Jimmy and Wilson followed suit. They left the canoes there, loaded a travois onto the mare and piled the remainder for Wilson and Judith to fetch to the cabin. Wilson shook hands with Jimmy, Charlie and Nelson, giving each a small measure of tobacco, then offered his hand to Tommy. "Thank you my friend. I have a gift for you as well." He gave the older man the remainder of the tobacco.

Jimmy had taken his share with a curt nod and moved over to where the mare was waiting. He patted the little horse and spoke quietly to her, scratching her neck. Judith watched, and then she moved closer to him. "We'll take good care of her, Jimmy. I promise."

The young man turned to her then, looked at her and nodded his head. "She's a good horse. I'll miss her." They turned back toward Wilson and Tommy, and Judith saw a shadow cloud the young man's face. It was on the tip of her tongue to ask what he had against her husband, but she thought better of it and bit her lip instead.

Tommy was shaking Wilson's hand. "I thank you for the gift, and wish you well. We will stop by on our way back this fall to see how you are making out." Tommy slapped him on the back. "You are pretty good for a greenhorn."

They laughed, and then Wilson turned to dig through the heavy pack in the travois. He located the ammunition he'd bought for Tommy's old rifle, and a box of #6 shells for the shotgun. "I bought these for you. I'm hoping you're a good enough shot to get some birds. If you get fine caribou, you can bring me some when you come by. If you're lucky enough to get more than you need, that is."

"I will do my best, if luck is with me." He grinned and turned to Judith. "Take care, Missus. Keep this greenhorn in check. He's a tricky one." Tommy's dark eyes sparkled as he nodded to Judith.

Judith blinked back tears, trying to keep her lips from quivering, "Give Sue my love. I didn't get to thank her or to say goodbye. I learned a lot from her. Good luck on your trip and on your hunting, but something tells me you don't need luck to get your caribou."

She thrust her hand in Tommy's direction and he took it, covering it in both of his old, calloused palms. He nodded and turned without another word, stepped lithely into a canoe where the others awaited and, without looking back, sent the canoe skipping along with the current and was soon out of sight.

5
The Inheritance

Dampness and pungent wild sage perfumed the air as the structure came into view around the bend in the creek where scruffy bushes and spruce had hidden it. Forever after, that particular blend of scents would stir in Judith a strange mixture of anticipation and foreboding.

There was no roof. A warped door hung drunkenly from one hinge. Dry, lanky weeds peered in through the south window at their spindlier relatives inside. Within the window frame only a few shards of glass remained, pointing accusing fingers at each other. A stone chimney stood stiffly at attention against the taller north wall of the weatherbeaten, slate grey logs of the cabin. But for the lichen encrustations it might have been erected recently, in disdainful contrast to the rubble to which it appeared to pay little heed.

Judith rubbed calloused palms over her denim-clad thighs and surveyed the upper branches of scraggly pines that pierced an incredibly blue sky. Below them, tangled willow and birch, with swollen leaf buds, appeared anxious to burst forth in emerald display. Then, once more, she studied Joe Daniels' cabin.

This rubble with the elegant chimney was to be their home for the next three years. What were they thinking?

"Well, we may as well take a closer look, darlin'. Though I don't think it will look any better up close."

"At least we're here now, Wil. No more paddling, hiking and camping."

Wilson tipped his head to the side. "Well I think we're going to be camping for some time yet."

They waded, hand in hand, through weeds, forest debris and shrubs, through dry brown, flattened grasses and stubby bushes, to the remains of his father's cabin. It looked worse and worse with every step the couple took.

Wilson wrenched the door open and propped it ajar, thrusting out his arm to delay Judith. "Wait. Let me check it out first." After ensuring there were no unwelcome inhabitants, he motioned for his wife to join him inside, where an even more unprepossessing sight awaited her.

A three-legged table leaned haphazardly against a rough log wall by the chimney, while the one and only chair sprawled on its side, two legs missing, weeds poking through a split in its back. The east wall sported a warped wooden cupboard, its upper doors jammed closed, its lower ones missing to display two unopened tin cans, rusty and without labels. A heap of grasses and twigs in one corner indicated some type of rodent had claimed possession at one time. What once must have been a bed hunkered against the opposite wall. All that remained was a rough log rectangle supported by the wall and one leg, with rotted pine boughs filling the interior. A musty smell of decaying wood, mixed with the scent of dry grasses, dust and pine, filled their nostrils.

A sudden rush of wings startled the young pair as a small bird fled skyward. "I wonder if it has a nest in here somewhere?" asked Judith, before she realized her husband had gasped.

Wilson turned away momentarily, as though to calm his nerves, then turned back to look into his wife's eyes. Seeing despair in Wil's face, Judith knew she had to show faith they could turn this hovel into a home. "The walls look fairly solid and the chimney's nice and straight. We can make a new roof, can't we?"

"Oh, darlin'. What have I gotten us into? I wanted so much better for you. I didn't think it would be this bad." Wilson shook his head slowly.

Judith's green eyes sparkled teasingly as she tossed a long, light brown braid over one slim shoulder. "Well, Mr. Wilson Andrew Daniels, you have brought me to a lovely cabin in the woods where we'll make our fortune." She turned to him, grasped his hard, calloused hands and looked deeply into his shadowed eyes. "As long as I have you, I don't much care where we live. And besides, I agreed to this, remember? And it's only for three years. Remember all that money we'll get after?"

Wilson sighed. "Let's put up the tent and have some supper," he said, trying unsuccessfully to keep despair from his voice. "Maybe it won't look so hopeless after a good night's sleep." He squeezed her hands and tried to smile. "And you, Judith Aileen McClosky-Daniels, are all I ever wanted and all I'll ever need."

"Is that so? Can we skip supper then?" Judith grinned mischievously.

"As much as I love you, my darling wife, and want you, I insist we have some food and an early night. I'm starving for some beans and your fresh bannock. Let's get a fire going, then while you rustle up some food I'll set up the tent." Wil gave Judith a playful pat on the backside. "At least we're here. No more paddling and hiking," he added.

He tried to look on the bright side. If there was one, he thought. If only the cabin had been in better shape. He wondered if they were really up to this task they'd set themselves. All at once doubts crowded in. This was going to prove much more difficult than a mere camping trip. The journey with Tommy's people had shown them how little they knew about living off the land in a wilderness where civilization was days away. How long would their supplies last? At the rate they had gone through food as they travelled, it wouldn't last as long as they needed it to last. They would have to learn how to supplement what they'd brought with wild meat and vegetation. He hoped Sue had been able to show Judith some of the ways to gather food from the wild.

He turned to watch as she bent her tall frame to collect dry twigs. Her well-rounded and very alluring back end covered with sturdy denim was remarkably sexy. Judith had lost some weight on the trip to the cabin, and it suited her. Wilson chuckled and turned to collect his portion of firewood before his thoughts led to other, more satisfying pursuits. Again he dismissed his wish he'd come alone and then gone back to her. He needed her. She kept his demons at bay – demons that haunted his dreams, demons that made him panic when the bird flew up and startled them. He'd half expected enemy soldiers to open fire. How long? How long would those experiences haunt his every hour awake and asleep?

Judith refused to look beyond the present. They had made it to the cabin, they would repair it together, and they would enjoy this time as a married couple, away from the emptiness that seemed to haunt Wil in Calgary. Here he had work to do that had meaning, he was outside in the fresh air, and he had regained some of the sparkle in those deep blue eyes that used to mock her when they were kids. This was best for Wilson and for her. They were working toward a common goal, to gain the inheritance his strange father had left, and they would be rich once the three years were up.

In a short time, a crackling fire heated the canned beans while Judith carefully prepared the biscuit dough she would wrap around a green stick the way Sue had taught her. It would bake nicely over the hot coals while she turned it carefully. With the help of Sue Lightfoot, Judith had learned quite efficient camping skills.

As Wilson approached the fire, she allowed her eyes to devour the long muscular body of her husband. How she loved that man. If he'd asked her to live in a slum house in the worst part of Calgary, she wouldn't have hesitated. As long as they were together, they could manage to do the impossible.

After filling the blackened coffee can with water from the stream, Wilson returned to get the tent up. "It looks like there are berry bushes along the stream, and maybe we'll be lucky enough to catch fish there as well as at the river." He glanced over at Judith, and his attempts at optimism were not lost on her.

"We'll be fine and it's only for three years, Wil. Supper'll soon be ready." Judith never doubted Wilson's love for her or their ability as a couple to survive. Used to being surrounded by family and friends, she wondered how they would manage so far from others now that they really were completely on their own. She missed Tommy's group, especially Sue and Libby, and even the surly Jimmy. She wondered why he had such animosity toward Wilson.

"Wil, honey, do you have any idea why Jimmy hated you? He treated me OK and he was pleasant to the others. It was only you he couldn't seem to stand."

"In the forces, it was the same way. For some reason one of the crew would strike up a hatred for another fellow. There was never a reason that you could say; they just seemed to hate on sight. I don't recall ever saying or doing anything to set Jimmy off, except maybe he really didn't want to part with his mare and Tommy kind of forced the issue."

"I suppose that could be it. He seemed to really like the mare and he said he'd miss her. I promised we'd take good care of her."

Wilson pushed his hand through unruly black hair kept short to control the waves and curls. Whiskers peppered his strong cleft chin and determined jaw. He had threatened to grow a beard, as shaving had become a nuisance in the muskeg and marshy lands they had traversed, but so far he'd continued to shave every morning.

"Maybe he'll have gotten over it when we see them again. I have to hoist the supplies up into that jack pine. We were lucky Tommy showed us that, since we don't have dogs to warn us now. A bear would really mess things up for us."

"That one the dogs were after that night sure left in a hurry when Jimmy shot over his head." Judith laughed at the memory of the skinny bear bounding away, his rear seeming to try to pass his front end.

Wilson attended to the necessity of securing their supplies as Judith removed the beans and biscuit roll from the fire. She added some damp vegetation for a smudge to discourage the nasty, biting blackflies and mosquitoes that were becoming a real nuisance. Powdered milk made the coffee more palatable and a little healthier.

This was their first night on their own property. At least soon it would be theirs, and then they could sell out. Three years wasn't so long, she kept reminding herself.

✳

Later, they were cuddled into their sleeping bags. The musty smell of
the canvas tent mixed with the perfumes of sage and pine needles. From
outside, the wavering tones of a lone wolf echoing across the night
chased shivers up and down her back. She turned to her husband. "Your
father lived here all alone. What kind of man was he?"

"I don't rightly know. He left when I was only a few years old, four,
maybe three. I don't remember him much. Mother never had a great
deal good to say about him. One time I caught her crying over a photo
of him that she kept tucked away in her dresser drawer. She got angry
when I questioned her, so I let it drop. I learned not to ask too many
questions."

"Why did he leave his family like that?"

"Mother said he was untamed, like a renegade cowboy. She said he
refused to try to get a job in an office and work like a civilized man. The
last thing she told me is that he was living in the 'cowboys and Indians'
days like a kid who'd never grown up. Granddad seemed to think he
was a pretty good fellow, that he had tried to change to what mother
wanted but couldn't. I believe good guys don't leave their kids without
a backward glance. He didn't even keep in touch after he left. I never
knew what had become of him or where he went, and didn't know he'd
died until the lawyer contacted me."

"Yes, I remember when we were doing the wedding invitations. I
wonder why he insisted we live here for three years before you would
be allowed to have the money he'd saved." Judith puzzled over the kind
of man who would father such a wonderful son and then abandon him.
Wil never said much, but it obviously hurt. This was the first time he'd
really talked about how his father's abandonment had felt.

"Ten thousand dollars isn't an enormous fortune, but it's a lot more
than we have right now, and more than we could save. It would take
most of our lives to earn that much. Once we get the money, I'll build
you the most beautiful house, with water, a gas washing machine, a

telephone and everything you're going to have to do without for these three years. I'll make it up to you, Judith."

"Oh Wil, you have nothing to make up. I'm here with you because this is where I want to be. It'll be fun. We'll be together. Together we can do anything. In that lovely ceremony we promised for better or worse, for richer for poorer. Well, this is the worse and the poorer. We'll get the better and richer later."

"I believe that too. We'll see what tomorrow brings."

Judith pondered things for a while, and then turned again to Wilson. "The cabin hasn't been lived in for a long time. Your father must have lived here only when he first came. I wonder where he lived before he died, since the lawyer said it was only, what . . . about six months earlier?"

"You're right. The cabin could not have deteriorated this much in such a short time. I don't know any more than you, darlin'. Maybe we'll never know. Perhaps my father will always remain a mystery."

As they lay on the ground cover beneath the canvas tent, lights from a thousand twinkling stars spangled across the heavens, Wilson reached for his wife. He nuzzled her neck, then worked his way to her mouth. She eagerly accepted his caresses, and they made love as enthusiastically as they had before this adventure began. "I've missed this. I've missed you," Wilson murmured.

Only once while travelling had they made love, and the knowing looks of their companions the next morning caused Judith to refuse Wilson's advances until they had privacy. While he tried to change her mind, protesting that others in the company continued their relationships, he knew she was shy. Respecting her need for privacy was trying, however, and he was grateful when the exertion of their journey brought sleep early.

"It's not that I didn't want you to make love to me," she said now. "I just couldn't, not with the other people knowing."

"It's OK, as long as you're fine with me making up for all the times we didn't."

"Enough talk," she said. "Show me."

※

Later, snuggled together, sated with lovemaking, their minds drifted to the events that had brought them so far from home and all that was familiar. The snorts and shuffling of the horse, the croaking frog chorus and the lonesome echoes of wolf song provided a perfect accompaniment to their wandering thoughts.

Judith relived the lovely wedding. Her gown and trousseau were packed away with the wedding gifts, not to be seen for three years. Her thoughts turned then to the Indian people she'd so feared while in Sherridon, and how she'd learned so much from them, and had come to admire them. She really missed their companionship. Especially Sue, she thought.

Wilson's thoughts were on the time they'd spent in the lawyer's office and the events that had brought them to this broken-down cabin. He wondered if he'd ever understand what his father really had been like. He knew his mother well enough to realize her version would be coloured strongly in her own interests.

He had asked her one time why she had married such a wild, irresponsible person. That was the last time he'd questioned her about his father. It was wiser and safer to keep his questions to himself. He thought of the reading of the will, and the lawyer's remarks. There was a mystery here. Things didn't quite add up.

6
Homesteading

Morning sounds of rasping ravens, twittering songbirds, raucous jays and the increasing cacophony of waterfowl gradually replaced the monotonous but soothing frog chorus of the evening. These, plus the snorting of Jazzy, the mare, roused the sleeping couple at sunrise. Jazzy was not the name Jimmy had given her, but Judith had no qualms in renaming her. By now they were used to these wake-up calls. They arose stretching and scrambling to get a fire going for breakfast.

Early morning mists rose, hovering over the rocks and scraggly pines surrounding the cabin. Shimmering sunlight gave the entire scene a utopian aura. "Isn't it great to be alive?" Judith murmured, snuggling up to Wilson and breathing deeply of the moist, pine-scented air. "Doesn't it look just heavenly this morning?"

"It does in this light, but we have a lot of work ahead of us, darlin'."

After a quick, filling meal around the fire, the young couple entered their soon-to-be home once more. Wilson inspected the table and said by adding a fourth leg and cleaning it up it was salvageable. The chair would make firewood, as would the sounder parts of the collapsed roof that hadn't succumbed to rot. The southern wall was a few feet lower than the north one, but little useable material remained of the cabin's once-slanted roof. He wondered aloud if that was the reason it had fallen in so completely. "I think a peaked roof would last longer. What do you think, Judith?"

"It likely would, but if we're only going to be here for three years do we need to do it that way?"

"It would take a lot longer, I think, and be tougher to do. And you're right – a shanty lean-to roof should last longer than three years. We have to think of how much time we'll need to get ready for winter as well. I believe it comes earlier this far north." He spoke his worries aloud.

"OK. That's decided. What say we get this rubble out of our new home?" Judith was eager to get at it. They began sorting out what was salvageable and what was not, the latter ending up being the largest pile by far. A lot of it required the both of them. It was hard, dirty work, accompanied by a lot of grunting and straining, but without a word of complaint.

Once the heaviest work was done he made an announcement. "I'm going to look for sturdy pines that are long enough and straight enough to go across the cabin. I think we should make the north wall a bit higher as well, to help the snow slide off. Otherwise I'll be shovelling off the roof after every storm to keep it from caving in on us."

"You take the rifle with you then, Wilson, in case you run into a bear or something we can eat, OK? Will you take Jazzy as well?"

"No, not this time. Once I have the trees cut I'll need you and Jazzy to get them back here, but Jazzy will stay with you. She'll alert you if anything comes around. You'll have the .22 as well." He pulled Judith's firm body close and pressed his lips hard against hers. "I'll be back well before dark for supper. You make use of this worthless timber to keep a fire going. I'll be worried about you while I'm out there. Hopefully, no more foraging bears will scent our supplies and come looking, but it's best to be safe."

Judith watched her husband's tall form disappear amongst the scrub pines. Taking a deep breath, she entered the cabin. For a moment she stood there, wondering where to start. From outside she heard the mare searching the tender new shoots of grass and mosses and snorting gently from time to time.

Jazzy was an Indian pony, used to eking out a living in the wilderness. The animal would fare well here; Judith wished she could say the same, and wished she were used to such tough conditions this remote location imposed. Even with the largest part of the debris cleared out, the cabin looked far from promising.

Alone, she stood in the mess of what she was supposed to turn into a home. How could she spend three years here? A dirt floor. No one lived on a dirt floor. Even her dad's farm animal buildings had cement or wood for flooring. A window without glass, a door that hung like an old drunk on a corner, no furniture unless she counted a three-legged table and a rotten bed. She was supposed to fix this up so they could actually live here? Could she do this? Was it possible? What if she became pregnant? How could she have a baby out here? How could she raise a child here so far from civilization? Her husband had worked as a medic and an orderly, but he'd never delivered a human baby, or animal either for that matter, and though they both had witnessed animal births she was sure it would not be the same thing. Who could they call on?

Having been raised in a Christian home, Judith turned to prayer whenever things looked bleakest. She prayed for strength and courage, and most of all not to get pregnant until the three years were up.

After her brief prayer, as always, Judith felt renewed strength and determination. She decided to try to see how much of a difference she could make before Wilson returned. Picking up a stick, she dug a mess of dry grasses and mud out of the north wall, but stopped in dismay as a hole opened up to show the world outside, like a peephole. She gasped in consternation, realizing that was how the gaps between the logs had been filled. Knowing it was as good a solution as she could find, she determined to mix up some more to plug the hole she'd created as well as others she could see.

Judith took her teapot pail in hand and hiked down to the creek to get a mixture of gooey bottom sediment and sand. She hauled the mixture back to the cabin and began to collect dry grasses and moss which she mixed into a big mud pie in the centre of the cabin floor, stopping now and then to add more wood to the smouldering fire. She then plugged many holes and reinforced some wobbling globs in the existing holes, packing the mess into spaces that would allow air, mice and other undesirables entrance. By the time her mixture was depleted, Judith was spattered with muck up to her elbows and across her face where she had brushed her hair back. Now she looked and smelled much like her disgusting teapot.

Wondering if she could ever clean it well enough to carry water for drinking and cooking, she picked it up, went to get Jazzy, who snorted a greeting, and headed back to the creek. Jazzy would appreciate a drink, and she needed to clean herself as well as her teapot before Wilson got back.

Judith rinsed her teapot, using clean sand to scour it, and threw the rinse water away from the creek before she allowed the mare to drink. Then she gently led Jazzy down to the water. The little mare sank into the soft mud as it approached the water to drink its fill. Jazzy seemed comfortable in the water, having spent so long wading and swimming with the canoes they had transported from Sherridon, and the water in the creek was a lot warmer than in the lake. Judith thought about Tommy, Sue and her son Jimmy, Georgie Bighawk and shy young bride Libby, Nelson, Bruce, and the rest of the band of Indians who had accompanied them so far on their journey. Tommy had assured them all they had to do was follow the little stream and it would bring them right to the cabin. It had taken the two of them with Jazzy two more trips to carry all the supplies up to the door.

Thinking back, Judith wondered at the reluctance of their native friends to go close to the cabin, but supposed she had only imagined their aversion. Perhaps they hadn't wanted to see disappointment in the young couple once they saw the condition of their new home. Or maybe they really did have to hurry north to the bush where their settlement was to meet the migrating caribou. She chuckled to herself as she remembered the two canoes speeding away from the shore, on their way to catch up to the rest of the band. The journey with the Indian band was not only an adventure but also a learning experience. She'd enjoyed the little children and the two babies as well and the women, elderly and young. They dressed strangely, and their customs were different, but she'd soon felt at ease with them, becoming accustomed to their ways. She smiled as the thought of how different she'd felt at the beginning, dressed like a lady with refined manners, and how they had just accepted her the way she was. It hadn't taken too long before she'd relaxed and joined in the teasing and easy camaraderie of the others. Wilson had adjusted much more easily than she. She'd changed from fearing them to accepting them and finally to admiring their ways of coping with their way of life. Down deep, she thought, all people are just people after all, whether dressed in fine fabrics and sporting the latest hairstyles or wearing long scruffy skirts, shirts and blankets with their dark hair in braids. They certainly knew how to make a living in the wilderness.

Being lost in her thoughts while she cleaned, she wasn't prepared when the mare threw its head back, snorted and began a nervous dance. Jazzy's eyes were wide and rolling while the mud sucked at its feet. Tommy taught her that noise was the best way to drive a bear away. Grabbing her teapot in one hand and the bridle in the other, Judith yelled and banged the pot on a rock, continuing to shout as she forced the nervous animal to accompany her back to the cabin. She heard crashing in the bush behind the cabin, the noise extra loud in the eerie silence that usually surrounded this isolated spot. Whatever the creature was, it sounded awfully big. Judith's heart was hammering like a runaway train in her chest. She continued to make as much racket as she could, banging the tea pail on rocks and yelling. The little mare was becoming as fearful of her as it was of the unknown animal.

Back at the camp Judith tied the mare and fetched the .22 before she threw several pieces of wood on the fire and stoked it much higher. She watched as the skittish Jazzy slowly settled and began to graze once more. She listened intently, but the only sounds she heard were the birds twittering, the wind moaning through the pines and the mare's mowing and chewing. Gradually realizing the danger was past, Judith relaxed. Seeing by the sun's descent behind the westerly trees that it was getting late, she dug out the frying pan, lowered the provisions from the tree and put some dried meat and onion flakes, dehydrated vegetables and rice on to boil slowly, as she waited for Wilson's return. She inhaled the tantalizing aroma of the cooking meal rising from the pot, ignoring the smell of Jazzy's piles of manure that mingled with the scent of pine, juniper and sage.

After taking a good, long look at the mare, Judith decided the animal had relaxed enough for a quick, safe trip to the creek for more water. She set the pan back from the main part of the fire. Deciding to move silently while listening for any commotion from Jazzy, Judith steeled her nerves and rushed to the creek. As she clambered up the slippery path back to the fire, her heart skipped a beat and she bit her lip to keep from crying as she heard the whistling of a lively tune. Wilson was back.

Thank heavens she was no longer alone, but it wouldn't do for him to see how unnerved she was. Judith rushed to the fire, placed the deep frying pan directly over the burning embers, and, taking a deep breath, turned with a smile to greet her mate. As he approached, she could not stop herself from running to him. He caught her close and snuggled for a moment before drawing back.

"Why, darlin' you're soaking wet. Did you fall in the creek? And what is this mucky-looking stuff across your cheek? What've you been up to?"

"Just you wait until you see what I've been doing, Mr. Daniels, just you wait. I'm so glad you're back." After another long hug, Judith drew back. "Did you find many good trees, Wil?"

"Well, not too many, but enough I think. Trees are pretty stunted and wind-stressed around here, but I think we can manage with what I did find. If not, we'll have to trek farther south to get more. We'll have to figure out a way to fill in the spaces between the rafters I put across. Is that stew I smell? I'm hungry enough to eat a bear."

7
Wolf Family

Cold light from the pale spring moon cast indistinct shadows on the still partially frozen earth, illuminating a large silvery form as it separated from the ground and stretched, nose testing the slight northerly breeze. A thousand odours wafted his way – scents he sorted with ease.

His mate stirred to complete wakefulness, rose awkwardly and stretched beside him. Her belly was swollen with pups soon to enter the world and join their lupine parents. A ripple of excitement stirred her blood as her mate, pale as an apparition, pointed his muzzle toward the thin high clouds and raised his voice in song. She joined him in chorus, their voices complementing each other and sounding like many more than only the two of them.

Wolf song, the song of the north, wavered high and low – long, curling notes stirring apprehension within the breasts of small night creatures. Five miles north, a huge moose raised his head and, snorting, flapped his ears before moving into deeper water.

The darker female licked her mate's muzzle then lowered her head, exposing the nape of her neck to his caresses, her tail wagging. After a few minutes the two wolves set out on the trail of a substantial meal. He knew she would soon take to her den to whelp and he would be alone to hunt until the pups were strong enough to survive without her constant presence. It was important that they find a large enough animal to feed them both for a time. A pair of wolves hunting could easily take a large prey against which a single wolf would have no chance.

Within a quarter of an hour the pair of timber wolves reached the marsh where the large bull moose regarded them askance. He knew he had nothing to fear from these two predators as long as he stayed in the water. He lowered his bulbous nose into the muskeg and came up snorting water, trailing fresh green shoots from his mouth, the liquid streaming from the vegetation and his muzzle. His tail swished and the skin along his flanks flinched, unseating scores of hungry insects. He shook his head, snorted again, flipping his ears and eying the wolves.

The pair of wolves continued, following the water's edge, heads raised to test the air. Again they scented moose, but with a difference this time, and waded across the shallow marsh to the island situated in the centre. The female had to swim part way, as her legs were not as long as his. They circled cautiously, coming upwind upon a cow moose about to give birth. The labouring cow had sensed their approach and turned nervously to run, but the huge white form launched itself, slicing the hamstring muscle of her right hind leg.

She floundered, bawling her fear and frustration. Striking in desperation with her sharp front hooves, she connected with the side of the darker wolf, and watched it tumble away from her. Before she could follow up by trampling the smaller form of the dark wolf, the white one had her throat. The cow lowered her head, and then thrust it high in the air, twisting, trying to dislodge the clinging, wraith-like form that gripped like a second skin. Thrashing desperately, she managed to connect again with the darker wolf and heard it yelp in pain once, before her front legs gave way and she ceased to struggle. One last rattling breath shuddered within, and then all was still.

Again, the dark female whined. Releasing his hold on the cow's throat, the male slipped over to where his mate lay panting on the trampled, muddy ground. He kissed her nose and accepted a return caress. Waiting and watching as his mate struggled to her feet, he silently supported her as she approached the fallen cow. Licking at the blood leaking from the ripped throat seemed to give her strength, and she knelt to feed, whining once or twice as she tore flesh from the carcass.

Once assured of his mate's condition, the male fed as well. The tender belly was ripped open, and the heart and liver devoured immediately. Then they set about gnawing the flesh from her haunches. Between the two predators, they managed to strip about 50 pounds of meat from the body of the moose before stretching out to sleep. She was restless, her sleep fitful, and it was not long before she arose determined to head toward the spot she had chosen for a den several weeks earlier.

It was 15 miles distant, and she had to cross the marshy area surrounding the island where they'd killed the pregnant cow moose. The male rose to follow.

She barely made it to the den before her strength gave out. The male waited by the mouth of the den, hearing her moans, whines and yelps. He waited, not knowing quite what to do, and howled mournfully, unsure exactly why he felt the need to do so. Once he poked his head in through the opening, but snarls and gnashing of her teeth assured him his presence was not welcome.

All night and on into the next day she struggled alone in the den, while he patrolled outside and intermittently raised his head in a long, mournful howl, hoping to encourage her. Finally he heard the whimpers of a youngster. He arose and paced back and forth, waiting. All was silent within. Then at last he heard another sound of a pup's snuffling breathing and the mother's coaxing whines.

The next evening she emerged from the den, thin and limping, carrying the small lifeless body of a cream-coloured male pup. She laid it down and licked it gently. He understood. Tenderly he took the tiny body in his mouth and trotted away from the den to bury it. He returned to find her waiting with the black body of a small female. This process was repeated four times, as he buried the bodies of three sons and his daughter. The fourth time he returned, his mate was in the den and did not come out. He sat outside, raised his voice toward the inky heavens and sent wavering notes of sorrow echoing through the wilderness.

❋

In the morning he again heard the snuffling sounds of a pup. This time it was nursing. He pushed his head into the den and was greeted by a snarling mate. Jerking back in surprise, he squatted outside the den, head cocked to one side in a quizzical pose, ears forward. With a short woof, he headed northward to the site of their latest kill. His long strides covered the 15 miles with ease, his effortless loping pace eroding the distance.

As he arrived at the island, a flock of feeding ravens arose, squawking their displeasure. He smelled coyote and fox. Both had been eating from the cow moose's carcass. The belly with the entrails was gone and little remained of the upper front and hind parts. Rich brown hair and some of her bones were strewn around, and the nearly bare ribcage extended eerily; a persistence of lung tissue waved disconsolately in the breeze. The head remained, but the eyes had been pecked out by the birds, and blowflies buzzed around in the warm sun, crawling in and out of the eye sockets and nostrils as well as the body cavity.

There was no sign of the calf, but there was still plenty to eat. He consumed more than his fill, engorging his abdomen with meat for his mate for he would regurgitate his stomach contents for her. Once replete with as much meat as he could pack into his stomach, he proceeded to urinate near the body, scratching the scent over what remained and attempting to bury the largest portion to keep it from ravens and other thieves.

Content to wait until she decided it was time for him to meet the sole living pup of the litter, he crossed the water separating the island from the mainland and carried his swollen belly back towards the den, a portion of meat clamped in his jaws.

8
Bear Summer

Very early one mid-April morning, Wilson and Judith were awakened by screams of rage and fear from the mare. As he kicked off the bedroll, Wilson reached for his rifle. By the faint light of a pale moon and countless stars, he spotted the large form of a bear rearing beside the terrified horse that was yanking at the tether and screaming. As he rushed out of the tent, his foot caught and he fell, hearing the rifle blast as he went down.

With a roar, the bear turned toward him, arriving just as Wilson scrambled to his feet. The speed of the enraged animal carried it past him, hitting the man with its shoulder and again knocking him to the ground. From his supine position Wilson fired again as the bear ripped the tent. He heard Judith scream just before he fired the gun.

He pumped another shell into the rifle as the bear spun toward him and rose towering over him as he lay on the ground. Wilson fired at the bear's huge form, rolling away as the massive shaggy body came crashing down in the exact spot he had been.

Judith was screaming for Wilson, and Jazzy was squealing, rearing and snorting as the sound of the rifle's blast echoed off in the distance. Wilson heard none of it. The last shot of the rifle had been so close to his head that he was momentarily deafened. As he felt Judith's trembling hands moving over his face and body, he sat up and wrapped his arms around her. He could feel her sobbing. Her hands cupped his face before continuing to frantically explore his body.

"Hush, darlin', it's over. I'm all right." He was bemused to note in some part of his mind that he could not hear his own voice. He captured her roving hands and kissed them. "I'm fine. I'm not hurt, Judith."

As he continued to soothe Judith, his hearing slowly returned and he was relieved to hear Jazzy. When the gun went off as he fell the first time he feared he had killed their horse. He didn't know how badly she was hurt, but she was still alive at any rate.

"Let's see to Jazzy, darlin'. I don't know if she's hurt or just plain scared."

They helped each other to their feet and moved toward the terrified animal. As Wilson reached for the mare, Jazzy jerked away, squealing. "I'll get a fire going so we have more light here. You try to calm her down, but don't get too close."

As Wilson started a fire, Judith spoke soothingly to the horse, but it continued to snort and pull against the tether. As the flames chased the darkness, they could see blood trickling down Jazzy's right front leg from four long gashes in her shoulder. "That looks pretty nasty, doesn't it? I'll get out the medical case and see what I can do for her." The mare continued to pull against the tether, the whites of her eyes reflecting firelight. She was rearing and squealing, her front feet pawing the air.

Once he managed to take her to the rear of the cabin away from the sight of her attacker, Wilson got the mare calmed down and was able to attend to her wounds, with Judith carrying a flaming torch so he could see what he was doing. Judith kept reassuring Jazzy with gentle words of encouragement. Later she had no idea what she had been repeating, but it seemed to do the trick. Over and over again in her mind her words to Jimmy replayed. *We'll take good care of her, Jimmy. I promise.* If the mare didn't recover, what would it do to their rocky relationship with Sue's son? Would he include her in his unreasoning hatred?

Using the torch as a light, Wilson and Judith went to the edge of the lake to get cleaned up. Wilson was covered with blood from the mare and mud from rolling on the ground, and both of them were chilled to the bone. Once the excitement and exertion were over, they built up the fire again and crowded close to it. The eastern horizon lightened as a new day approached, chasing darkness to the western reaches.

"I know a much better way to warm up," Wilson murmured into Judith's ear. He led her into the torn tent, stepping away from the bear's carcass. "I really need some loving."

The next time they left the tent, the sun was high, the air around the tent reeked of bear, and there was only a thin line of acrid smoke eddying from their huge bonfire of the previous night.

"We have to get a corral made for Jazzy, darlin'. She didn't have a chance against that bear, and a cougar could get her very easily, not to mention wolves. In a corral she could at least run around and we'd hear her before anything too bad happened."

"Yes, we need to take good care of her. I promised Jimmy. We have to move into the cabin, even though we haven't built the roof yet. I'm not spending another night just in the tent." Judith had made up her mind and was determined not to budge.

"About moving into the cabin I agree, but as far as Jimmy goes, he was very well paid for the mare and she belongs to us. The reason we need to protect her is because she's ours and we really need her. It has nothing to do with Tommy's miserable grandson. I'll have that door repaired today, and as soon as Jazzy's fit, we'll get the north wall built up a bit more and get a roof on. We still have to sleep in the tent, but we'll set it up inside the cabin until we have it ready for us to live in."

They had to deal with the bear carcass. Wilson decided to skin it, or at least he'd try. He'd skinned enough muskrats over the years trapping with his cousins, but this creature was huge, heavy and rank. Pausing for a moment, he surveyed the task before him, and remembered the animals he'd skinned – so many rats, and once a mink. He chuckled, remembering his pride when he'd saved enough from the sale of pelts and gopher tails to buy his own gun and some ammunition. He wondered if the old .22 were still at Uncle Mac's farm.

Well, he thought, the bear awaited. He cut around the paws, after deciding that keeping them wouldn't be worth the effort. He slit the hide down the belly from the chin to the anus, and then cut the underside of each leg to his cut around the paws.

Because the bear was big and heavy, he asked Judith for help. She looked at him, then at the carcass. "Why don't you tie the legs to trees for support? I don't want anything to do with that." She then busied herself with packing up all the supplies to move inside the cabin.

Wilson wisely said nothing. Taking her advice, he tied the legs on one side of the bear to a couple of spruce trees, and then hoisted it up off the ground on the one side. He was able then to separate the sinews holding the hide onto the musculature of each limb. He managed to give himself several nicks with the knife, none of which went too deeply. As soon as the skin was off the suspended legs, he struggled with the belly, and managed to sever the connecting tissue enough so that it was even with the leg hide. Next, he raised the carcass higher with the ropes. He began to pull the hide from the bear's back. Sweat was running down into his eyes, and he scowled as he brushed his sleeve across his forehead.

Ravens and magpies watched his antics from perches in the surrounding evergreens. Wilson wasn't sure whether their calls were an attempt to encourage him or if they were merely laughing at his efforts.

"If you know so much why don't you come and help?" he called out to them.

Judith heard and came to investigate. "Who are you talking to?" she asked.

"Them." He indicated the feathered audience. "This is a lot harder than I thought it was going to be."

"Well, I'm impressed. You have it half done already. How will you do the other side?"

"Hey, I did my half. The other one is yours."

"Oh, no. I'll leave it for the birds. I've never skinned anything in my life, and I'm not starting with that bear. Anyway, everyone knows the one who kills the animal gets to skin it. I have to get back to moving into our rural residence." And with that as her parting remark, Judith returned to the cabin to struggle with the removal of the one-time bed.

Wilson decided to finish, as tempting as it was becoming to abandon the task he'd set himself. He lowered the side he'd hung from the trees, tugged the carcass end for end so the opposite side was facing the bush, and suspended the remaining legs. It didn't take too long to accomplish the hide removal on this other side, and he only cut through the hide twice. He decided it was better to cut the hide than himself, and proceeded to attempt to remove the skin from the head. He'd seen bear hides with the head attached, mouths open and looking very impressive, but it wasn't long before he gave up and settled for a strip of face fur down the centre to the nose. Though he had been tempted to give up so many times during this task, he knew they would need to use whatever nature provided for them, and he was sure the hide would come in handy somewhere down the road.

Tommy had told them the lean and tender meat of a young bear, especially a young female, was delicious and made excellent pemmican as it was lean and tender. Although they knew this was not a young female but a mature male, they decided to try it. Once the skin was off, Wilson removed a roast from the thigh. They cut off strips to fry, but found the taste was too strong, with tough, stringy meat and a pronounced gamey flavour. They ended up burning the carcass, as they could not haul it away, except in chunks, and Jazzy was too terrified to tow it. The burning flesh smelled fairly appetizing, but they knew it was inedible except to the scavenging birds that managed to score a few free meals. Leaving the meat close to camp would encourage predators, yet burying it would be virtually impossible when the land was mostly rock.

Judith helped him build a frame stretcher on which they mounted the bearskin and propped it into the smoke from their fires whenever a wind was blowing. They knew if they didn't do something the hide would rot, and smoking was the only solution they could devise.

Together they built a sizeable corral for the horse, using rocks, logs, and standing trees. It was not attractive by any means, but it would be serviceable as protection for the horse and it would keep her confined. Once they put her into the corral, she was able to trot around and exercise her sore front shoulder so it wouldn't get too stiff.

May came and went, bringing longer days and maddening, buzzing hordes of mosquitoes, blackflies and deer flies. The only real deterrent was a smoky fire. They had to build smudges for the horse as well. Judith despaired of ever smelling like a lady again. More and more their odour resembled that of the bear hide. At night they draped netting across the portion of the cabin's interior where they slept, and that was helpful during the night. During the day they swatted continually until, maddened beyond endurance, they sought the smoky fire. Judith prayed they could last until the roof was up and the window was covered.

Wilson was impressed with the way she had chinked the cracks and holes in the walls. He helped with the gaps she was unable to reach, and soon the cabin's walls were weatherproof. Yet in the heat of the day, when the sun beat down and no breeze gained entrance, the cabin was unbearable. At night the air was stifling. Only their exhaustion allowed them to sleep.

With the long warm days of June came wood ticks. They were vexing to Judith, who could not seem to overcome her squeamishness where the small beetles were concerned. She decided that mosquitoes and flies were preferable because at least she could hear and feel their presence, while a tick could swell with her blood before she knew it. Slapping at them had no effect, as they flattened their bodies and clung tightly, like scabs. Digging with fingernails worked better. Wilson calmly removed them and placed them in the fire or picked them apart. Judith screamed, slapped and usually ended up crying as Wilson removed and destroyed the offending creature. He never made fun of her, and he tried to assure her that in time she would get used to them and be able to kill them the way he did. Judith could not see that happening. She said she was less scared of a bear than a wood tick. Wilson believed her.

As Jazzy's leg continued to improve, Wilson and Judith planned the roof raising they would need to do, but in the meantime they spent hours of toil hauling leaf mould from the forest, sand and mud from the river, and what little soil they found to make a garden patch for the seeds they had brought along. Their canned and dried goods were being used faster than they had anticipated, and they knew there was a long, cold winter to survive just ahead of them.

Judith, being raised on a farm, knew more than Wilson about food production and preservation, but she worried too that their supplies were diminishing too quickly. A garden would be one solution, hunting up natural produce another, and though it meant a lot of work, she felt it was possible.

"Do you remember how Tommy and his people reacted when they saw how much food and supplies we brought with us?" he asked. "Now I'm afraid we don't even have enough to last until next summer."

"Sue told me of the things their people ate. We need to start using what is here. I can plant the garden by myself. You should go hunting and see if you could get some meat. We can dry it the way Sue told me, and we have a natural icebox, a few feet below the surface."

Wilson took her advice and went looking for food in the forest. He brought along his shotgun, hoping for small game, but strapped on his rifle in case he saw a deer or moose. He made so much noise with the dry debris underfoot that larger game left the area, but he did manage to kill a grouse and a male mallard duck. He hated to have worried Judith about their food supply, but they had to be realistic. Somehow, they had to lay in provisions for themselves as well as for their horse.

It seemed every day that passed, the more he came to fear that they had untaken a much larger task than they were going to be able to manage. He was the man of the family, the proverbial breadwinner. It was his responsibility to provide for Judith. He wished they had bought excess service rations. They had been the perfect option for light travel

and sustenance. At the time, however he'd vowed never to eat another
bully beef, dried biscuit, canned cheese, cereal bar or bullion powder.

June and July were long days of toil, and short nights of exhausted sleep.
At least the cabin had a roof. The long poles reached across the roof
from north to south, with an overhang above the south wall in which
the reinforced door stood solidly, blocking forced entry from outside.
Over the long timbers Wilson spread pine boughs, weaving them this
way and that, building a fairly solid though springy roof over which
their tent stretched, and though it didn't cover the entire area, it certainly helped. They used the two canvasses that, together with the tent,
nearly covered the entire length and width of the roof. The material was
anchored with more poles around its perimeter to keep it from blowing
away, and pine boughs covered it from the sun. Wilson did not want
to nail it down, in case they needed the canvas again for something
else. Netting covered the window on fair days, and one of Judith's white
shirts was used to keep out wind, but not driven rain, which seeped in,
dripping where the two canvasses and the tent walls met.

Wilson had tried to make a wooden floor, but with only a handsaw
and axe he found it more work than he had bargained for, and they
ended up spreading pine needles over the packed earthen floor instead.
It provided a sweet-smelling carpet that was easier to keep clean, and
it protected them from the inevitable mud that would form whenever
there was a lengthy rainy spell. This carpet was changed whenever it
became too packed or dirty.

It was a rough dwelling, completely unlike the houses they were used
to. Even in the mining town of Sherridon the buildings were painted
and covered with shiplap siding and had real shingled roofs. Annie's
rough 12-by-28 (which was what the houses were called, referring to
their dimensions) now seemed like a palace compared to the cabin in
which Judith was living. The cabin's inside walls were rough, and the

cupboard was made of boxes in which their supplies had been packed. It added an extension to the original cupboard of which Wilson had repaired the doors, using strips of canvas for hinges. He had replaced the missing table leg and made rough chairs from willows. There was also a bench made from a log that he chopped fairly thin and supported on poles sharpened and forced into the holes he dug in the underside.

They slept on pine boughs laid over the bags of oats and flour, with their bedrolls on top. When it was chilly they used one of the rolls as a blanket. On the west wall, over the bed, they nailed the bear hide, where it looked rather fitting. Judith objected to the smell, which still clung to the fur, though having had it stretched out in the trees and smoked by the campfire kept out insects and added a tangy odour to the smell of bear. Wilson had spent a lot of time scraping all the flesh from it. There wasn't any fat, since it hadn't been long out of hibernation, but the hide remained hard and stiff, and was unusable for anything beyond insulation.

One night brought near disaster. They had both been in the deep sleep of exhaustion, when Judith was wakened by Wilson's whimpers and his restless movements. Suddenly he screamed, and just as she reached out to him, he towered over her in the bed, both hands locked around her throat. A sudden explosion in the fireplace caused him to whirl toward the sound, and Judith began gasping for breath. "Wil. Wilson, it's OK," she croaked.

"Oh my God, Judith. Are you OK? Oh my God, I could have killed you, Judith. I'm so sorry. Are you OK?"

Judith nodded her head just as Wilson broke down into great gasping, heaving sobs. He pressed his head against her shoulder, trembling with emotion. Judith held him, rubbing her hand over his shoulders and head and whispering comforting sounds.

Once he'd regained control, Wilson sat up and said, "I could have killed you. Maybe we'd better sleep apart."

"No. That's not the answer. You need to talk to me. Tell me what was going on in your mind. It was the war, wasn't it?" At his nod she continued. "Tell me about it, Wil. It'll help."

For a while he sat looking at her serious face, the face he loved so well, saying nothing. Then he slowly shook his head. "Judith, I've been to hell. I can't tell you about it. It's . . . it's . . . I can't explain it to you. I saw things, terrible things, things you cannot imagine. I heard sounds that I can't even describe, smells that are beyond description. Things are burned into my brain, into my soul, and there's no way I can undo them. There is no way. Telling you about it won't help me. It eats at me, sneaks into my dreams. If I share them with you I won't lose them, but you'll bear them with me, and two twisted souls is not the answer. I can't bear to share the horror with you. That's why I spent so much time on the way here talking to Nelson and Bruce. They know. They've been twisted as well. Do you understand what I'm saying?"

"I'm trying to, Wil."

"It's like you are this clear pool of sweet water and we've been filled with putrid waste. If I pour some of my filth into you, I'll still have it, but you will too."

In answer, Judith wrapped her arms around him and held him close. "I think I begin to understand. I'm so sorry you had to go through what the war did to you. I wish there was a way to undo it. I can't, but can I at least try to help you live with it?"

"You do."

And they snuggled together back into bed for what remained of that night.

Wilson continued to skin and stretch every fur-bearing creature he killed, using skills he'd learned from his Uncle Mac during the times he stayed with his cousins. He found himself drawing more and more upon his own ingenuity to create what he didn't have, such as the stretchers he made from willow branches.

Raccoons, rabbits, birds and squirrels took a toll on the garden. Judith hung tin can lids and strips of brightly coloured rags in and around it. That worked for a while, especially when the wind was blowing, but on calm days the pests raided their small patch. "All our hard work, and we'll be lucky to even have anything to eat ourselves," Judith raged. "We should have just eaten the seeds."

"I prefer to think we're fattening up the livestock so we can eat them," Wilson replied, attempting to lighten the situation. He understood her frustration, but realized getting angry didn't help. He knew that some of the garden was doing well. But they had worked so hard to get this far, and they depended on the fruits of their labour to survive, and the garden was Judith's pride and joy. Judith looked at him, not saying anything. "You've done well so far with the garden, darlin'. I'll see what I can do to protect it." The long hours of daylight seemed to coax their produce from the skimpy soil much faster than he had ever seen before. "It's as though the sun is pulling the shoots up on a string," he said. The corn and peas did not fare well, as the wildlife got them, the lettuce and radishes never materialized, but the onions, carrots, rutabagas and beets were flourishing. Besides, he thought, they were fortunate to have a garden at all with the amount of work the cabin had taken.

"I hate to share the vegetables with wildlife. We need them for ourselves," Judith said.

"The raiding rabbits have provided some meat for our stew pot and you've stored some, haven't you?" he asked. "And see how nice they've added to our pelt collection?" He pointed to the numerous inside-out hides he'd hung on handmade stretchers along the south wall between the door and their bedroom.

Judith nodded. "I dried rabbit meat, along with some other meat you've caught, but we need more than meat to survive. We need the vegetables. I was so hoping for carrots and peas. As far as the lettuce, we'll keep on trying out the leaves that grow here to see which ones are good to eat." She turned to Wilson. "I'm glad you cheer me up when I just feel like screaming."

Wilson put his arms around her and nuzzled her neck, whispering into her ear, "You do the same for me. We work well together."

One rainy day in August, Judith turned to Wilson as a thought crossed her mind. "Wilson, honey, what do you think your father would say if he saw this cabin now?"

"Well, I really don't know, darlin', but I can sure imagine what my mother would say."

Judith laughed. "Mine, too. But it's not so bad is it? I mean we're fairly dry, and after a few days the wet spots on the roof will dry out. The fireplace is great. And we have each other."

Wilson pulled her down onto the bed pile, and the next hour was spent rediscovering the best places on each other's bodies for intimate caresses. Judith pulled back long enough to say, "Thank the Lord above for these rainy days. It is the only time we have to spend together not working."

"Oh, there's work I could be doing, but nothing that gives me this much satisfaction." Then the time for talking was over, and together they reached heights of passion that left them relaxed and content, listening to the rain pattering against their shelter and dozing within each other's embrace.

9

Companions

September brought shorter days, longer evenings and more time spent together, working hard and sharing their love and dreams. Onions hung in long braids from the roof along with smoked meats and fish. As well as onions, they harvested rutabagas, beets and carrots from the garden, and stored them in a root cellar Wil had built in the northeast corner in the cabin. He had dug down almost to the permafrost, and layered in many thicknesses of cattail leaves, before placing the vegetables inside. These were covered with more cattail leaves and pine boughs inside a rough box that doubled as additional seating on the inside corner of the cabin, protected from frost and heat alike.

Against the north side of the cabin, not too far from the chimney, Wilson had dug a three-foot hole down into the permafrost, which they used to preserve meat and other provisions, and on the inside he dug a trench to reach them without going outside. A flat rock covered it inside, over a mat of woven cattail leaves stuffed with seed fluff to keep the cold from entering their dwelling. Outside, a pile of rocks and branches mounded the top of the excavation. He and Judith had gathered as much of the native grasses as they could in hopes it would keep Jazzy fed through the winter. They still used the oats as their mattress as they were saving them to supplement Jazzy's winter feed. They also stored cattail cuttings, particularly the white part that grew underwater. They knew it would likely not be palatable for humans after storage;

perhaps, though, the mare could eat them. Freshly gathered, they were quite good eaten raw or lightly boiled when added to the cooking pot. This was one of the many things Tommy and Sue had taught them on their trip together from Sherridon.

Jazzy had grown a thick, shaggy winter coat, but Judith and Wilson made a lean-to shelter for her, a shelter she used only on the coldest, wettest days.

Firewood was stacked against the east wall of the cabin, with another cord along the corral. The trees here were mostly coniferous – fur, pine, and spruce, with willow, birch and aspen competing for space and soil. Aspen burned fast and hot, birch was a slower, longer-burning wood, while the conifers, though plentiful, tended to throw a shower of sparks as they burned, sending perfumed heat through the room.

October 8th, by the calendar Judith and Wil kept, became a red-letter day for the Daniels. They had visitors. Tommy Lightfoot, his daughter Sue, and her son, Jimmy, Charlie Big Hawk and Libby, along with two young men called Louis and Ben, stopped by loaded with fur and meat on their return from the northern hunting expedition. The rest of the band had gone on ahead of them with the balance of the caribou hunt.

Tommy and the women entered the cabin with Wil and Judith, but the young men preferred to remain outside. Jimmy had entered briefly, lifted the end of the stiff bear hide, and snorted his derision as he went back outside.

"I guess Jimmy doesn't think much of my bear hide," Wilson observed. "Tell me, Tommy, how do you get the hide to soften up?"

"You get your woman to chew on it, like the people of the north do," Tommy offered.

"It is going to stay hard and stiff then," Judith retorted.

"He is joking. We tan our hides to soften them." Sue smiled shyly. "Did no one ever teach you how to tan hides?"

As Judith shook her head, Wilson said, "Neither of us had any idea what to do with them," referring to the numerous pelts of squirrel, rabbit, raccoon and fox held open with bent willow branches and displayed on the walls. "We've never tanned anything but our own skin outside in the sun. How is it done?" Wilson wanted to learn all he could to prove he could thrive in the wilderness. This cabin was comfortable, but it had only the one room, and was very primitive, not at all what he wanted Judith to have for a home, even for just three years.

"Save the brains. There is always just enough, for every hide you get. You would need to soak this hide to get all the dirt and blood out. I see you have scraped it, but there is a lot more on here that needs to come off." Tommy was looking at the underside of the bear hide.

"How long and where would I soak it, and what happens next?"

"In the river where water is running. Keep it down with rocks or something will eat it. Move the rocks every day. Then stretch it out and scrape it. Keep it a bit wet, but not too much. Then work mashed brains and fat into it. You have to work it in a lot. You leave it overnight. Next day work the brains in again. Three days you do this and stretch it and shake it, and dry it. You stretch it over a pole, back and forth," he said, demonstrating the way, "then you smoke it. Smoke keeps it soft. Keeps bugs out." This was the first time Tommy had spoken so much. He sat quietly for some time after.

Judith turned to Sue. "Have you tanned hides, Sue?"

"I have helped my mother and my grandmother. It is hard work."

"Everything out here is hard work." Judith could not keep the note of despair from her voice.

"But you have done well, my girl." Sue gestured to the tidy cabin's comfortable interior. "We can help with the window. Jimmy has a nice hide that would cover it well. It will be warmer for the winter. I will ask him for it."

Wilson overheard. "Thanks Sue, but we don't want to take advantage. I can just board up the window for the winter. It doesn't let light in anyway the way it is. I haven't done it yet, because when we get a nice day the netting works fine, keeping out insects but letting in light."

"The hide will be less confining, and it will allow an escape if you ever need to get out and the door is barred," Sue said. "I will ask for the hide."

"I never thought about the need to escape, but that is something to keep in mind. I don't mean to sound ungrateful, Sue, but Jimmy, well, he seems to have taken a real dislike to me, and I hate to be asking him for favours."

"You are not asking; I am. It is for Judith." Sue was insistent.

He capitulated, but with conditions.

"Maybe he will trade for this." Wilson offered one of his good skinning knives. He did not want a handout from the scornful young man, and would have refused, but did not want to offend Sue. It was a generous offer.

Sue took the knife and went outside to talk to Jimmy. Luckily, she had taken her warm robe, as it was a while before she returned. When she came back inside, she held out the soft hide, with a smile. "It is cured well so it will stay soft, even if it gets wet."

"Oh, thank you. And please, thank your son for us." Judith accepted the roll with a warm smile, rubbing her hand along the smooth, soft leather. "It's beautiful."

"I want to fish through the ice this winter, Tommy. Will the fish bite?" Wilson turned to his friend.

"They might."

"Any tricks you can give me?"

"Cut the hole big enough for the fish you want to catch. It goes best when the sun is highest. Use the hook I gave you. Use raw meat or pieces of fish for bait."

"Did you get many good hides up north?"

"Quite a few."

"All caribou?"

"Mostly."

"What other kinds, Tommy?"

"Bobcat, muskrat, a few good beaver, fox, but mostly caribou."

"Can we leave some of the caribou meat with these people?" Sue asked Tommy.

"We will leave some."

"Where are you going with the hides? Will you sell them?" He was thinking he might be able to get some pelts this winter to sell if there was a market for them. Some of the rabbits and squirrel pelts on the walls were caught with his snares. He could set snares this winter, when the furs would be in a more prime condition.

As a kid, he had run a trapline with his cousins several winters, and they had made enough money to buy themselves each a gun and some ammunition. He remembered how grown-up he'd felt, buying something of which his mother did not approve, with money he'd earned by his own labours. His mother would never have agreed to purchase him a gun, but she couldn't stop him from owning what he had earned through his own efforts, and he made sure to leave it at his uncle's farm.

"At Sherridon, the man takes our furs and hides. He sends them to the big city. He trades us for supplies and traps and stretchers. We can make our own, but this is faster. We sell caribou meat, too."

"Judith, we'll have to add that to our list of things we need when we go back to Sherridon. I wish we had some now. I could trap this winter and we'd have a bit more money for supplies." Turning to Tommy, Wil added, "I sure wish I knew how to make traps and stretchers myself. I can set snares well enough."

Tommy left Wilson several handmade traps and stretchers, explaining how to make them, admiring the ones he had fashioned, and showing him how to improve upon them. He added a few of the factory-made ones they had gotten from the trading post. Wilson agreed to settle up with him when Tommy's people made the northern trek once more, although Tommy protested the ammunition Wilson had provided before more than paid for what he'd given.

While Sue, Libby and Judith remained inside the cabin, Wilson, Tommy and Charlie went out to join the other men and build a storage area for the caribou meat. They stowed some of it in the storage cairn on the north side of the cabin. There was sufficient meat to necessitate creating another cache a few yards from the front of the cabin, close to a big old pine. A log roof and heavy rocks would keep scavengers out. It was cold enough now that the meat would stay frozen, without digging far down into the permanently frozen layer below the surface.

Nelson helped with the excavation, while Bruce and Charlie went to cut timber to build the box. Tommy was supervising while Jimmy was walking around, surveying the work Wilson and Judith had done over the summer and inspecting Jazzy's shoulder.

He spent considerable time with the little mare, and when he returned to where the others were busily constructing a meat cache, he spoke to his grandfather in the language of their people. Tommy, busy with a hammer, responded in English. "Ask Wilson. He'll tell you."

Jimmy spoke again in his native tongue.

Tommy stopped what he was doing, put down his hammer and looked Jimmy in the eye. "You want to know? Ask Wilson. I don't know, and I don't want to know. You ask."

Jimmy found other things to occupy his attention, and Wilson ignored him, until finally the young man burst out, "What happened to the mare? Her shoulder's been hurt."

Wilson straightened up, looked at the younger man, ignored the anger reflected in his face and said, "That bear hide's what's left of the one that attacked her." He returned to work, ignoring Jimmy completely. Whatever the fellow's problem was, Wilson wasn't pandering to his bad mood. Out of the corner of his eye, he saw Jimmy stride toward the creek where their canoes were beached.

Back in the cabin, Sue also gave Judith some pemmican, explaining it would keep well inside and would be handier. "You can eat like it is, or throw it in a pot of boiling water and make a good stew with it. Like the old people did. Tex learned to like it. He even learned how to make it. Your man Wilson reminds me a lot of Tex, my girl."

"Tex?" Judith questioned.

"My husband. He hadn't eaten pemmican before we met. He didn't say much about it at first, but he came to enjoy it."

Judith remembered eating pemmican as they made the trek to the cabin site many months before, and though it was not her favourite food, she did recognize the value of its portability and nourishment. She asked Sue how to make it.

"Dry your meat well, then pound it into a powder. Mix it with fat and berries and it will keep for a very long time. It is light to carry and is very good food."

"How long has it been, Sue, since you've been alone?"

"Over a year now. It seems much less than that."

"You must miss him a lot," Judith said, noticing moisture fill Sue's eyes.

"I do. We were together for 21 years. Seeing Wilson reminds me of the good times we shared. You are lucky, my girl. Enjoy these days with your husband, even the disagreements." Sue had a twinkle in her eye.

The next morning, when their friends left before the sun was up, Judith could not help feeling abandoned. She stood, waving bravely, refusing to submit to the tears she could feel prickling her eyes as the small party left. Since the waterways were freezing up now, they would have to walk most of the long distance to Sherridon, and until the land was frozen solid there would be many detours. Biting her lip, and turning back to the warmth of the cabin, Judith felt like a prisoner, a lonely prisoner.

Once back inside, Wilson was enthusiastically going over the traps and stretchers Tommy had left behind. He was sure he could make some like Tommy had, and was planning to go out as soon as it was light enough to get the best materials. He was whistling cheerfully and did not notice the stiff set of Judith's back and shoulders as she stood in front of her cupboard, surveying its meagre contents, trying to stifle her sobs.

Lord, I need your help now, before I say something I shouldn't. I don't want Wil to see how unhappy I am. I hate this country. I hate it. I wish we had never come here. Help me, Lord; help me, she prayed silently over and over.

"How about that, darlin'? I'm going to become a trapper. If we're lucky we'll have lots of pelts to trade for supplies when we make the trek in the spring. We'll even buy you a book, darlin'."

Judith thought she would explode. A book, she thought. A book. He's going to buy me a book. A book, when we don't ever have any time to read except at night, and then it's too darned dark to see. She felt like walking over and hitting him. Then the thought was so ludicrous that she stopped. The thought of how he'd react to that made her snicker. Would he ever be surprised! What had Sue said about enjoying this time with him, even the fights? They weren't fighting yet, but if she didn't gain control of her emotions war was going to break out.

Judith got busy tidying the cabin, not trusting herself to reply. Wilson was so engrossed in his plans, his traps and his stretchers that he didn't even seem to notice. Well, she felt caught like a trapped hare in this forlorn country, and her patience was stretched thin as well. She couldn't blame Wilson for that, though. She had agreed to this venture, but how was she ever going to make it through winter in this place?

The short days were going to get even shorter, she knew. The nights longer and colder. The loneliness more unbearable. Without warning, Judith burst into tears, threw her dishtowel onto the cupboard and rushed toward the bed.

Startled, Wilson dropped what he was doing and caught her in his arms. She struggled against him, hitting his shoulders and crying.

"What is it, Judith? What's wrong? Tell me, darlin', what happened?"

"Oh Wil," she cried. "It's no good. I hate it here. We can't do this. You go hunting, trapping and travelling around and I stay here all alone in this miserable old cabin, and work and work and never get anywhere."

"Oh, my sweetheart. I didn't know you felt that way. Look, we have to talk this over. If you want, we'll leave, go back to Calgary and take the $5,000. That's enough to give us a start. I'm so sorry, darlin'. I didn't know." He held her, rocking and rubbing her back, kissing her neck and loving her until her tears subsided.

When she finally sat up, wiping her tear-streaked cheeks with the back of her hand, and sniffling, she said, "It's OK. I'm OK now."

"No. We're going to talk this out. You can't stay here hating it and resenting this place. It'll tear us apart. You mean more to me than life itself. I only wanted the money for you, so I could provide a really nice house for you and dress you like a fine lady. We'll pack up and follow Tommy's people out. I can get work in the mines to earn enough to get back to Calgary and we'll carry on from there."

In a small voice Judith answered, "I don't want that."

There was silence in the cabin, broken only by the logs snapping in the fireplace. Wilson waited, unsure of what to do or say. One part of him felt like yelling, "Then what the hell do you want?" He bit his lip.

"I'm sorry, Wil. I'm sorry. I don't know what I want. I think I just miss Sue so much now they've left, and I know we won't see them or anyone for months now. I don't want to go back to Calgary."

"It tears me apart to know you're unhappy. What can I do? Tell me. I'll do anything for you."

"Take me hunting?"

"If you want to come hunting, sure. Do you want to shoot? Have you ever handled a gun?"

"I shot gophers with your Cousin Mickey's .22. I got pretty good until my mother found out and stopped me hunting with the boys."

So it was arranged that Judith would go with Wilson on some of the hunting jaunts, but she had to agree to skin what she shot and do the dirty work he did with game – the plucking and the dressing.

What kind of man, Judith wondered, would sentence his son to a life up here for three years? She guessed it was the kind of man who would marry a woman, father a child then abandon them both. How could such a man father a wonderful son like her husband? She knew Wil's mother and knew it was not because of that woman's influence he had turned out so well. Her mother-in-law was a selfish woman who thought of life in terms of how it affected her first and foremost. She had even talked as though the war was a personal affront to her, taking her darling son off like that. And you'd think no one suffered the trials war had put the country through as much as Marjorie Daniels.

Suddenly, Judith realized she was thinking just like that woman, and she blushed at the pettiness of her thoughts. She and Wilson were in this together, she reminded herself, and she had been in full agreement. Grumbling when the going got rough was shameful. Times ahead would be no easier, but if she acknowledged her bitter feelings while remembering what mattered, she would get through it all OK too. In less than three years from now they would be rich and she'd be able to live wherever they wished, do what she liked and have plenty of company every day if she so desired. She knew she should be thankful for the visit from her friends rather than bitter about their leaving. They'll be back, she told herself. They'll be back and we'll be better off than we are now. She began to think of things she could do to help her husband, and the first thing was to experiment with making pemmican. Sue would be proud of her.

10
Wolf Pup

The white alpha male and his mate rose leisurely, stretched and playfully sniffed each other, tails wagging, circling and rising on their hind legs, forepaws braced along the other's shoulders. They interacted, mouths open, nuzzling and playing until the pup joined them, nipping and licking at their jaws in hopes of getting fed. Tiring of the relentless badgering of their offspring, the adult wolves decided it was time to begin their daughter's education. Although the pup was young, only 2 ½ months old, there were no other pack members to babysit her, and she was larger than many wolves her age, with no littermates with which to compete for food.

The large white timber wolf set the pace, with the female following and the young pup just managing to keep up. When the pup fell behind, a woof from the female told her mate to move more slowly until their offspring caught up with them.

Catching the scent of deer, he turned to signal his dark companions. He sank low and glided to the right of the deer, making use of rocks, bushes, low growth and trees to conceal his ghostly form. The dark female crouched low and drifted to the left, her near-black coat blending with the rocks. The pup sat down, regarding the adults quizzically, head held at an angle. Finally deciding to follow her mother, she gave a short woof and bounded after the female in a rather sideways, gambolling gait. The deer, ever on the alert, raised her head, tail flapping madly as she eyed her surroundings. After a few nervous movements the deer was unsure which direction to take.

As the young wolf caught sight of the deer, she woofed and sprang toward it in leaps and bounds, causing the frightened doe to run in the direction of the unseen male, who pressed his body flat to the ground, tense muscles in his haunches quivering. The short bushes hid him, and since the breeze was in his face the doe was unaware of his presence. Then a small sparrow burst from the willows, causing the deer to veer off on a tangent, and he leaped from his spot, giving chase.

Running on his toes, wolf fashion, enabled the male to swiftly reach close to 38 miles per hour. The doe still had the advantage of speed, but the wolf caught her rear haunch with his solid body launched at top velocity, and he knocked her to the ground. Before she was able to scramble to her feet, he grabbed her throat.

As the terrified and desperate deer struggled to stand, attempting to dislodge the timber wolf, the adult female reached the scene and launched into the fray. The wolves brought the doe down again. A brief struggle, then she was still and the blood ceased gushing from the rip at her throat. The wolf's snowy muzzle was gory. The two predators began their feast.

The pup came running to share the bounty, but the alpha pair refused to allow their daughter to feed until they had consumed their fill. The pup saw and smelled blood oozing from the warm flesh. It came crawling on its belly many times, whining submissively and salivating, only to be threatened with growling, snarling and snapping until she backed off.

After the adults withdrew, grooming themselves and each other daintily, the pup sneaked to the carcass and began to gnaw on the remainder of the still-warm body of the young deer. She growled in imitation of her parents until she, too, was full of fresh meat and covered with blood on her front parts.

When all had eaten their fill, the adults circled the remainder of the carcass, defecating nearby and scratching their scent around to discourage scavengers while sending dirt, leaves and needles over the remains.

Scanning their current surroundings, they spotted a long esker that, with its elevated vantage, would give them a clearer view of the area. Loping easily, they covered the few miles and scaled the slopes, sniffing around to learn who else had frequented that locale.

Having decided it met their present needs, both adults proceeded to mark their territory with urine and feces. The pup was busy sniffing, uncovering many different interesting scents. She tried to dig where she could smell rodents had made a burrow, but her small forepaws did not make much of an impression on the gravelly surface. She wasn't hungry, just curious and playful, and soon forgot her digging to pounce on a branch that was waving in the stirring air. As the youngster investigated their new rendezvous, the adult timber wolves flopped onto their sides, stretched out their limbs and proceeded to take a well-earned nap.

The meal they had eaten was sufficient for several days for the adults, but the pup needed daily feeding, and nursing was not enough. Thus she returned often to the sight of the kill with her mother, to gnaw on the now-reeking remains of the young doe. The flies, maggots and beetles were no deterrent; they became additional nourishment. The adult wolf dragged some of the carcass back to the rendezvous area for the pup to chew on while she and her mate relaxed.

Summer slowly changed to fall and the pup grew, gradually taking a more active role in hunting. She was a fast learner, and never again went charging after their prey the way she had done at first. Most of the time the wolf pack of three fed on rodents such as mice, voles, rabbits, ground squirrels, raccoons, muskrats and beaver. Often they managed to flush a small flock of ptarmigan and with luck and speed were able to catch one. Yet a ptarmigan was never enough to feed three, and hunting larger animals was difficult with only three wolves in the hunting party, and one of those an inexperienced youth.

As the alpha female came into her season again, the adults spent more time together, re-establishing their relationship. When the pup's playful antics interfered with their bonding, they would rebuff the youngster. The adults played at chasing each other, with the female leading in a flirtatious manner, coaxing him to follow. Often they roamed far from the rendezvous area where the pup chose to remain. As her parents playfully and lovingly cemented their relationship, the youngster, bored and inquisitive, met with trouble.

Deciding to try her luck at hunting, the young female set off in a southerly direction. Following the esker, and then catching a scent on the westerly breeze, she veered off to investigate. She came upon a slow, waddling porcupine on its way to another tree, and cautiously circled it, intrigued as it curled itself into a ball. She approached, sniffing and woofing, wondering what this was. The porcupine kept its rear toward the circling wolf, slapping its prickly tail, rattling the quills. Finally, tiring of this game, the immature wolf leaped onto the curious creature, receiving a face, mouth and paws full of quills.

She yelped, mad with agony. She rubbed her face along the ground to dislodge the quills, but managed only to work them in deeper. Her front feet and legs were covered in quills. Her delicate tongue and nose were pierced. Quills stabbed close to her eyes. In agony she limped back to the rendezvous area, where her parents, sniffed her in sympathy, and licked her neck and cheek. They were helpless to do more.

Days passed. The pup couldn't eat, could hardly drink and grew thinner and weaker. Eventually, it gave up completely. The stench from her infected wounds worsened, and she barely whined whenever the adults approached with a plump ptarmigan or choice bits of game. One morning she was stiff and cold.

Her parents howled their grief, stayed with her body for several days in mourning, and then moved on. Already the next litter was growing inside the body of the black female and they needed to locate another den for the birth of her pups in the spring.

11
Trapline

October arrived, bringing snow by mid-month, and Wilson joyfully began work on his trapline. Judith remained in the cabin, building stretchers for his catch, following the patterns of Tommy's samples. With the increasing cold she was content to remain inside, though Wilson often invited her along, fearing another tearful episode. In the evenings she helped skin the bodies of the animals he caught. She became accustomed to the sight and odour of the inside-out pelts hanging along the higher northern wall.

Some of the meat she dried and made into pemmican or cut up and placed in the cache outside, where it would keep frozen until they needed to eat it. Some creatures, she felt, were not really edible. Whenever Wilson flushed a flock of ptarmigan they enjoyed a special treat. The plump little birds, like prairie chickens, were delicious stuffed with rice, wild sage and onions and roasted slowly over coals.

They saved the brains of all the animals and froze them with hopes of salvaging the bear hide and the other pelts adorning their walls. Wilson used entrails and parts of the carcasses as bait in some of the traps. He caught a few coyotes and, once, a young grey wolf. Tommy had told him the RCMP used to pay 20 dollars a pelt for wolves, and though the price had fallen they were still worth trapping. There was even yet a bounty paid for wolf tails, as wolves were considered a threat to the caribou population.

Sometimes when Wilson was away, leaving her alone in the cabin with her work and her thoughts, Judith found it impossible to believe she was eating the creatures they ate. She was sure her students in Calgary would be horrified to learn what her life had become. To them she was a modern young lady, very proper in her attire, speech and behaviour. At times it caused her to smile at the wilderness person she had become, and other times she looked at her clothes, which consisted of slacks, sturdy denim jeans, green army coveralls and men's shirts, wondering if she would ever regain the dignified persona to which she'd once laid claim.

Judith recalled the time spent with Annie Mills discussing fashion and helping Annie roll her hair into a fashionable 'do. Now her own hair was either tied back in a tail or braided out of the way. She looked down at the battered denim pants she wore and the faded work shirt that had been Wilson's. She spun around in a pirouette, making a curt-sey, and said, "Behold the princess of the bush." The lovely outfits she'd left for Annie would have been very out of place here, and would soon have looked as shabby as she felt now. But what did it matter? What did it really matter? Once the three years were over and the money secure in their possession, she would be able to dress like a fashion model. She would give Betty Grable a run for her money, all right.

Other times tears would fall unchecked, as feelings of loneliness and despair threatened to overwhelm her. Three years could seem such a very long time. It would never do to let Wil know how unhappy she often felt; she remembered how upset he was when she cried after Tommy and Sue left.

It was different when he was with her in the cabin. She loved him, and he praised the stretchers she made, the skinning and stretching that she helped with as well as the meals she was able to concoct from their supplies, which, while plentiful, were certainly limited in variety. It was only when she was alone for long periods of time that depression became her companion.

The pelts on stretchers were suspended from the overhead poles that formed the rafters of their roof. As the pelts dried, they were removed from the stretchers and placed in a corner where, after a time, a fair pile accumulated. Wilson kept shifting the pile to keep them evenly dried and to ensure they were preserved properly. They were light, thin and like stiff paper. Inside the pelts the fur was luxurious, and Judith often ran her hands over the soft covering of the bodies of the creatures before they were skinned, feeling a slight regret for their deaths.

One day in November Judith decided she did not want to stay alone anymore. As they sat after supper, checking the few carcasses of musk-rat, the one beaver and a mink waiting to be skinned once they thawed, Judith turned to her husband. "Wil, honey, I want to go with you tomorrow. I want to go on the trapline. I need to get out and get some fresh air and exercise. I feel claustrophobic in here all day."

"You want to . . . darlin', I'm sorry to hear you feel that way. But the trapline? It's long and really hard. I'd love to take you with me, but not for the whole trapline. It's tough work and too far, and there is getting to be fewer and fewer animals in the traps. Have you noticed how many stretchers we have empty now? Besides, it's cold and you don't have warm-enough clothing." Then he noticed her scowl and the stubborn set to her jaw. "But I'll tell you what: tomorrow I'll stay home with you. We'll go for a walk. I'll have to see what we can do for warm clothes for you."

"I can wear some of your things over mine. The moccasins Sue gave me keep my feet warm. I know I could do the trapline with you."

"Let's just do this slowly, darlin'. A walk tomorrow, then we'll take it from there." As his wife acquiesced, Wilson thought of how tough it was plowing through the drifts, how that cold wind could slice right through heavy clothing, and he knew Judith would not be able to do it, though she was a stubborn little thing and he admired her spunk.

✳

The next day dawned clear and cold, and by the time the sun was high they had finished caring for the previous catch and Judith was bundled in her winter gear, with her husband's larger clothes bulked over her own. She felt like a toddler, barely able to move with all the layers. By the time they got outside, after ensuring the fire was banked in the fireplace so it would not go completely out while they were gone, Judith was sweating and itchy.

The cold hit her like a sledgehammer, but she laughed and tried to run, only to fall rolling in the snow. She was unable to find her feet for the laughter that seized her. When Wilson reached to help her up she tripped him playfully. They rolled around in the snow like a pair of puppies, tossing snow at each other and laughing.

Finally, panting and giggling, Judith allowed Wilson to help her to her feet. They trudged all around the perimeter of the cabin, stopping to chat with Jazzy and pat her shaggy neck. The corral was marked with her tracks from trotting around and digging at the snow to get to the feed underneath. Thinking of the bags of oats and other bulk commodities upon which she and Wil slept, Judith promised to give up some of their 'mattress' so the mare could enjoy more oats.

Judith was amazed at how much snow had piled along the north side of the cabin in such a short time. On the south side, their frozen cache was now completely invisible under a huge bank of drifted snow, though it was plain to see where Wilson had an opening dug. "It gets pretty tough to dig out this door sometimes," he told her. "But if anything ever happens to me, you need to know where things are out here and how to get at the food and the firewood and Jazzy's hay, what's left of it."

A fist tightened around Judith's heart, squeezing as she tried to take in what he had said. She felt light-headed, as though she might faint. "If anything . . .?" She grabbed the front of his parka. "No. Wil, don't say that. I couldn't bear it if anything happened to you. You promise me it won't. Promise me, Wilson."

"Oh, darlin', of course I'll be careful. I'm always careful, but just in case, I need to know you'll be able to take care of yourself and Jazzy until I get back."

Wilson led Judith a short ways into the surrounding forest. He laid a trail for her to show her how tough it was. "I go for miles like this," he said. "The trapline is about 10 miles long, and it's pretty tough going the whole way, and then you have to walk back along the river."

Judith was panting with exhaustion and was quite glad to turn back, though she wouldn't admit it. It had been wonderful to get out of the cabin for a change, and they'd had fun being silly in the snow. She breathed in the fresh air, as bracing as a drink of cold clear water. Wilson's talk of being prepared unsettled her, however, and she was unable to shake the feelings of dread he had awakened.

12
The Encounter

Muscles rippled under the thick silver coat as his tireless stride carried him across miles of tundra, the stunted trees and thin undergrowth of this northern plain not impeding his rapid pace. Spring was gradually elbowing the long hard winter off the land. Most of the deep snows had melted, runoff waters gurgled among the hummocks, and northbound geese sliced the skies into pie-shaped wedges as their clarion calls echoed off the rocky esker.

The timber wolf had been hunting since first light, but had only unearthed a family of lemmings. The small rodents were not enough to sustain his huge lanky frame, and merely whetted his appetite. With a quick snap, he had ended the female lemming's life and daintily swallowed the squirming, hairless infants. Now his yellow eyes scanned the horizon through the short growth of tree-line timber as he travelled ever southward.

An efficient predator, the wolf had confidence in his prowess. No other creature threatened him, unless he happened upon a grizzly bear, and he was much too alert to be surprised by such a slow-witted animal. He knew he could outrun his other foe, a wolverine, which was smaller but strong, voracious and vicious. His mind was concerned solely with the hunt and his responsibility.

The dominant male of the wolf pack thought of the seven squirming pups deep in the recesses of the den in their own esker. They had been born just four days previously, and his mate needed food to feed her ravenous body in order to supply the needed milk for their pups. He'd listened to their suckling noises before he'd left that morning.

Nighttime was approaching and he had nothing yet to bring her. He had not even happened onto a flock of ptarmigan, usually plentiful in this area. In a few months the pups would be old enough for his mate and him to train. The pups would spend the summer growing and learning how to hunt, then the family would become an impressive pack well able to provide for themselves during the tough winter ahead, but for now it was his responsibility to provide food. Since the birth of the pups, the alpha male had had to hunt alone, and with spring being late this year, game was scarce.

He raised quivering nostrils, ears pricked forward intently. There it was again – a definite aroma of rabbit. Another faint odour unfamiliar to him threaded delicately through the heady scent of arctic hare. On the southerly edge of his regular hunting territory and close to trespassing into another wolf's domain, he was doubly alert. He decided to follow up cautiously the scent carried on the southerly breeze. No wolf fragrance reached his questing nostrils as his tireless stride rapidly closed the distance.

The smell of the hare was strong now, mingled with blood, the odour of death and a wisp of that unknown scent. The wolf slunk to the ground, inching forward, his large white form blending with the light skiff of morning snow covering the terrain. His eyes caught sight of the lifeless body of a hare, dangling from a willow branch. His stomach rumbled, but he knew the hunger of his mate feeding their greedy pups would be much greater. He glided forward, taking advantage of the slight cover provided by a stubby growth of ground juniper and willow. Every sense alert, he noted the sleepy twittering of chickadees in the willow stand, soft rustling of lifeless brown leaves remaining on the bare bushes and the inauspicious slithering of snow crystals skittering across the still-frozen ground. He crouched, muscles twitching, and then launched his lithe body toward the rabbit.

There was a sudden snap as the wolf felt steel jaws crush the bones above his forepaw. A single yelp issued from his throat. He jerked backward, lunging again and again, each time forcing the metal teeth deeper into his flesh. In desperation, he began to chew at this thing that held him. Blood seeped from his foot and from his gums. The ground around the scene became a churned mixture of mud, snow, and blood. In the fading light, he sank exhausted to the earth, knowing it was useless to struggle. He needed to use his wits now, not brute strength, to outwit this metal object with its merciless teeth sunk deeply into his tender limb. He had rested only a few minutes when he was alerted by the sound of something unfamiliar approaching upwind of him. It was making no effort to approach in silence.

An upright creature stepped into sight and stopped abruptly. Rising to his feet, the alpha wolf felt, rather than heard, the low rumble deep within his massive chest. He lowered his head, eyes riveting the unknown being, and a mixture of apprehension, rage and challenge swept through his quivering frame. The man and the silver wolf stared intently into each other's eyes. Minutes passed.

The vertical being sank slowly closer to the ground, assuming a non-threatening stance, and gentle, soothing sounds reached the wolf's ears. What was this? He remained alert, ears forward, every sense intent on the softly crooning man's figure as it inched forward, seeming to be submissive yet intrusive at the same time.

He watched as the strange being came within range, but something held him back from the lunge that would surely end the creature's life. The man knelt in front of the wolf, each a fine specimen of his kind, and each in the prime of his life. The man, careful to make no sudden moves, slowly reached toward the jaws of metal.

The wolf whined as the steel jaws of the trap were released, and the sound of his own voice jerked him to awareness. He leapt backward, ran several yards on his three uninjured paws, and then stopped to gaze at the strange creature that had released him. It was upright again, on its back legs, like a rearing grizzly. Their eyes locked for another moment, and then the wolf melted into the brush.

Out of sight from this strange upright creature, the wolf followed, keeping a respectable distance, but led by avid curiosity to learn more of its habits. He watched the man follow a trail, stopping periodically to collect game and the metal monsters that had done the killing. Some of the animals were alive, but they were quickly dispatched and added to the collection of game that would have provided well for his family. Many times the creature that travelled on two legs added the metal hunters to his collection, though they had caught nothing.

Finally, travelling non-stop for several miles along the frozen surface of the river, the upright creature led the wolf to a structure made from trees piled sideways like a carefully constructed windfall. There was smoke coming from the top of it, where a tall structure of rock protruded. As the pale wolf watched from behind some bushes, the man creature pulled open part of the log structure and went into it, leaving his sleigh load of metal hunters and their prey outside.

For several long minutes the wolf continued to survey this strange scene, then, becoming aware of the absence of daylight, he turned to the north, knowing his hunt must continue until he caught something with which he could return to the den to feed his mate and their young.

He knew he would cross paths with the man again, and was determined to learn more about the strange creature. This had been a very unusual and painful encounter for the huge predator, and one that would leave a lasting impression on the man. But for now, the wolf would spend the night nursing his foot, while travelling slowly back to familiar territory in hopes of catching game to bring home to his family.

As the wolf returned to its base, the man inside the cabin attempted to relate his story of the encounter to Judith. "I can't do this anymore.

Today I met a fellow creature and I saw what I have been doing and I don't like it one bit."

"What do you mean? What creature?" Judith had never seen him look so full of remorse and guilt. "Sit down, I'll get you a bowl of hot soup and you explain what happened while I get started skinning your catch."

Wilson told her how he followed the trapline as usual, until coming upon the wolf. He paused. "I stopped in my tracks. The size of him, white as the driven snow, and he looked right into my eyes." Wilson looked at his wife, tears in his eyes, as his voice lowered. "He knew, Judith. There was intelligence in those yellow eyes of his as he stared at me. My God, Judith, I felt guilty. A wolf made me feel guilty. Does that make any sense?" He told Judith about the look of intelligence in those animal eyes. "He knew, Judith. He knew and he accused me. And I couldn't kill him."

"What did you do?"

"I released the trap from his foot."

"Wilson, he could have killed you." Judith's face went ashen with the thought.

"Yes, he could have killed me, and I could have killed him, and we both knew where we stood. I had to release him. I have to find another way. Trapping isn't for me, and there isn't much in the traps anymore anyway. I hated to kill the other creatures and I hated to collect the bodies. That's the last of it. I pulled up all the traps."

"But Wilson, the pelts are going to bring in money. We eat meat from the catch. What are we going to do? How will we survive?"

"I don't know, but at this point the thought of making other creatures suffer just sickens me."

Judith, raised on a farm, had long ago come to terms with the necessity of killing animals in order to provide meat for humans, but she knew she had to approach this carefully with her husband. "You are absolutely right, Wilson. Other creatures shouldn't suffer that we might live. Let's just leave it for the time being. We have sufficient food on hand now. When we start to run low, we'll look at this again." She knew too well they needed to kill wildlife in order to survive out here. But she also knew her husband had seen too much cruelty at the hands of humans on the other side of the world. It was time to reconsider things. Wilson needed peace, an absence of bloodshed, and a healing of his mental wounds right now.

"It's OK. We'll find another way. You did the right thing, Wilson. We'll be OK. We have quite a pile of pelts there now."

Wilson pulled his mate into a close embrace, loving the clean woman smell of her.

13
Slaughter

As he travelled slowly, favouring the foreleg that had been mangled in the trap, the large white wolf was fortunate to surprise and kill an arctic hare that thought itself so well hidden it had remained motionless until it was too late. Now he had food to bring home to his mate, and he covered the distance as rapidly as he was able.

He lay quietly nursing his foreleg, listening to the dark female devour the hare. He knew he would have to leave for more sustenance for her very soon.

With game so scarce, the alpha pair became lean, as hunting was less successful. To compensate, he expanded his territory more than half a square mile, so that, even wounded, he managed to provide enough to keep his family fed and growing.

The pups had been leaving the den for a few days now, tussling with each other, and playfully pouncing on his tail, which wagged happily as he watched his offspring. When the large white female pup got too close to his injured leg, he got up and limped a short distance away. He stretched his mouth wide, tongue lolling out the side as he enjoyed the sight of the pups rolling over and climbing on top of each other. They snarled and yipped as they tugged pieces of fur from the hide of a ground squirrel caught some weeks before. This type of play prepared them for hunting when they were older.

These seven pups, raised and trained with their parents, would become a formidable hunting team – a wolf pack. The pups were now walking around, and knew enough to scramble back into the den for safety, so the female was able to forage with her mate, as long as they didn't venture too far.

Soon the pups would be moved from the den as they began to eat meat and need less milk. The wolves had chosen a good spot on an esker about five miles due east as one of the rendezvous places to finish weaning and training their pups.

On a sunny warm day in early June the move was accomplished. The pups continued to thrive on marmots and lemmings, and once an unwary beaver caught too far from his waterway. Most of the pups had begun to imitate the howls of their parents, and when the whole pack started singing they made quite an impressive chorus.

With both wolves hunting, they were able to ambush larger prey at times. One day in early May, they managed to separate a cow moose from its calf and the male killed the calf as the female distracted the mother. Had it not been for the trees hampering the cow's movements, they may not have been so lucky.

Again, the alpha male's mate had been injured in the hunt. As she rolled out of the path of the trampling hooves she twisted her right front paw, spraining the ligaments. Once the calf was dead, the cow turned and strode off into the bush, snorting and bawling. The female limped to the kill site and began to feed beside her mate, both wolves growling and snarling as they tore tender flesh from the still-warm carcass. Tender inside parts – the liver and heart – were eaten first so they could begin to be digested as both wolves stuffed their stomachs in order to transport food for the pups. The white wolf also carried a rear haunch in his mouth. Limping badly, the female brought the head for her pups to chew and fight over.

Once they got to the rendezvous the pups swarmed over them, licking at their mouths until the entire contents of both adults' stomachs were emptied. The alpha female stayed with her pups at the esker to lick at her injured forepaw while the male returned to the moose calf's carcass for more meat.

As he gorged himself, he became aware of a distant droning sound that came closer and closer. Looking skyward, he spied the metallic glint off a huge mechanical bird that snarled and roared as it swooped and turned, back and forth through the sky, now higher, now lower, eventually flying off in a southerly direction. The wolf had never before seen anything like it, but soon dismissed it from his mind.

After eating everything off the carcass, he loped back toward the esker. He expected to hear the sounds of his family, but all was deathly quiet. He found the pale body of his largest pup, a female, first. He sniffed her small body, smelled the fear she had felt, her blood, but nothing else. He tested the air with his delicate nose. That odour hung over all.

One by one, he inspected their bodies, and found one little black female, still alive but badly injured. She whimpered when he touched her. He whined, begging her for response, but she was not able to do more than raise her head slightly and lick toward her father. He sat beside her and raised a mournful song of sorrow. The next morning she, too, was dead.

Meanwhile, 59 miles away and 1,864 miles in the air, the mechanical bird, a Fairchild F-11 Husky single-engine plane, headed back toward civilization. Two men in the aircraft entered an additional eight in the log they kept, bringing the count to 56 – the number of wolves they'd killed that day. This was a government policy to manage caribou herds by reducing predators, so ensuring the increase in the number of caribou available for human hunters.

The lone wolf decided to abandon the area where an unknown instrument of death had deprived him of his mate and their offspring. His tail, usually held aloft in a show of superiority, now hung low. Ears close to his head, head low to the ground, he moved farther south. This move would inadvertently put him in the vicinity of the human who had trapped and then released him.

He still had a slight limp as a result of the trap wound on his forepaw, and as the winter set in, it became harder and harder for him to hunt. Alone, he was relegated to searching for only small game, and that was scarce. Though he often flushed a flock of delicious ptarmigan, he was not swift enough now to catch one. He was unable to run down the odd arctic hare and had to settle for mice, lemmings, frogs, grasshoppers, crickets and berries. He became lean and hungry most of the time, and was morose at the loss of his mate and their litter.

14

Blizzard

March eventually elbowed winter over and let spring peep through the crack. The 14th dawned bright and clear with no wind. It was a gorgeous day, and Judith took advantage of the break in the winter to spend time out of doors with Wilson, visiting with the mare, listening to the foraging chickadees and just enjoying being alive. The scent of moisture and hint of warmth in the sun heralded an early spring. What a delight after so many months of being stuck inside, cold and more cold, week after week with short days of wan sunlight. Judith had an urge to fling out her arms and run, feeling as free as a kite with a broken string. She grinned at the noisy "Ack, ack, ack" of the skinny black and white magpies that spread wide wings overhead.

"Isn't it wonderful?" she said. "It makes me happy to be here with you right now, in this place."

Wilson grinned back at her, enjoying her delight.

That night, he went out to bring in more wood, returning with his arms full. After he had placed the logs in the area by the fireplace, he turned to Judith. "Come on, darlin', get your outdoor clothes on again. You have to come outside."

"What is it, Wil? Is it the wolves howling again?"

"Just get dressed. You have to see this."

As he would give her no idea what she was to see, Judith found warm clothes quickly. With a million questions, she hurried ahead of her husband. The sky above was radiant. It was as though they were under a huge umbrella, spinning with rippling waves of dancing colour. Aurora borealis – the northern lights were putting on a wondrous light show. Judith pushed the hood off her head to see better, turned slowly in a full circle, arms akimbo, and then stood stock-still. "Oh, Wil," she breathed. "Listen to them!"

Wilson listened to the hiss and swish of the lights as they darted across the sky, playing out a scintillating rhythm all their own. It was glorious, like nothing they had ever seen or experienced before. Wilson wrapped his arms around Judith and together they revelled in the magic of the mysterious and awesome panorama above.

Finally, bursting with the experience, they went back inside to warm up. "Never, ever, have I seen or felt anything so wondrous," Judith whispered as they went to bed.

"Me either. It really was spectacular, wasn't it? This north country gives you extremes of the best and the worst. Surely this would qualify as one of the best." Wilson nuzzled his wife's neck. "This is another," he murmured.

As they settled for the night, they talked about what they had accomplished since coming here in the spring. The cabin was livable again. A corral protected and contained the mare. They had meat frozen and dried to last for a while yet and their vegetable stores were still holding out, though those supplies would not last for long. Wood for the fire still flanked the eastern wall of the cabin as well as the near side of the corral, and they were comfortable and happy. Experience showed them clearly what they needed to survive, much more effectively than well-meaning advice from others.

The following Monday, flakes the size of quarters began to float down lazily from a brooding sky. What began as a gentle drift gathered quickly in thickness and velocity. With the steady snowfall, the winds picked up, causing a blizzard that lasted for five days without letup. The contrast to that early taste of spring couldn't be greater. It was hard to believe they were in the same locale.

Judith asked Wilson to open the hatch in the cabin for a chunk of meat from the cache. He had to tell her it was empty.

"We're out of meat?" she squeaked.

"No, we have meat, but not in this cache. I should have moved some into this bin. And we need more wood, too."

Wilson dressed in his outerwear and opened the door, only to be met by a wall of white that whipped his breath away. He quickly ducked back inside and slammed the door. "If I go out in that without a rope I may not make it back inside."

The only answer was to fashion a rope from their clothing. He tied one end to his wrist and the other to the door catch, and then he ventured outside. He ducked his head to try to protect his face against the fierce bite of the wind, but it blasted him, sucking his breath so he couldn't inhale. Gasping, he raised an arm to deflect the force. The blinding swirling snow obscured everything, but he played out the rope and moved slowly, going by instinct and memory until he stumbled over the pile of snow that blocked the opening to the food cache. He dropped to his knees and began to dig at the snow, but the swirling, screaming wind was filling it back in almost as fast as he was able to dig it out. Snow pellets scoured his face, causing his eyes to tear up and ice to form along his lashes. Snow packed his beard, and his nostrils stung from the cold. What little air he drew into his lungs burned like fire. Many times he had to stop long enough to hold his mittened hands in front of his face while he laboured to catch his breath. He couldn't quit. With his own bulk for a windbreak he clawed and swept at the snow until at last he pried off the rock that secured the cache. He dug inside and grasped some type of meat, which he jammed under one arm before he forced the rock back in place. He checked for the rope around his wrist. He wrapped it around his bent arm from elbow to hand, using his thumb as an anchor, taking up the slack as he made his way back to the cabin. He bent double against the force of the gale, and in the back of his mind he kept repeating, Rope, don't let go. Finally, to his aston-ishment, he was at the cabin door.

He kicked the snow away from the door, and with Judith's help from inside he forced it open. As soon as he had the door shut he pawed at the snow on his face and beard.

"Don't go out again," she begged.

"We can't afford to let the fire die," he said, gasping. "I've got to go back out. That one stick there isn't going to last very long."

Wilson shouldered the door open again. Once he was outside he grasped the rough side of the cabin and moved along, afraid to let go. When he stumbled and fell he threw his arms before him to break his fall, and he lost the wall. Panic struck, and his first instinct was to stand and windmill his arms out around him, feeling for something solid in the choking, swirling snow. He made sure not to take a step in any direction, lest he distance himself from the cabin. Nothing – there was nothing substantial within reach. Terror threatened to overcome him, and he had to stop and tell himself to think. The cabin wall was close. It had to be. By bending at the waist he extended his reach slightly, and the back of his knuckles connected with the log wall. He moved in that direction, rubbing the rough surface with both hands, almost hugging it. As soon as he calmed down enough to continue, he moved his right foot ahead. He tested it to ensure it was secure before he brought his left foot forward. So he moved, cautiously, along the side of the cabin to the woodpile. With his shoulder braced against the cabin he dug out an armful of logs before inching back to the door once more while keeping his right elbow sliding against the cabin wall.

As soon as he was inside he stamped the snow from his clothing, shaking his head and filling the entry with icy white lumps of snow before making his way across the floor to the fireplace, where he stacked the snow-packed logs to thaw before adding them to the fire, which was now burning rather low.

Judith rushed to assist. "It won't help for you to get wet," he said. Yet he let her help him out of his frozen outer clothes. "It's really rough out there. Like nothing I ever saw before, and I've seen some bad blizzards."

"How long is this going to keep up, Wil? I hate the wind and the cold. I hate it that you had to go in it. All I could hear was the howling of the wind." Judith noticed his tight face and knew he, too, was scared.

"I don't know. I've never seen anything like it."

"Are we going to be all right?"

"I hope so. It can't last forever." He frowned. They were not the only creatures facing this blizzard. Wilson spared a brief thought for the wolf he'd encountered and released, wondering how it was surviving, but never said anything to Judith about the matter.

The wind shrieked and moaned, day in and day out, making the cabin frosty although the fireplace was working all the time and the crackling flames sent light and heat into the one room they shared. They layered clothing, and even resorted to wearing their outdoor clothes inside. The only time they were warm was when they were crowded close to the fire.

Judith felt as though they had entered a period of permanent night-time and isolation. She felt like screaming at the wind, and it was only through talking with her husband that she didn't go crazy. Could this truly be the same country that had given them that tantalizing glimpse of spring and the expanse of the glorious auroras just a few days before?

Day after day, the only light they had was the fire, and it gobbled wood at a rapid rate. Wilson had to make more forays out to bring wood in, terrified each time that he might become disoriented and be lost to the fury. The shrieking wind ate at their nerves. Once, Judith ran to the door and beat on it with her fists, screaming back at the wind. Wilson wanted to shake her and rushed over to grab her, but she turned to him and wept. "I'm going crazy, Wil! I'm going crazy."

He realized it was harder on her. As dangerous as it was, his trips for wood at least gave him something to do. Suddenly he got an idea. He led her to the fireplace, scraped a smooth place in the dirt floor and, taking a couple of twigs, drew a tick-tack-toe game. They played that for a while, and then each revived other games they'd enjoyed as children to pass the time.

Late on the fifth day, the wind stopped. A weak sun shone briefly before setting on a changed world. A white landscape took a rosy tint as the banks of pristine snow reflected the dying rays of the tepid sun. Many trees broke under the weight of snow. Snowbanks reached above the height of the cabin's roof, and Wilson had to spend the greater part of the evening and the next day digging out the cabin door, clearing off the roof, finding and tunnelling down to the meat cache and digging Jazzy out of the lean-to. The corral was so far under the snow that Jazzy was free to go where she wanted. Fortunately, she wanted to stay where the oats were, so she never strayed far.

Their woodpiles, completely buried, were dangerously low, and Wilson had to make a foray into the bush for more. He harnessed the mare to the sled he'd made like a travois, piled the wood onto it and hauled it back behind the horse.

On his second trip Jazzy began to act nervous, so Wilson reached for his rifle. Bears would be still hibernating. It had to be some kind of carnivore or the mare would not so skittish. He kept checking behind him. There, following in the tracks made by the travois sled, was the lean shape of large white wolf. The animal favoured one front leg. He didn't want to shoot it, as it didn't seem threatening. At times it would sit and watch their progress, getting up to follow when they got far ahead of it. Wilson kept a wary watch nonetheless as they made their way home.

The wolf followed them back to the cabin, never getting too close, and melding into the bush or sitting on its haunches whenever Jazzy became too nervous. Wilson was sure the mare was in no danger, but just in case, once he unloaded his wood and poured her the ration of oats, he opened the meat cache and took out two rabbit carcasses, which he left at the edge of the clearing. Somehow he sensed that this was the same animal he'd released from his trap. It was so lean. Surely, he thought, his snare and the injury contributed to that.

Entering the cabin with an armload of wood, Wilson stomped the snow off his boots and pants, and took off his heavy outer clothing. "Judith," he said slowly, "I think I have just witnessed one result of my handiwork. I think I was followed home by the big white wolf that made me stop trapping. He's so thin now." Wilson ran a hand tiredly across his forehead, around his ear and across the back of his head. He pushed back the thick wavy hair that was far too long now, and then let his arm drop to his side.

"How could it be the same one, Wil? How can you be sure? What besides his colour would make you think that?" Judith hated to see her husband feeling so down.

"He's favouring his left front paw. That's the one my wolf had caught in the trap, and even though he's thin, he's big. If he were to stand on his hind legs he'd be nearly as tall as me."

After half an hour, the wolf floated over the snow to the meat. He checked carefully for the scent of metal. Sensing none, he snatched up one frozen carcass before dashing back to crouch under the boughs of a pine to gnaw it until it was gone. He then returned furtively for the other.

15
Spring 1949

As the end of March came and went, the longer days and warmer sun thinned the huge piles of snow, turning them into icy streams that began as tiny trickles, burbling and rippling, and then built gradually into torrents that tumbled and roiled on the way to the rivers and lakes that fed Hudson Bay. Icicles formed along the front of the cabin. Distant sounds of returning swans and geese heralded the coming warmth of summer, deciduous tree buds swelled with burgeoning growth, and it became a vibrant, pulsating land. It was glorious, not warm enough for the myriad of biting insects yet, and a heavenly end to the long, dark days of winter.

Judith felt like a prisoner newly released from jail must, free to run and jump and play. All the bedding was hung out to freshen. The hide was removed from the window, fresh pine boughs were brought in to perfume the cabin and clean melt water was heated to scrub the creosote and grime from the inside. Judith enjoyed cleaning away the dirt of winter's isolation while she planned for the busy days of spring and summer. It seemed they had gained a new lease on life.

The Lord had given rebirth to the land, and Judith accepted this as a sign of rebirth for her faith that they were where they should be, and things were right with her world. Together Wilson and Judith Daniels were going to be just fine. They had survived their first winter in the north, they still had some food left, and the warmer, lengthening days made everything seem possible.

Wilson busied himself with spring cleaning chores outside, planning as he worked how to prepare better for the next winter. He understood Judith's energetic welcoming of spring, and though he shared her enthusiasm, he wanted to ensure the following winter would not be so difficult. If they were going to stay here for two more years, he wanted his family to thrive, not merely survive.

The lone white timber wolf also survived the winter, though he was often forced to rely on handouts from the two-legged ones. While the blizzard raged he was curled tight beneath a blanket of heavy snow, his nose buried into his bushy tail to preserve his body's warmth.

The balmier days of spring brought about better hunting, and he thrived on smaller animals. It was proving a good year for mice, which he found in their tunnel networks beneath the deep snowbanks; they were a quick meal. The wet spring forced many smaller burrowing animals like lemmings, voles, ground squirrels and marmots out of their burrows, and they provided the wolf with plenty to eat. He had competition from owls, foxes, coyotes and other predators, but there was enough to go around. He began looking for a mate, but found no willing female wolves close. The distant pack he often heard presented no invitation to a lone male, and he was in no shape to battle for hunting rights with a younger wolf that would be in much better condition than he was.

He stayed fairly close to the humans, watching them and finding them a strange species. There seemed to be only two of them – a big male and a smaller female. He watched them digging in the soil, caring for the large moose-like animal and moving long poles of jack pine around the land by their wooden den.

One day he followed the male into the forest and watched as the man killed a young moose along the shore of the lake by making a sharp noise. He could not fathom how the death had occurred, as the upright being had not even been close to the moose when it fell. There were many things about these creatures that were beyond his comprehension.

When the moose had been left in the shallow water while the male returned to his den the wolf followed and watched as the man led the animal that was somewhat like a moose, but wasn't a moose, back to the shallow water where it was used to haul the real moose's body to the den of the upright creatures. He watched the man with the animal haul the body of the moose up into a sturdy tree, to hang by its head. The upright creature then cut open the belly and removed the soft inside parts. He took the outer covering off the body, and removed most of the flesh.

There were parts he hauled a distance from his wooden den and abandoned to the ravens and foxes. After a short time when no harm befell the scavengers feasting off the entrails and other discarded parts, the wolf rushed in, scattering the others and devouring the remains. It might be to his advantage, he decided, to continue his surveillance of these bizarre beings.

Unaware of their lupine audience, Wilson and Judith were busy planting a garden and building a better corral, a container for their wood alongside the cabin, and also an outdoor toilet. The moose was cut up and stowed in the ready-made freezer permafrost created for them. Wilson took Judith hunting for waterfowl and later on collecting eggs from their nests, but never cleaning out any nest completely. They enjoyed the change fresh eggs made from their usual breakfasts of oatmeal, boiled ground wheat or stew. Bacon and ham had not lasted very long, and the canned Spam and fish were but a distant fond memory.

Judith looked forward to washing their clothing in the stream and drying it in the sun. She loved the fresh scent of clothes dried out-of-doors. All winter their clothing received very few launderings and were dried in front of the fire, giving them an odour of jack pine smoke and creosote.

The creosote nearly cost them their lives once when the chimney caught fire. Luckily Wilson was able to smother the flames with snow from the roof, and from then on they made sure to clean the chimney every month. The black, sticky substance leaked down and dripped into the fireplace, adding its rank smell to their clothing, hair and everything in the cabin.

Because the fireplace was their only heating and cooking device for the cabin, he needed to ensure the chimney was kept clean and wood supplies were never low. One day Judith paused in the never-ending cycle of sleep-eat-work-sleep. "Before we came here, did you ever, in your wildest imagination, think we would be doing this and becoming good at it?"

Wilson grinned. "We are doing well, aren't we? I'm a lot hairier than I used to be, but I think a lot stronger as well. And, you know, I haven't had a nightmare for some time now."

"I love your beard. It suits you."

"It might be hot in the summer, because it sure helped keep my face warm this past winter." Wilson scraped mud and pine needles from his winter boots. "I hope this soil soon dries enough that we can put our garden in." The snow that lingered in shaded spots added a chill to the air, but it was warm enough that they were able to work with lighter clothing as well as lighter moods.

As melt waters continued to pour, the creek rose to the edge of the bank and kept on rising, churning and tumbling, flooding the willows and berry bushes in the low-lying areas. Wilson and Judith kept watching the water level, and as it neared their cabin they began to pack up their things and prepare to move onto higher ground. The water continued rising, reaching almost to the door of the cabin. And then, where the stream entered the river, the ice jam let go, and the freezing water sped on, twisting, swirling and rushing to enter the river system and eventually join Hudson Bay.

"That was scary," Wilson admitted once the danger was past. "We were lucky this time. I guess all that snow the blizzard dumped on us the first part of March is responsible for the high water and the ice jam."

"Yes, that plus the fast melt," Judith added. "Do you think we should move our cabin to higher ground?"

"That's a pretty tall order. I think by the looks of things the water doesn't often rise that high. We should be OK here for the time being."

They looked at each other and began to laugh. "It almost sounds like we intend to stay here permanently," Judith said.

"Would that be so bad?" Wilson wrapped an arm around her waist and drew her close to him.

"We only agreed to stay here three years." Judith frowned, and her body stiffened. "This first year is just about over. We're still alive and in good health. I'm pretty sure now that we'll make it for two more years, but I can't see staying longer than that."

"Is it so awful out here, Judith? Do you really hate it so much?" He looked deeply into her eyes, holding her within his embrace but leaning back to watch her expression.

"No, I don't hate it." Judith sighed. "It's a lot of hard work, though. And we've had some close calls with the fire and the blizzard. There are lots of dangers here. We can't pretend there aren't."

"Yes, but we haven't been beaten, darlin'. That should count for something. It makes me feel like anything's possible if we want it badly enough and are willing to work for it. If you don't hate it here, tell me what the best things are."

"Oh, Wilson, the very best thing is we're here together. I can't imagine my life without you. And on days when the weather's fine, when the birds are singing like this, or the night of the northern lights, or even after the blizzard, the way everything was so peaceful and still, then this is the most beautiful place I've ever seen." Safe within the embrace of her strong husband, looking on the fruits of their labour and secure in their love for each other, Judith felt content. There was really no spot she would rather be than right here.

"This place has gotten a hold on us, that's for sure. I'm glad it's not just me that sees the beauty here. I know it gets pretty lonesome for you."

Wilson noticed another frown flit across her face. "Out with it, woman. What are you thinking? What bothers you about living here?"

Judith took a moment to gather her thoughts. "It's more than the loneliness, Wilson. I don't feel like we're getting anywhere. We're just marking time. Is that what it's all about, putting in the time until we can get the money your father left?"

"I guess that's most of it. But I feel much closer to you since we've come here. I feel more at peace with myself, maybe because we're so busy I don't have time to remember the wartime horrors. Maybe that's why I'm able to sleep better, too, because I'm so darn tired by the time we get to bed."

She nodded. "I've noticed. I guess I enjoy working at the same tasks as you, rather than working in a job far removed from yours. If only we weren't so far from other people. We can't even . . . I miss my family, Wilson. I miss listening to a radio, getting the newspapers, hearing about the rest of the world. We are so isolated here. Don't you find that?"

"I'd rather be isolated here with you than living in Calgary or Winnipeg or even Sherridon. In two years' time, we'll be able to live wherever you want, darlin'."

"Wherever we want," she corrected.

"Soon Tommy and Sue and the others should be coming by," he reminded her.

"It will be so good to see them again." Judith's eyes sparkled with anticipation.

"The waterways are open now. They'll bring news from Sherridon."

"It'll be so good to see Sue again. I learned so much from her when we were travelling, and I know she could teach me so much more. I wish they could stay with us for the summer, or at least for a week."

"Me too, but they have their own commitments. I wish I knew more about the natural remedies they use. And I would like to get Tommy's take on that wolf. There is a lot we still need to learn about this country, and they have the knowledge of survival out here. We're learning, though, darlin'. And we're one-third of the way to gaining our fortune. Have you thought of what you want to do once we have the money?"

"It seems like a mirage, wavering just beyond our reach right now. I'm almost afraid to count on it. Sometime when we have nothing else to do, we need to talk about it, but right now, as always, there is too much to do."

Wilson leaned down and kissed her. Then, arm in arm, they returned to the endless chores that always needed attention. They had to build an outdoor toilet, a box to hold logs cut for the fireplace, and a better, higher corral for Jazzy. It seemed no matter how much they did, there was always more to be done.

All through April Judith didn't feel well. She wondered if the food they ate was to blame, but Wilson wasn't affected. She felt tired and moody when she wasn't sick to her stomach. Wilson asked her if she thought maybe she was pregnant, but she said she didn't have morning sickness, but rather all-day sickness. She worried that she had contacted scurvy or some other illness. One day she complained of an aching head and upset stomach and refused to get out of bed. Wilson brought her some hot broth made from boiled rabbit meat, and she gagged, and began crying.

"Oh, darlin'. I think you're pregnant."

Once Judith began to count up her days, she realized she was indeed late with her cycle. About two months late, in fact. "We've been so busy, I didn't even . . ." Panic set in at once.

"I can't have a baby out here, Wilson. How can I? We're having a hard time with just the two of us." Judith sat on the bed, tears streaming down her face. "I don't know how to have a baby. I don't want this. Not now. I'm scared."

"It'll be all right, darlin', I know we can do this. I'm going to be right here with you all the way. People have been having babies since the beginning of time, Judith. You'll be OK. And it's not going to happen tomorrow. We'll have time to get ready. Just think, a baby. Our baby. A darling little girl like her mom."

"Or a sturdy, dark-haired boy like you." Judith grinned through her tears. Then she began to cry again. "Or a frozen little thing that we won't be able to keep warm."

"We will keep him or her warm," Wilson assured her. "I'll make a cradle and Sue will help you. If you like we can go to Sherridon. There's a hospital there, with a doctor and nurses and everything."

"If we do that, we won't be living here for the three consecutive years, will we? It's no good, Wilson. It's no good."

"I'll take of you and the baby. We'll be fine, darlin'. Don't you worry." Wilson backed away slightly and looked into her eyes. "Trust me, Judith. OK? Just trust me."

In a few weeks Judith began to feel better, but she felt tired most of the time, and her moods were still unpredictable. She became angry over small things, burst out crying over minor problems and caused her husband to puzzle over the changes in his usually serene, predictable mate. Judith herself could not understand where the volatility came from, but eventually her emotions became more even. Wilson was pleased to regain a wife that wasn't about to explode over the most minor problem.

"If this is a girl, let's name her Aileen Maigrette, for my mother and your grandmother," Judith suggested as she nestled up to Wilson in bed very early one morning in late July. Wilson had his hand on her tummy, enjoying movements of his child inside Judith.

"And if it's a boy, how about Angus Charles or Charles Angus?"

"Hmmm, Angus Charles Daniels, Charles Angus Daniels. I like Charles Angus better, but his initials would be CAD. Do we really want a cad for a son?" Judith asked, laughing.

"Would we end up calling him Chuck or Gus?"

"How about Gus Chuck?"

"Well, that's better than Up Chuck," he said.

"Oh, you!" Judith playfully smacked Wilson. "If I remember anything about babies, there'll be plenty of upchuck."

On that note, they got out of bed and prepared to face another long day in the north country.

One early afternoon, Wilson and Judith were enjoying a wonderful day. The wind gently whispered through the willows, and birds were busy preparing nests trilling their various songs. Killdeers floated along the clearing repeating their plaintive cries. Their garden was sown and some early plants were poking a few leaves above the surface. Suddenly they were hailed from the river. "Hallo, the cabin!"

Judith and Wilson halloed back, and up the stream came a flotilla of canoes with Tommy and his family, Nelson, Bruce and Sue with Jimmy. Judith saw Charlie and Libby, who were waving to her. There were a few more they recognized, and others they didn't remember well. "Welcome to our camp," called Wilson as he went to help them draw their crafts up out of the water. He shook hands and clapped Tommy on the back. It felt good to see people again.

Tommy handed them a package with mail in it. Judith wanted to tear it open at once, but her good manners held her back. She cuddled it under one arm.

"Any news from civilization?" Wilson asked.

"If you mean, Sherridon, there is talk of the mine closing," Tommy said.

"What will happen then? How will the people make a living? Most of them work in the mines, and they're what keeps the town going." Wilson was concerned with those people he and Judith had met on their trip in. He was especially worried for Clarence and Annie Mills, who'd been their hosts for those weeks in Sherridon. Annie must have had her baby by now. Then it struck him – what would it mean for Judith and him? How would the lawyers get information about their whereabouts?

"The people will have to move," Tommy said.

"Well, come on. Let's have a cup of coffee or tea and share our news," was Judith's contribution. She was itching to open the package and see what they had for mail. She wished they had sent some back with Sue and Tommy in the fall; their families must be worried sick about them. But oh how happy she was to see her friend Sue again. Because the cabin was so small, only Tommy and Sue accompanied Wilson and Judith inside.

As they led the way to the cabin, Judith and Sue talked. "I see you have some very important news." Sue observed. "When is your baby due?"

"We think late in November." Judith couldn't wait to share her fears with Sue, since this was her only chance to talk to another woman. "I'm scared. How can a baby survive out here?"

"Our babies often do," Sue reminded her.

"But I don't know much about babies. I've never had one before."

"I only had Jimmy. And he was born out here. It will be OK. You'll see. Tex, my husband, was so good the way he helped me and I know Wilson will take good care of you."

"I don't think Wilson knows much about babies, either. He was an only child. At least I had some experience helping my mother with her babies. But they were all born in the hospital, and my aunt came and stayed with us for a long time, until Mother was able to be on her own. I doubt if Wilson has ever changed a diaper. And what am I going to do about diapers? We have nothing for a baby."

"Babies don't need much, Judith. As long as they are fed and warm and loved, everything will be fine. A couple of towels will do for diapers. We use the soft mosses and the fluff of cattails to soak up the wetness. If you put it between the layers of cloth, it will work fine."

"Wilson said he would make a cradle."

"Don't worry so much about things, girl. You take care of yourself and get rest and things will work out just fine."

"Is Libby expecting yet?" Judith asked.

"I don't think so," Sue told her. "I am happy for you and Wilson. A baby will be nice. We will be coming back before the time you have the baby. I will stay with you and help, if you would like."

"That would be wonderful, Sue. Thank you so much. I feel better already." Judith felt a thousand fears melt away. Impulsively she gave Sue a hug, which Sue returned warmly.

They shared coffee and news. Judith made a batch of biscuits and Tommy suggested a bonfire outside where they could cook up some of the big jackfish and walleye they had caught. Jimmy had caught a good-sized whitefish and several trout, so everyone ate well. The young man still held himself aloof from Wilson, though he was polite to Judith, who assured him the little mare was in good shape. When she invited him to look at the horse to verify for himself, Jimmy gave a half grin and went to the corral and whistled. Judith smiled when Jazzy galloped to the rough fencing to welcome her old owner. "Our horse still thinks she belongs to Jimmy," Judith told Sue.

"Yes, Jimmy is good with animals. His father was, too."

Impulsively, Judith blurted, "Why does Jimmy hate Wilson?"

"I don't think that he does. You know, sometimes it takes people a while to get to know what makes others act the way they do. Time usually answers all questions." Sue's response was not very enlightening, but Judith knew that she had said all she was going to on the matter.

After a day's visiting, catching up on the winter news, everyone prepared to get some sleep before the people left early the next morning. Nights were only really dark for about six hours at this time of year so far north, but travellers and pregnant women needed rest.

Jimmy continued to address his grandfather and the others in the native language, although the others all responded in English. Whenever Tommy and Sue asked Jimmy to do the same, Jimmy left the circle to spend time with the horses – especially Jazzy, who was excited by the proximity of the other pack animals. Before he left with Tommy's people, however, he spoke to Judith. "Be careful. Take care of the baby," he said, looking at her belly.

Judith bit back a retort that Wilson would see to it the baby and she were all right, and instead smiled gently at the young man. Jimmy reminded her of her younger brother, who could be in a foul mood when things didn't suit him. She wondered what it was about Wilson that Jimmy didn't like. With her, he seemed shy and a little protective. He didn't seem to be attracted to her romantically, so Jimmy couldn't be suffering jealousy or envy.

She smiled again at the young man and attempted to open a conversation. "How long did you have Jazzy?"

"You mean . . ." He told her the name he had for the horse. It was a name Judith could not get her tongue around.

"Yes. I can't say the name you call her. I call her Jazzy."

"She was born to my black mare. I helped when she was born."

"I've never seen a foal born. It must be very special."

Jimmy nodded and looked away, seeming embarrassed. He didn't respond, so Judith decided to end the conversation. "I hope you have a safe and productive summer, Jimmy. Take care of your mother and Tommy, and be careful yourself." Again the young man nodded, and then moved away. Judith stood still, a thoughtful look on her face as she watched his lithe movements as he rejoined the others.

When the visitors left the next morning, Judith was nearly as morose as the last time, but this time she had mail. She opened the package anxiously. As well as a dozen copies of various newspapers, there was a letter from Wilson's mother, one from his grandparents and one from Judith's parents. Every writer expressed worry, and only his mother failed to wish them the best. Wilson's mother hoped they would come to their senses and return home. They read each letter three or four times.

"We need to write home, Wilson. We can send the letters back with Tommy and Sue in November. That will be at the end of the first 18 months. We'll be able to go with them. We can buy a thousand dollars worth of supplies. That's what the agreement said, right?"

Wilson watched as the thought of a trip to civilization brought a flush of excitement to her face. Her eyes lighted with enthusiasm. His mind filled with thoughts of what lay ahead for them, and he didn't answer right away.

"If we just go for supplies," she continued, "it won't mean we aren't staying here, will it? The time will still count, right?"

"Of course it will. Don't you worry, darlin'." Wilson thought of the approaching birth of the baby and made no comment. Judith would not be able to travel either with a new baby or so close to her due date. She would not be going to Sherridon. He didn't want to say anything to dampen her euphoric mood. There was time enough for the truth of the situation to sink in. He worried about what was going to happen. He couldn't leave her just before or soon after the baby's birth, and she was certainly going to be in no condition to travel. They did need to get the supplies, but just how he didn't know. Judith had not told him Sue was going to stop with them when the group returned on their way to Sherridon. Had he known Sue planned to stay and help Judith as she neared the time of the birth, he would have been less concerned. There was no way for either of them to know how much worse things were going to get.

16
Dark Days

Summer came bursting upon them, bringing long hot days and humid nights. Judith got heavier, more awkward and prone to backaches. By mid-July she was finding it increasingly difficult to get around on her swollen ankles. Backaches dogged her when she was awake, and her sleep was fitful as she kept waking with the need to pass water. Her discomfort was amplified because she didn't know what lay ahead of her in pregnancy. Certainly, her mother had shared scant insight, as such a topic was not for the ears of children.

Judith's moods became unpredictable. Little things she would normally have laughed off assumed gargantuan proportions, and tears were seldom far away. She fussed about her clothing not fitting as her tummy swelled with the child, and though she tried to alter the pants and shirts she was not satisfied with the results. This was one time she was happy to be where no others would see her, but if she were with others, she reasoned, she knew she would be able to get properly made maternity outfits. Wilson wondered many times what had become of the sweet, level-headed woman with whom he'd fallen in love. One time she flew into a rage because there was no water in the cabin for her cooking. Another time she threw the entire meal out the door because it didn't smell right. Wilson tried to reason with her, but she yelled that he never understood what it was like to labour over the hot fireplace for hours only to make a mess of the meal. In complete confusion and frustration, Wilson grabbed the shotgun and some shells and took refuge outside.

"That's right, Wilson Andrew Daniels! Run off to hunt and leave me with all the mess!" Judith screamed after him. Wilson put his head down and walked faster.

Left alone to work out her anger, Judith threw herself on the bed and wept. She knew it wasn't fair to her husband. Her mother would have been shocked to hear her yelling like that. "But I get so mad!" she cried.

After her storm of tears cleared, Judith felt a bit ridiculous and wondered what Wil thought of her. I'll make him a nice meal, she thought, but then she realized the ingredients for what she considered to be a nice meal were nowhere to be found in their abode. It will have to be stew again, she thought. She would add bannock to the stew to make it special.

As the stew bubbled merrily over the fire, she stirred up a batch of bannock dough and pushed the pieces into the stew. The pot was soon near to brimming, but she pushed on the lid and went to clean up her kitchen area.

She heard Wil whistling and decided to go out to meet him. Maybe she would apologize for her tantrum. He smiled as he held up a couple of ducks. "Fancy duck supper tomorrow, darlin'?"

"Sounds lovely. Will you get them ready?"

"I sure will. Are you OK?"

Not trusting herself to speak, Judith nodded.

"Whoa!" Wilson looked to the open door of the cabin. "What's burning?"

"My supper!" Judith wailed. She rushed back inside the cabin. The boiling stew had overflowed the pot. Damp, stew-soaked clumps of dough had fallen into the fire, and the stench of the burning mess was dreadful. She tried to grab the pot, miscalculated, and seared her hand.

The pot dropped to the floor. Yet it landed on the bottom, fortunately, and the spillage was not as bad as she feared.

Wilson propelled her to the water pail, where he submerged her burning hand. Fearing another outburst, Wilson cuddled her, told her how much he loved her, and vowed supper would be just fine. Despite the accident there was more than enough stew left in the pot for both of them, he said, and added that he'd have the mess cleaned in no time. Judith let her tears flow. She felt she was an incompetent fool, but at least one who was loved.

"I still have about four months to go," she said. "I have so much to do and I feel so useless. I'm sorry, my love."

"You have nothing to be sorry for," he said gently. "I'm managing just fine. Don't forget I'm the reason you're in this condition. Sit there and I'll finish getting the meal on the table."

Once the meal was over, Wilson told her how delicious it was and how clever she was to think of making it that way. "We just need a bigger pot, that's all," he reasoned. Judith had to admit it did taste pretty good, even though the air hung heavy with the reek of burnt bannock and stew.

"I don't know what gets into me, Wil. I get so angry sometimes. I'm sorry. I don't mean to be like that."

"You take it easy. Maybe this is just a bump in the road." Wilson tried not to show his concern, but he was worried.

"It's a bump, all right," Judith said, laughing, "but not in the road." She patted her protruding tummy.

"Hey, you in there. You're making Mommy uncomfortable." Wilson admonished his growing child.

"Mommy," Judith echoed. "I didn't know how sweet that word could sound, Daddy."

Wilson grinned. Though he looked forward to seeing his child, he was quite concerned for Judith. He couldn't leave her alone, and he could not bring her anywhere with him. He wished Sue had stayed. He wished they were somewhere close to a doctor. This was a hellish time for them to have a child on the way.

August 9 was a cold, miserable day. The wind tore leaves off the willows and beach trees and flung them around the clearing. It moaned through the pines, sounding like myriad tortured spirits. Howling mournfully around the sides of the cabin, it seemed to be trying to tear the leather away from the window and wrench the door open. Thunder growled across the skies and grumbled away until it died in the distance. Judith huddled on the bed, back aching intolerably, trying without success to find some way to place her body that didn't hurt. The pain continued to intensify throughout the day, and by evening she was crying, no longer trying to stifle her moans and screams.

"Something's wrong, Wil. Something's wrong with me and the baby. I can't stand this pain! Oh, I feel like I'm going to die!" Judith's screams tore at Wilson's heart. He felt so helpless. All he could do was rub her body where he could reach it through her thrashing, and try to talk calmly to her. He doubted she could even hear him. All through the night, Judith alternated between screams of pain and brief moments of exhaustion where she lay back like a lifeless doll. Wilson used a wet cloth to wipe her face, and tried to calm her though he was terrified himself. He had no idea what to do in this situation.

Just before dawn, a baby was born. It was a little girl. Her tiny body was blue. Wilson tied off the umbilical cord, and tried to get the baby to breathe, but she just lay limply in his hands, her thin, brittle-looking limbs sagging away from her tiny blue, blood-streaked body. Wilson wrapped her carefully, holding her against his large warm frame. She fit into the palms of his hands. Such a small, pitiful little creature. Tears poured unchecked down his cheeks as he cuddled his daughter. "Poor little baby, poor little thing," he murmured. "You never stood a chance, did you?"

Judith was barely conscious. He placed the infant's body beside the fire as if to warm her and went to care for his wife. He delivered the afterbirth, knowing it was important that it come out cleanly. Then he carefully cleaned Judith and tried to make her comfortable.

After a long while, Judith began to stir. "Did the baby come?" she whispered. "Where is it? Where is the baby?"

"The baby's here, darlin'. It's a little girl. She's so tiny. She didn't make it, darlin'. I'm sorry, I'm so sorry."

"Give her to me. I want my baby." Judith became so distraught that Wilson got the baby and handed her to her mother.

"Here she is," he said. "See how tiny she is."

"She's beautiful. She's going to be all right. You're going to be all right, Aileen Maigrette. You're going to be just fine. Mommy will take care of you." Judith held the tiny body, crooning to her, rocking gently.

"Let me take her now. You need to rest." Wilson tried to remove the little body, but Judith refused to let go.

"She needs her mommy. Isn't she lovely, Wil? She's just beautiful."

"Yes, she is precious. But we lost her, Judith. She came too soon. She isn't breathing. She never did breathe. She was born dead. I'm so sorry. I tried, I tried to get her breathing, but . . ." He was crying openly.

"No, no. Don't cry. She's OK. She's our baby, Wil. See her? She's our little girl." Judith pulled the child's body close to her own and wrapped the down-filled sleeping bag around them both, blocking out the cold reality of a death her mind refused to accept.

Wilson rose, and put his hand on Judith's head. "Are you going to be all right for a few minutes? I have to go out, but I'll be right back."

Judith didn't answer. She was concerned only with the baby she cuddled.

❋

Wilson got the material for the cradle he was building and formed it into a small casket. Through his tears he prayed for the words to convince Judith to let the baby go and get through this. Shaking his head and wiping away tears, he prayed for the strength he needed as a husband and father. He wondered whether he was still a father though the baby hadn't lived. Taking a shaking breath, Wilson rubbed his hand over the casket and, choking back his sobs, tapped home the final nail.

Once he finished the little box, he took it to show Judith. "Look darlin'. I made this with all the love in me."

Judith looked up at him. She frowned to see his tear-streaked face, wondering why he was so distressed. She then looked at the box. "But it looks like a coffin. Why would you make a coffin?"

"Oh, darlin', I wanted to make a cradle. Oh, Judith . . ."

Judith began to cry. "Is she . . .? Is our baby . . . dead? No. Why, Wilson? Why? What did I do wrong?" She took the tiny body from under the blanket, slowly removed the wrap Wilson had used, and checked over the tiny fingers, toes and thin little limbs. The thick umbilical cord was still attached to the tiny belly. "Why did she die, Wil? Why couldn't she live?"

"She was born too soon. The Lord called her back. We have to let go. Wrap her back up and we'll make a nice place for her." Together they placed the tiny body gently in the wooden box.

"Where, Wilson? Where will we put her?" Judith leaned back to look into his face. "I don't want her to be dead."

"I know, darlin', I know. On the little hill in back there's a place where wild roses grow. We'll bury her there. I'll make a cross to put on her grave, and when you're better we'll say prayers there for her, OK? It's a really pretty place."

"I don't want to bury my baby," Judith wailed.

"It's not what I wanted either, darlin', but we have no choice. You know that, don't you? We have to do what we have to do. We'll visit her and she will live on in our hearts."

Judith's sobs slowly changed to hiccups and jerky gasps as she nodded miserably. "Can we make a little fence around it?"

"We'll make a pretty little fence around it."

Things came to pass as they had planned. The little coffin was placed to rest on a hill where wild roses perfumed the air and birds sang hymns. Wilson built a little fence around the site and a sturdy cross was erected. Inscribed were the words:

Aileen Maigrette Daniels
August 10, 1949
Our Daughter
Safe in the arms of Jesus.

17
Farewell

By the middle of September, Judith was well enough for a ceremony by the gravesite. They offered prayers for their tiny stillborn daughter, and asked the Lord to bless and keep her until next they saw her.

"God bless you, my baby. Mommy is so sorry. I'm so sorry." Judith was crying.

As Wilson put his arm around her waist and led her back to the warmth of the cabin his mind was troubled. "Why did you tell the baby you're sorry?"

"Because it's my fault she died, Wil."

"How can you say that? It's not your fault. You're not to blame for our daughter's death." Wilson looked into Judith's face and wiped her streaming eyes. "Don't blame yourself."

"It is my fault. I asked God not to send us a child while we're living out here. I knew it would be hopeless. It's all my fault."

"And God always does what you ask? Your prayers are the most powerful and always answered the way you ask? You really didn't want the baby?" Wilson forced Judith to look him in the eyes.

"I wanted her. I did want her. I wish I hadn't asked for no baby." Judith wept big, gulping sobs. She buried her face into Wilson's shoulder. "Just hold me, please. Just hold me."

"First off it's as much my fault as yours. It's my fault we're out here. And you know that you had trouble right from the first days you became pregnant. There had to have been something wrong, darlin'. God doesn't make mistakes. I don't know why the baby didn't live. I don't know why this happened to us. But I do know that things happen for reasons we don't understand. We just have to have faith that eventually everything will work out the way it's supposed to." He rocked Judith gently, loving her, hurting for her and with her. "She really is safe in the arms of Jesus, you know. She is."

Judith nodded.

"You have to know it's not your fault. You do know that, don't you?" He pulled back, searching his wife's face.

"I guess you're right, maybe. But I just feel so empty, Wil."

"I know. Me, too. I'm just so glad I still have you. I don't know what I would have done if I'd lost you, too."

Daily hard work was a good antidote to grief. Though Judith needed to take it easy for a few weeks, they had to spend the rest of September and most of October preparing for winter. There was little time for reflection. More storage room was made for their meat. Their skimpy harvest from the garden was stored carefully in the root cellar, and as much hay as they were able to gather was set aside for Jazzy. The mare's lean-to shed was filled with wood cut into lengths for the fireplace, and smaller branches and twigs were packed in the wood box. Judith gradually resumed more and more of her share of the workload as she regained her strength. She often found herself thinking of her daughter, but had to push the thoughts away. "Later," she said aloud to herself. "Later there will be time to think of you, my baby."

They had reached the 18-month point in their stay and they were able to purchase another thousand dollars' worth of badly needed supplies. Wilson was still puzzling about the trip. If they left the cabin, the vegetables would freeze. They couldn't leave Jazzy unattended, so the mare would have to come along with them. The tent would have to be packed as well, and that was when he remembered it was now part of their cabin roof.

Toward the end of October Tommy Lightfoot's group returned on their way back from the caribou hunt. Their friends shared their sorrow over the loss of the child. Sue shed a few tears as she held Judith in her arms. Although she didn't have any words to offer, her closeness and shared sorrow said more than mere words could. Jimmy's anger was apparent, but he chose to ignore Wilson rather than exhibit his usual rude behaviour. The group regaled the couple with news of the hunt, and worried aloud over the couple's poor timing for the necessary trip. The waterways would be frozen soon; already, there was ice along the sheltered areas. This would enforce overland travel that would be much slower and harder.

Tommy told Wilson that during the hard winter months the stronger young fellows were hired by the mines to cut and haul wood for the mining camp. This, plus the sale of their pelts and caribou hides, provided money for his people. Tommy suggested that Wilson and Judith travel with them and spend the winter in town. Wilson could probably get work in the mines, and maybe Judith could find work in the school.

Wilson turned to his wife. "What do you think? Would you like a taste of civilized life this winter?"

Judith was sorely tempted, but they had discussed the ramifications of abandoning the cabin. She would not leave her little daughter alone here. In her head she knew it wasn't terribly sensible, and hesitated to voice the concern. They did need supplies, as the stores they had accumulated were not sufficient to see them through another winter. She thought of Annie and Clarence. They would have the baby they'd been expecting. If Annie had a successful pregnancy and birth, the child should be about a year old now. It would be great to see her friend again, but not if she had to abandon her own baby.

"No. I don't want to leave the cabin, Wil. We worked too hard to put up the vegetables, and if we leave here for any length of time we'll have to start those three years all over again. It's been too hard to have to do over. I'll stay."

"But I can't leave you here alone, and we need to get supplies. You know that. Come on, darlin', let's go back with Tommy and Sue. We'll come back in the spring with them and start over."

"I don't want to go."

"Be reasonable, Judith. It's the sensible thing to do right now. We can wait another year to get the balance of the inheritance. We can do it."

"I'm not going, Wilson, and that's final! And it won't be a year; it's a year and a half." Judith took a deep, calming breath. "If you go now with Tommy, how soon could you be back?"

He looked to his friend. "Tommy?"

"You could fly back if you have enough to hire a plane. There are planes flying out of Sherridon a lot. That would be quicker."

"How long will it take your group to get there by the waterways?"

"About four days if the weather holds."

"See, it won't take long," she said. "I'll be fine here for five or six days. You go with the group, get the supplies and fly back. That's the best way – the only sensible way." Judith had made up her mind; she would not leave while her baby was left behind.

"I don't want to leave you," he said.

"I can't go and leave you here. I can't travel with them. I'll be fine if I stay here. It's the best way, Wil. You know we can't leave the cabin." Judith refused to budge. "You must see that. It's the only thing that makes sense. I wouldn't be much help to our friends if I went instead of you, and I'd have a harder time to get back. Please, you go, Wil."

"I know it makes sense, but I don't want to leave you alone." Wilson was torn. It did make sense, and Judith wasn't really up to travelling so soon after having lost her baby. She still was weak, and tired easily. He was aware they had enough provisions for her to be all right for a week. He ran his hand tiredly around the back of his head, clenching his jaw.

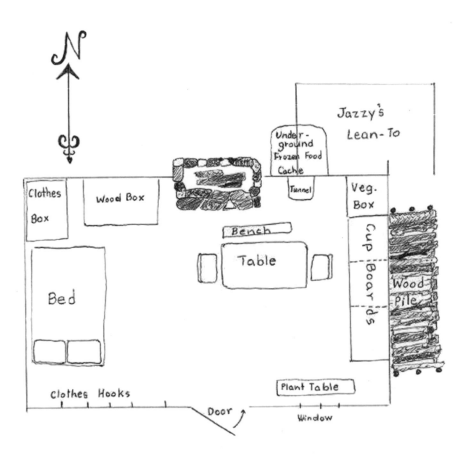

18

Alone

Wilson left with Tommy Lightfoot and his band on October 28, and by November 3 they reached Sherridon. The trip had taken three days longer than they had planned. Cold weather had arrived earlier than usual, choking the waterways with ice, and what was treacherous for walking was lethal in a canoe. Tommy and his people were forced to travel on land for the final days of the journey. Wilson carried with him the pelts he had accumulated, and the letter from the lawyer that allowed him to take provisions worth a thousand dollars, with the written assurance the storekeeper would be paid as soon as the bill was received in Calgary.

The owner of the local store was an understanding man who agreed to buy his pelts and give him enough cash from the balance of the supplies budget to hire the pilot of a Canso, a small plane used in the north, to fly Wilson and his supplies home to Judith. Had the shopkeeper not heard about a young woman left alone in a cabin this may not have been such an easy deal to make.

Along with the canned and dried goods and ammunition for the three firearms, Wilson bought a real glass window that was packed securely within a wooden frame and padded with yellow flannelette material patterned with tiny green ribbons. As well, he bought needles, an assortment of thread, a warm parka and several books for Judith, extra socks, vegetable seeds, more oats for Jazzy, a new skinning knife for himself and a hoe and shovel, plus 50 feet of rope.

Wilson met Fred Coulter, an ex-RCAF pilot, a short, stout man in his 50s. Fred's love of flying and his bravado led him to become a bush pilot, one of the best available. The two men talked about their war experiences, respecting the roles they had each assumed during the war. When Fred learned that Wilson needed a pilot to fly him into bush country where a young wife awaited alone, he insisted on being the one to accomplish the mission.

They pulled out maps of the area and determined Rat Lake provided a promising landing strip. Fred flew a Balanca, a high-wing monoplane, big as bush planes go, with a 750-h.p. Radial engine and a three-bladed propeller that stuck out in front like a cigar. Fred said it was one of only two still in service. Two struts on each side connected the wing to the floats and the floats to the fuselage.

Fred got Darcy, his mechanic, to assist with the removal of the floats so skis could be installed. The struts were wide and shaped like airfoils, evidently designed to provide some lift. As Fred and his mechanic worked on the skis, Wilson asked, "How much lift do you get from those struts in comparison to the wing?"

Fred studied the struts a moment and drawled, "Well, I don't really know; we've never tried flying her without the wing." The mechanic nearly fell off the ski laughing at Wilson, who joined in the laughter, agreeing that it was a question that couldn't be answered.

"As long as it gets me home, I'll be a happy man." Wilson added.

Close to shore, the ice would be thick enough to support the plane, and since it had been bitterly cold without insulating snow cover, and not windy, the ice was likely to be quite smooth. Wilson would need to haul the provisions himself from the landing spot to the cabin, as the plane would need to return to Sherridon at once.

The morning they were to fly out, it began to storm and the plane was grounded until conditions improved. Fred told Wilson he was sorry but it was out of his control. Wilson worried about Judith. The early freeze-up had delayed his return already, and here was a further delay. Pacing and letting anger eat at his gut was not the answer, but Wilson was hard-pressed to remain calm. It reminded him of the many times in the services when they had been ready to pull out, only to be informed the unit was grounded until further notice. Frustration dogged him, but he had to hold strong.

It helped to visit with Clarence and Annie Mills, their first friends at Sherridon. Their baby, Charlie, was a little more than a year old, just learning to walk, and a good-natured child. Wilson also spent hours at the Club, which was open 24 hours a day to give the bachelors a place to spend time off. He asked Clarence and Oscar, the huge old guy he'd befriended on the train on the way into Sherridon, about the rumour Tommy had told them, and both miners informed him the ore was indeed running out and the town would be relocated 150 miles north to where a promising strike had been found.

Oscar showed him Cats – huge machines that would drag the 12-by-28s over the frozen land and waterways. Wilson was amazed to think of moving a town in this manner. The tractor swings, as they were called, took four days to make the one-way trip, barring accidents or break-downs, Clarence said. The families would be flown to the new site once their homes were in place on basement foundations.

"Tell me about this new place, Clarence. What is it going to be like?"

Clarence told him it was a promising site for mining nickel and would be called Lynn Lake, after Lynn Smith, the mine's Chief Engineer. Evidently, about 50 men had been stationed there for the past four years, since 1947. "We were concerned there for a while that since the ore field here was failing, we were going to be laid off. That happened before, from 1932 to 1937. We're lucky that we can continue to work.

We love it here in the north. It's a great place to raise a family." Clarence winked at Annie, making her blush.

Wilson used one of the four camp phones to place a call to his grandfather to let his family know that all was well, and promised that he and Judith would send more news when they could. Doc MacDougal agreed to call Judith's parents to let them know how their daughter was faring. Then Wil settled down to learn what was happening around town, while awaiting better weather so he could fly back to his wife.

Oscar explained the tractor train move would take several winters as SGM, the mining company, ceased operations in Sherridon and moved to Lynn Lake. Canadian National Railway had agreed to extend the rail line to the new location, some 140 miles due north, and was to be completed by 1952. Oscar loved mining, and if Lynn Lake panned out, he would be able to stay there for the rest of his working life. There would be an airport at the new site, and Canadian Pacific Air Lines would be making flights from Winnipeg three times a week. There would no longer be a need to order a year's supply of groceries in advance.

Wilson was pleased to note this rail line would be much closer to the cabin, shortening the distance for them to make contact with the outside world. Judging by the map, Lynn Lake was quite a bit closer to the cabin site than Sherridon was, about a third of the distance in fact, though it was uncertain what the terrain between the two locations would be like.

The first families were ready for relocation as soon as ice on the lakes was thick enough for the heavy tractor trains. Annie and Clarence would not be leaving until next year. Their friends were packed and awaiting the news the houses were relocated so they could be flown in. The families that were relocating were living with others while their houses were being moved, and though they were excited about moving found the wait quite difficult. Usually the men accompanied the tractor swing so they could assist in getting the houses onto the basement foundations and get things readied for their wives and children to arrive by plane.

The glacial winds howled along the empty streets of Sherridon, blowing sand and snow that blasted anyone foolish enough to be outside. Wilson waited along with the pilot for the storm to abate. Gusts of wind moaned through the stressed pines, sounding like restless wailing ghosts of the long dead. Anyone going out for the necessary wood and other supplies went out at a risk of their lives.

Alone with her thoughts, and only the mare for company, Judith kept busy. She counted on the days flying past, which they seemed to, but the nights were so long, dark and lonely. When it became bitterly cold, Judith took some extra oats out to Jazzy. The crunch of snow beneath feet, the mare chomping the grain, and the odd popping of frozen trees – little interrupted the eerie silence. Frost sparkled on the tree branches lit by the twilight in the southern sky, looking like a thousand candles lighted on sparkling Christmas trees.

Even the air was still, as though holding its breath, but the cold stung her exposed flesh. Then, far off in the distance, came a lonely wavering call of wolves, echoed and answered by others in the opposite direction. The notes rose and fell, died out and arose again, sending chills up Judith's back. It was beautiful but eerie and she loved the sound – the music of the north.

Synchronized with the fading light of the sun, the northern lights began their dance across the heavens in weaving bars of pink, orange and green. Judith wrapped her arms around her body, leaned into the mare, and remembered sharing the magic of the lights with Wilson. He had been gone six days now and should be back tomorrow perhaps, or the next day. "Where are you tonight, my beloved? Are you thinking of me? I miss you, Wil." Judith spoke her thoughts aloud and the mare stirred restlessly, snorting and stomping its hind foot. Judith patted the mare on the rump, and after wrestling some chunks of wood from their pile returned to the cabin, where she shut the heavy door, barring it against the approaching darkness.

✵

Unknown to Judith, a white form rose silently and padded away along the edge of the stream. The wolf had been observing the two-legged ones, and saw the male leave in the hollow logs with others of his kind. He wondered at the male leaving the female and the moose-like creature alone. He had watched her feed the mare, heard her speaking and saw her re-enter her den and close it.

He was distracted by the scent of beaver. He hoped to catch an unwary one away from the water, but heard a loud slap of a tail on open water followed by several liquid sounds of bodies slipping back to safety.

He sensed something behind him and twisted off the path he was following, and then slipped into the reeds along the edge. He caught sight of a big, slow grizzly. Had it been following him? The white wolf crouched in the bulrushes as the bear came abreast of him, moving its immense head from side to side, sniffing to locate the wolf.

With lightning speed, the wolf darted out and grabbed at the bear's rear quarters, bit quickly and deeply and then darted off to one side, out of reach of the massive paw that swept toward him. The bear roared and lunged at the wolf, which again darted off to the side and dashed towards the bear's rear.

Knowing there was no point in carrying the battle further, each combatant faced the other warily and then backed off. It was time for the bear to look for a place to hole up for the winter. He was fat and lazy and not in the mood for a senseless battle with a very large, if somewhat emaciated, wolf.

The wolf ate a few late berries he found, unearthed a mouse, and surprised a mink that had just emerged with a fresh muskrat. The wolf took the muskrat away after a brief skirmish, leaving the mink unscathed. Knowing he could have killed the mink as well did not bother the wolf. The muskrat was in excellent shape, and proved quite filling. He got it easily, without wasting any of his energy reserves. He sensed a change in the weather, and knew he had to prepare. At least now he'd have a fairly full belly.

Before Judith climbed into her down-filled sleeping bag, it had begun to snow; gusty blasts of glacial wind hurled stinging ice pellets against everything in its path. When she awoke the next morning a howling wind wailed mournfully around the cabin. It tore at the hide covering on the window, stealing warmth from the dwelling, and battered the roof as though daring her to step outside to face its fury.

Judith wrapped herself in the warm blankets. She stirred up the embers and carefully placed bark and thin branches in the fireplace, adding several slim logs as soon as a steady flame was licking at the fuel. Then she added a couple of large logs and hooked the pot of water over the flames. Once she had hot water, she made some coffee, added some to the cold water in a basin to wash and put the rest back on with some oatmeal, though it was getting pretty stale. Then she prepared to trudge outdoors to take meat from the cache, wishing she had done so the previous night. The wind whipped her breath away and she could see nothing but white, swirling flakes. She backed into the cabin, pulled the door closed, and knew it was wiser to wait until the storm died down.

The blizzard continued for two days without letup, and when it was over, the weather turned bitterly cold and clear. Judith bundled warmly, determined to get outdoors. For two days she had eaten nothing but stale oatmeal.

The door wouldn't budge. Snow had piled against it, barring it securely from the outside. "Oh, sometimes I just hate this country!" she shouted. "I will not be a prisoner in here. I won't." Judith stomped over to the window and began to pry off the leather that covered it.

Once the leather covering was off, icy air swirled into the cabin, displacing the warm air inside, which sailed out as a cloud of steam.

Judith dragged a chair over to the window and pushed her way out of the opening. Then she plowed through the deep drifts to the door and began the process of digging it out. Eventually she was able to get it opened enough to go back inside, recover the window with the hide and add more wood to the smouldering fire. The inside of the cabin was filled with smoke, as the opened window had created a downdraft. Judith knew the warmth from the fire would pull the smoke out if she left the damper wide open. She was exhausted with the effort it had taken so far and she still did not have any meat in the now-freezing cabin.

After a brief rest beside the fire, she went back outside and began to dig out the meat cache. Once she succeeded in opening it, she discovered to her dismay it was nearly empty. She felt an urge to scream, and then she felt like crying. Wilson hadn't told her that they were so low on meat. Why hadn't he asked Tommy and Sue to leave more than one small haunch? Wil and his damned pride. "Damn you, Wilson Daniels. Damn you," she whispered again, battling tears of fury and fear. She pulled out the single piece of caribou venison left by Tommy and Sue, looked in vain for more, placed it on the snow beside the door and started to close the opening. Then she stopped abruptly, holding her breath as an eerie feeling of being watched came over her. A tight strip of stretched rubber encased her heart, encased it and squeezed it, hurting, tightening so that it was hard to breathe.

She felt a prickling sensation run through her body as she sensed danger. She spun around, catching a glimpse of a white form as it dissolved into the bush behind her. She hurriedly replaced the door and the rocks that blocked the cache, and then scrambled with the heavy haunch until she was on the safe side of the door. Her heart pounding like a war drum, she leaned her back into the sturdy door Wilson had repaired, and fought to slow her breathing.

She decided to take a knife with her the next time she went out. The gun was above the door, where it was always kept, but there was little ammunition left. Wilson should have borrowed some from Tommy before they left, but as he'd had to leave so soon, they hadn't thought of it, and besides, he was supposed to have been back days ago. She had to admit she wasn't confident enough to make good use of a rifle. A .22 she could handle, but not such a powerful weapon.

Judith quickly set about preparing a stew with the meat, deciding to use the last of the carrots and onions. She stirred up some of the ground stale oatmeal with a bit of water and baking powder to drop into the rich broth. It would make a disgusting type of biscuit, but that was the best she could do with what she had. As she dropped spoonfuls of biscuit dough into the broth, she heard snow crunching outside the cabin. Her heart stopped. Had the creature that had been watching her returned? It could not get in through the door, but the hide window was easily accessible, especially with the snow so deep just outside.

Judith rose slowly to her feet. Carrying her remaining dough with her, she moved to the cupboard and withdrew a large knife. She placed her bowl on the table and moved behind a chair. A burning stick from the woodpile could serve as a weapon. She inched toward the woodpile, all the time keeping an eye on the window.

There was movement outside the door. She heard scuffling sounds and thumping. Just as she thought she was going to pass out with fear, she heard, "Darlin', are you OK? Judith, you in there?"

With a whoosh, the air she had been holding in her lungs exploded. Judith dropped the knife and dashed to the door. Wilson squeezed in though the small opening, as she pulled at him. "Wil, oh, Wilson!" She was laughing and crying with relief and joy.

They spent some time holding each other and reuniting with joy, before they collected all the supplies Wilson had dragged with great difficulty to the cabin.

"I have a whole pile more down on the lake where the plane let me off," he said, panting. "We need to hitch Jazzy to the travois and go get it as soon as we have some daylight. But for now, I just want to be here with you. The supplies I left there will be fine until tomorrow."

✳

Judith helped Wilson take off his snow-covered garments, and then they shared a closeness both needed, shedding clothing as they made their way to their bed, where they took each other to heights of ecstasy. After several hours of lovemaking, they became aware of a delicious aroma that stirred their hunger.

The pot was dangerously close to burning and would have, had not the fire nearly gone out. After the stew was made, the half-baked biscuit dough fully cooked and their stomachs full, the happy couple stoked the fire and again returned to bed, snuggling into each other and falling into an exhausted, contented sleep. They knew morning would arrive late and daylight hours would be short, forcing them to make a hurried trip to the lake where the supplies awaited. There would be time enough later to share their separate adventures during the time spent apart.

19
Reunion

Before sunup the following morning, after a brief, satisfying session of togetherness, Wilson and Judith arose and dressed. They stirred up the embers and added more firewood to produce a crackling fire over which they reheated the stew. As they ate, they talked. Judith informed Wilson she was accompanying him to the river for the supplies. All his objections fell on deaf ears.

Once finished eating they donned their outerwear and headed outside to hitch Jazzy to a travois, on which Wil insisted Judith ride, as the return trip would be taxing enough for her. Jazzy snorted a greeting and stood patiently as they attached the long poles over a hide blanket and anchored it to her body. She tossed her head, snorting her displeasure at being asked to work without being fed first. "Don't worry, old girl," said Wilson, patting her withers. "You'll get some nice fresh oats once we reach the supply cache."

He turned to Judith, whose face was tight in apprehension. "OK, darlin'. It's your turn now. If you don't ride, you don't come." Wil helped settle his wife onto the travois before going to the mare's head to lead her.

Judith laughed. "This is fun. I just hope Jazzy doesn't crap on me."

"What did you just say? Crap? Darlin', I'm not used to hearing such words coming from you."

"Well, bowel movement would be ludicrous, don't you think? And poop is poop, no matter what you call it."

By now Wilson was laughing so hard he could barely walk. "You hear that, Jazzy? No crapping on the missus."

Judith joined in the laughter. "Should I apologize for my word choice, oh proper one?"

"No. No apologies are needed. You're not in the classroom now. Tell me how you made out on your own, Judith. I know it couldn't have been easy."

"You left me with one small haunch of caribou venison. I could have starved. I was really mad at you, you know. And there was only one shell for the rifle. Why didn't you ask Tommy for more meat and ammunition?"

"Ah, darlin', Tommy doesn't have the same type of rifle we have, and his shells wouldn't work. I was sure I'd be back long before you ran out of meat, but I'm truly sorry to have put you through all that."

It was a fair distance to the river. The goods were packed in wooden crates, and Judith saw new makeshift cupboards and spare lumber for shelves. Wilson said he hoped there would be enough wood left to build a proper floor for the cabin. Together they piled the goods onto the travois. He let her help with the lighter loads.

As they walked back they shared their experiences each had while apart. He told Judith of speaking to his grandfather, but added that he hadn't told the man of the loss of their daughter. He had felt that a phone conversation was not the best way to handle such news, especially when there was no privacy for him. "I would have ended up crying, darlin'."

"I know. I miss her, too. She was the real reason I wouldn't leave here with you. I didn't want to abandon her."

They paused and gave each other a consoling hug. "Granddad said he would call your folks and let them know we were doing OK."

When Wilson shared his news of the Mills family and the little boy they had, Judith said, "I am happy for Annie. Am I being selfish to wish we had our little daughter?"

"No, I wish we had her too. I told Annie and Clarence, and Annie cried."

"Annie cried?" As Wilson nodded, Judith bit her lip to hold back her own tears. "How long is it going to hurt, Wil?"

"I don't know. I just don't know. Maybe it will always hurt, but we have to go on. We can't let these feelings overwhelm us. We still have to go on living and trusting in the Lord and in our love. Maybe she's an angel now. She'll always be with us in a special place in our hearts. The pain will lessen in time, though I doubt it will ever be completely gone. We have to believe she's safe now and happy."

They were silent for a while, each deep in thought.

"Wilson, there is something I haven't told you yet. When I got the meat, I got a creepy feeling of someone watching me. I looked around, and though I never got a good look at it, there was a big white animal in the bush staring at me. I was terrified. I think it was stalking me."

"I'll take the rifle and go check out the tracks when we get back. It was likely that wolf that followed Jazzy and me. I doubt it could be a polar bear this far from the sea, but we'll make sure."

"Did you buy any type of meat? I've used all we had."

"I brought some bacon and a ham, but I'm afraid that is about all the meat we have right now. I'll set out some snares and get some rabbits, maybe trap some muskrat."

"I thought you weren't going to trap anymore," she said.

"Not for furs, but it's different if we're going to eat what we trap. We need food, no matter how we have to get it. I won't trap what we can't eat, though. We'll save the pelts, because to waste them would be a shame. I hate to have to do it, but we have to eat."

"I guess it does make a difference, all right. I would rather you got the meat by hunting, though."

"Well to make the killing more humane, I bought some Victor stop-loss traps and Conibear ones instead of the leg-hold type. They're designed to kill within two minutes if used correctly. I hate it when I find only a leg in the trap, because it means the animal had chewed off his leg rather than die slowly. It just sickened me, even before I caught the wolf."

"Life is hard out here. It forces us to do things we would never have dreamed of before."

"That's for sure. I wish I'd have asked for more caribou, but I was certain I'd be back within the week. I'm sorry." Wilson glanced ruefully at Judith. "Now that we have all these provisions, I'll be able to shoot some game and we can fish through the ice. We'll soon have more to eat, darlin'."

It was getting late once they got back to the cabin, unhitched and fed Jazzy. Judith grinned as they opened one of the crates. "I feel like a little kid at Christmas."

She was thrilled with the glass window and her new parka, but when she saw the two books, tears came to her eyes. She clutched them to her chest, then jumped up and ran to him, throwing her arms around him. "Thank you, thank you, thank you. I'll read them out loud to you, one chapter a night, so they will last longer."

Together they put away the supplies, using the bags of flour and oats to raise their bed again, and Wilson nailed the window into the wall of the cabin. The extra light was a welcome addition, although it was not as warm as the leather from Jimmy had been. "We had better keep the leather to use for a night covering to save our heat, I think. Can we do that?" Judith knew how cold the cabin became once the leather was removed.

"We certainly can. Maybe if we nail it to the top and tie it up during daylight hours we can drop it when it's dark. Would that work?" He was anxious to fulfill her every wish, and was pleased to see Judith smile and nod.

"What do you think of the kerosene lantern?" he asked. "If we use it sparingly, the kerosene should last us all winter. You can read to me by the light of the lantern."

"Well, it's getting pretty dark now. Maybe tonight can be our first meal by lantern light and Chapter 1 after supper?"

As her husband nodded with a twinkle in his eye, Judith flung her arms around him, saying, "Oh, Wil. Thank you so much. I love you, husband."

And so began the first of many enjoyable evenings spent involved with the Whiteoaks in *The Building of Jalna*, by Mazo de la Roche. He'd bought it from Mrs. Tyner, the wife of the mine foreman, who was happy to pass it along to someone who might draw as much enjoyment from it as she had.

After they blew out the lantern that night, Wilson told his wife what he had learned about the future of Sherridon. He explained the best he could about the powerful Linn tractors that would move the buildings. When the railway was completed in 1952, they would be much closer to a large centre and have a way out of the wilderness, as the new mine would be less than half the distance for them than Sherridon was.

"What about the people?" Judith asked. "They can't be moved like the buildings and machinery. How will they get there?"

"The same way I got here," he said. "They get to take an airplane ride. Sure hope they manage OK."

"Why wouldn't they? Did you have trouble?" Judith suddenly had an inkling there was more to this story.

"I didn't think so. I was relaxed and enjoying the flight. I thought it was pretty neat that we were flying lower and lower, and I figured the pilot was following the river systems and needed to watch for the cabin. It is a beautiful country from the air. I could see where a fire had gone through some time ago. The trees are about all gone, just a few poles leaning haphazardly here and there and bare rock. I wonder how long it will take for the land to recover. When we landed, I learned the reason for the low altitude was because of all the ice buildup on the wings. It took us a while to knock it off, and when I left to get back here Fred was still working on it. I was about halfway home when I heard the plane take off on the way back to Sherridon.

"Wilson Andrew Daniels. That's a terrible story. You could have crashed. Then what?" Judith had sat bolt upright in bed.

"Hey, lay down, woman. You're freezing me. If we had crashed it sure would have been a waste of a window and all the supplies." He could sense Judith was about to explode, and he added hastily, "I could feel your prayers carrying me home to you. I was fine. Didn't you feel my prayers with you?"

"Well, sometimes I guess, when I wasn't scared out of my wits thinking a bear was breaking into the cabin," Judith admitted in a small voice as she lay down again and cuddled against him.

"Tell me about this bear." It was his turn to feel alarm.

"It was a great huge beast. It frightened me almost to death. It had me backed up to the fireplace with a knife in my hand ready to fight for my life. It had a name. It was Wilson Andrew Daniels." Judith finished with a giggle.

"Judith Aileen, you deserve a spank for that." Wilson laughed as he pinned her to the bed. The wrestling match that resulted was very satisfying to both contenders.

Just before he went to sleep, Wilson remembered her telling about the white animal that had been watching her. It was worrisome. He decided he'd have to check out the tracks in the light of day. It had been too late when they got back with the travois of supplies. He wondered what it could have been, and if it was the same wolf he'd seen before.

Tomorrow, he thought, tomorrow I'll take the rifle and find out.

20

Winter of '49/50

As soon as he had eaten, Wilson took his snares, an ice chisel and shovel, his hook and line and some meat scraps for bait, along with the rifle. After telling Judith he was going to fill their larder, he left to check out the tracks where she'd said the animal had been the day after the blizzard.

There were tracks all right – the huge paw tracks of a wolf. Wilson was almost convinced it had been the wolf he'd released from his trap. There was only the one set of tracks, and wolves usually travelled in packs. This had to be a lone wolf. Was it hunting? Why would it be watching the cabin? It certainly was a big one, judging by the size of its feet, and the wolf he released had been huge. The last time he'd seen it, the wolf was thin and travelling alone.

Deciding not to say anything to Judith, but to be alert to the possibility of a predatory wolf on the prowl, Wilson went into the bush to search for rabbit trails on which to set his snares. He had to replenish their fresh meat. Snares almost always killed rabbits outright, and their meat was good eating. The hides once tanned were very soft.

Once he had his few snares set, he headed for the river to try his luck at fishing. Chopping a hole in the thick ice was hard work, and he remembered to make it as big as the fish he wanted to catch, as Tommy had joked so long ago. That was a joke, but it sure would be disappointing to catch a fish too big to bring up and to lose his hook at the same time. He decided to use the lucky bone hook Tommy had given him on the way to Sherridon. He had bought a few metal ones from the store, but the bone would be best, as it wouldn't collect ice as metal would.

Fortunately the sun was still high when he had finished the hole. Wilson baited the hook and carefully sent the line down, jigging it up and down gently. Before long he felt a tug, and jerked the hook, setting it into the fish, and then he coaxed the fish to the surface with firm, steady movements, playing the fish, releasing the line when it pulled hard and gradually reeling it in. The water in the hole rose as a big pike came to the surface, twisting and pulling, trying to break free. Wilson fought with it, finally hauling it out onto the top of the river ice. He raised the ice chisel and with a quick rap ended the fish's struggles. "Oh boy, are you going to be good fried for supper," he said, chortling. He tried a few more times but without luck, so he packed up his gear and looked at his catch. The pike, which had come from the lake slippery with glistening scales, was now coated with white rime as the cold began to freeze its body. Wilson tied the fish tail-first to his bundle of belongings and set out to follow the tracks he'd made on his way out. Along the way he checked his snares. All remained empty. He wasn't too surprised, as rabbits, being nocturnal creatures, were usually more active after dark. He looked up at the pines, whose tapered tops pierced the clouded sky. Just as he was coming to the clearing, he saw a snowy owl glide swiftly and silently from the top of a jack pine near the cabin. It was a glorious sight. He wished Judith could have seen it.

Wil entered the cabin, carrying the fruits of his labour, and proudly held the pike high for Judith's admiration. "Look what I got, Judith. Just take a look at this beauty." She already had supper started, so Wilson headed and dressed the fish to add to the meat cache outside. He looked at the head and insides, and then took them out to the edge of the clearing, where the wolf tracks were still visible in the twilight. If it were the wolf he'd injured, perhaps it would enjoy some fish as well.

The window, of which they were so proud, had grown a layer of frost at least an inch thick. It did nothing for visibility, just became a light spot in the southern wall, but the illumination was welcome. They knew it would be more useful once spring came. It did add a cheery note to the cabin, one that Judith sorely needed.

The new coffee did not agree with her, and so she switched to drinking hot, powdered milk with a touch of sugar. Soon, she began to notice she was feeling more tired and irritable than usual, and her breasts were aching and tender. Judith thought she might have caught a cold in them by not being dressed warmly enough when the door was opened for a while. She knew she couldn't be pregnant, as she'd had a period last month. She must be coming down with something, she reasoned. Food didn't taste right, and she had to drag herself out of bed in the mornings, and when Wilson left the cabin, she often would crawl back into the comforts of the blankets. One day he came back as he'd forgotten something, and caught her in bed.

"What's wrong, Judith? Didn't you sleep last night? Did I wake you with a nightmare again?"

"I just don't feel well. You didn't have a bad dream, and I think I slept OK, but I just feel so tired."

"You didn't eat breakfast either. Are you sick?"

"I don't know Wil, I just feel like I can't get enough sleep. Food tastes awful and I'm not hungry. I guess maybe I am sick."

"Do you think I brought back some kind of bug from Sherridon? Were you OK before?"

"Maybe that's it. I don't know."

Not knowing what ailed her, he checked her temperature and found it normal. He decided he would watch her carefully, hope for the best and keep his worries to himself. What would they do if she were seriously ill? They were on their own, miles from any other people, with no way of making contact with anyone.

✳

After a few weeks of feeling ill at odd moments Judith counted up her days, and she was sure she'd had a period three weeks before. It had been a light one, but she'd had to use her flannels as usual. But as time went on, she began to notice other signs. Smells of food made her gag, often she felt better once she'd vomited, and her breasts were very tender. Panic set in. "Wilson, my darling, can you come and sit with me for a while? I need to talk to you." Judith tried unsuccessfully to hide her worry.

Wil searched her face. Something was amiss. This was unusual behaviour, and concern stirred deep within his belly as he sat down beside his wife. "What is it? What's wrong?"

"I'm pregnant and I'm scared."

"What? When? How did that happen?"

"Oh, I think you know very well how that happened, husband," she snorted. "And it likely happened the first night you got home from Sherridon. That was quite the little bug you brought me."

Wilson was not able to remain seated beside her. He leapt to his feet and began pacing. Worry for her and the baby overwhelmed him. He wanted to get her to a doctor, to get her to where people were. He didn't think they could go through another experience like the one they had with the previous baby.

Judith began to cry. "What are we going to do? I'm so scared."

"Me, too, darlin', but what can we do? We're stuck here. You'll never make it back to Sherridon, especially if you're pregnant. Even using Jazzy, it's too far. And I'm not leaving you again. I won't do that."

"I'm scared to lose another baby."

"Darlin', I want you to think about the last time you were expecting. Remember how you felt then. Is this the same?"

"I wasn't so scared then. But I remember feeling sick at most food smells, and I was so tired all the time. It's hard to say if it's the same. Maybe it won't be so bad this time. I'm scared, though."

Judith's illness was not so hard to bear once they knew the cause for it. By eating small amounts and more often, getting Wilson to help with the cooking and going outside for brief periods of fresh air every day possible, Judith got through the first three months, after which her stomach settled.

Wilson checked his snares daily and often came home with one or two large hares and sometimes even a couple of plump ptarmigan, which they both loved. They had agreed not to disturb the muskrats unless it was really necessary to vary the diet of bacon, ham, fish, rabbit and canned fruit and vegetables. He always left the parts they didn't eat at the edge of the clearing. That refuse soon disappeared, and often he saw fresh wolf tracks.

Jazzy and Wilson hauled more wood to add to the dwindling pile on the east side of the cabin, and it wasn't long before the spring breakup silenced the sound of small planes passing off to the west of them.

"I wonder how many of the buildings have been hauled from Sherridon now," Wilson speculated aloud.

"I wonder how soon it will be before we see Sue and Tommy again." Judith was more concerned with people than with mining companies, even though relocating an entire town was certainly a novel idea. She had managed to record a few major events that she hoped at some point to share with her family back home, and the morning illness had become a thing of the past.

"Don't you think we should ask Sue to stay with us this time, darlin'?" Wilson didn't want anything to go wrong.

"I feel great. I feel so different than I did the first time, Wil. I really think we'll be just fine. This baby is due in August late. Or early September." Judith really felt very calm and relaxed about the coming birth. She noticed the scowl on his brow and added, "We could ask if Sue and Tommy could come back earlier than the rest of the hunting party if it would make you feel better, but I'm sure we can manage. You did great. I feel comfortable with you handling this baby's birth. I really do, Wil."

"Well we don't have all summer to think about this. We need to know by the time they come through. We'll talk more about this later, OK?"

By the end of April the snow had almost gone. With no ice jams in the stream there was little danger of flooding this year. Everything looked as though this would be their best year to date. They brought in soil in empty tin cans so some plants could be started indoors to give them an early and longer growing time. A beaver dam provided a fair amount of soil, which in this rocky land was difficult to find. The lumber of the crates had gone into more cupboards and an additional narrow table by the window, from which the thick layer of ice had melted, allowing additional heat and light to enter.

They had saved the pelts from every rabbit caught in the snares, along with the brains of each so they could tan the hides in the spring. They placed the pelts in the icy water of the stream. Those pelts would surely make a warm bed for the baby.

On the first day of May their visitors arrived as they were busily working on the pelts. Tommy inspected their work and approved. Libby, Charlie's wife, was huge with child. She was expecting to have her baby in mid-July. Judith congratulated her, and said their baby should be born in early August. "I'm glad Sue will be with you, Libby." Judith exchanged a telling glance with her husband. Wilson drew a deep breath, but said nothing. Then the three women went into the cabin together. Libby and Sue looked around at the improvements he and Judith had made.

It was clean and neat. Fresh spruce boughs carpeted the floor, the cupboards were enlarged and the kitchen area was filled with sunlight, thanks to the new window. A new, narrow table under the window supported numerous tin cans with sturdy seedlings poking above the surface of the soil.

"This is a nice home you have here," Libby said. She smiled as she ran her hand along the table's satiny top.

"Wil and I like it. It was a real mess when we first got here, though. He's been working so hard to get everything the best he can before the baby comes." Judith bit her lip.

"My husband, Tex, also wanted everything to be right before Jimmy was born," Sue said gently.

"Sometimes babies don't wait until everything is right." Tears filled Judith's eyes as her thoughts centered on Aileen Maigrette, the tiny daughter who never lived.

Sue reached out and hugged her, causing the tears to cascade down her cheeks. "It's very hard to lose a child. Have you given yourself time to grieve?"

Judith didn't know how to answer that.

"She is your guardian spirit. She watches over you. She will watch over this new baby." Sue's hand stroked Judith's swollen tummy.

"We buried her on the hill at the back where the roses grow. Her birth and death aren't even registered yet. We just wrote it in our Bible."

"You buried her body. You cannot bury a spirit. Her spirit is with you. Neither of you is alone now." Sue reached for Judith's outstretched hand and held it firmly. "But you must allow yourself to grieve."

"There just is never enough time for that. It's just work, work, work. Day in and day out." Judith shook her head at the way thing were.

"You should write a letter to her, or a poem or a story. Put your feelings into words. I wrote a song for Tex when he died and it helped. Can you do something like that?"

Judith attempted to smile through her tears. "I will try. Yes, I will try. I'll write a eulogy for my little daughter. Thank you, Sue."

✳

Outside, the men talked as they worked on the pelts. Wilson decided to make the first move to try to get Jimmy to relax a little and stop the hostility. He turned to the younger man. "Sue is your mother, right Jimmy?" Jimmy nodded curtly, and Wilson continued. "Where is your father?"

"Dead." Jimmy scowled and turned away.

Wilson persisted. "Oh. I'm sorry. My father, too, is dead. I never got to know him." Wilson refused to be put off by Jimmy's curt and cold attitude. Maybe by sharing like this he could find some common ground with the young man. "Tell me about your father. What was he like?"

"My father was a good man. Brave and true. He was strong and he taught me many things." Jimmy's tone was argumentative. It sounded almost as though he were defending his father against Wilson's questions. Without warning he took the piece of wood he'd been holding and threw it into the fire.

Tommy turned to Wilson. "Tell us about your father, Wilson Daniels. What do you know of him?"

"Not much actually. He left when I was very young. He must have been a real bastard to leave a wife and small son the way he did. All I know is what my mother told me, which wasn't a whole lot, but my grandfather seemed to think kindly of him. I do know he left us without a backwards glance. He never wrote or sent money, not even a birthday card."

"Why do you judge?" Tommy asked gently. "You do not walk in your father's moccasins. You do not know the path he followed. Maybe he did what he had to do."

"I don't know. Perhaps you're right, Tommy. Granddad would agree with you, I think. I'll never know though, will I? It's too late for me to get to know the man he was."

"Spirits talk. But you have to listen. Maybe one day you will know your father."

As Tommy spoke, Jimmy rose. He walked a distance and then stood still, shoulders stiff and head held high, his back turned to the men.

"Why is Jimmy upset? Did I say something to anger him?"

"Jimmy waits for you, Wilson. He has not yet learned patience." Tommy's brown eyes twinkled with mischief as he tapped Wilson on the shoulder. "You, too, could use more patience. Jimmy is young. He has only 18 years."

"I don't understand. What's he waiting for me for? That doesn't make any sense."

"That is not for me to say. You will know in time. Patience, young Wilson."

21
Summer Trials

The weather, which dictated so much of their lives, was idyllic, and the entire forest area burst with new life all around. Wild geese, sandhill cranes, swans and many different ducks, from the noisy hen mallards to tiny teals, built nests and laid eggs. Seagulls screeched and mewed as they swept the skies. Hundreds of shore birds waded along the banks of lakes, rivers and the stream, wading and then flying briefly to land and wade some more. They darted here and there, discovering morsels of food. Mud hens or coots clucked like domestic chickens, swam with their heads bobbing back and forth and built their nests on pushups made by muskrats. Wilson harvested eggs from various nests, careful not to take too many from any one, and they had boiled, scrambled and poached eggs to add to their diet.

Birds and squirrels enjoyed the bounty of the garden until Judith hung all the tin can lids and strips of material around the garden plot. On windy days these were quite effective, but soon the thieves ignored the fluttering items, so Wilson created a life-sized scarecrow that made them both laugh. Judith called it Wilson Junior. "You just wait, darlin'. Next year I'm going to make a lady one and we'll call her Jude. I'll save a few brown pelts for her hair and we'll braid them like yours."

The plants were fairly tugged to the surface, coaxed upward by the heat and strength of the sun and long hours of daylight this far north. Wilson enlarged the root cellar in anticipation of a bountiful harvest of vegetables.

Judith decided to gather as many berries as they could and cook them up, preserving them in the icy depression they had created. Some, of course, would be dried for the pemmican she never failed to make now.

He had planted some of the oats so Jazzy could have green oats to eat, and if they produced as well as it seemed they were going to, then the grain and green stalks plus the leaves would certainly add to her feed for the winter. The meadows were thick and lush with tall grasses, and he knew they would have plenty of hay stored away for the winter. He varied the locations where he tethered the mare, always making sure the tether was long enough that she was not an easy target for foraging carnivores, but not close to bushes or shrubs that would snag the rope. In this manner he saved the most abundant growth for the hay crop. Judith would not be able to help much with the harvest come fall, as she would be getting close to her time to give birth. He didn't want to take any chances with her or this baby.

Early one morning on his way to the outhouse, Wilson heard splashing and snorting from the stream and ventured cautiously to have a look at what was creating the commotion. As soon as he spotted the cause, he quickly but quietly made his way back to the cabin, and summoned Judith in a whisper. "You have to see this. Be very quiet and follow me." He took his rifle along.

Judith followed Wilson, refraining from asking a single question. Her curiosity was burning as she inched along behind her husband, carefully placing her feet where his had been. When he stopped behind the reeds and motioned her forward she held onto his shoulder for balance and stood as high as she could.

"Oh, Wil," she breathed, her eyes wide. "They're amazing."

A cow moose and her calf were feeding in the stream. They waded slowly, their heads sometimes partly submerged. Whenever their heads came up, water streamed from their long, bulbous noses and plants dangling from their mouths. Wilson and Judith remained watching for several minutes, and then he motioned her to follow him back to the cabin. "Why did you bring the rifle?" she asked. "Were you thinking of killing them?"

"No, of course not," he said, "but if that cow had seen us and thought we were a threat to her calf, she may have charged us. I needed to be sure we'd be safe. I won't hesitate to shoot that calf this fall if I see him again. He'll look great in the meat cache, and moose pemmican is my favourite. Oh, those haunches will taste wonderful roasted slowly over the fire."

Judith shuddered to think of the cruelty of life in this land. It seemed a shame to kill the little calf, but their need for survival had forced many tasks on them, tasks she would not have believed possible while living and working in Calgary. She saw their beauty, their wildness and the bond between mother and offspring. Wilson had seen primarily food and the danger the cow could have presented. Raising animals for food seemed different when she was growing up on a farm. Perhaps her pregnancy brought forth a stronger maternal instinct.

Judith and Wilson harvested green and yellow beans and several feeds of green peas from their garden. "I'm so glad Wilson Junior saved our peas and beans for us this year. These fresh ones are so much better than canned or dried."

"Of course he's good," Wil said. "With a name like he has, he's bound to be great."

Happy in the prospects of a bountiful harvest, and with Judith's belly protruding more every week and them sharing the movements of a strongly kicking baby, the young couple felt their world could not be better. "Do you have any names picked out for junior?" Wilson asked one morning in mid-April.

"No. Call me superstitious if you want, but I'd rather not name this baby until I'm holding it in my arms."

"OK, darlin', but let's not call him Wilson Junior, all right? We already have one of those."

"What makes you so sure it's a boy? It may be another girl. Sue said Aileen is our guardian spirit, Wil. I think I believe that. I feel very confident and relaxed about this baby." Judith rubbed the palm of her hand over her abdomen. "I'm not at all worried anymore."

May 10 dawned bright and clear. Not a cloud was on the horizon as far as they could see, which, with the bush and pines all around, wasn't all that far. It was quite hot for this early in the year. Judith went out to check on the beans and peas. Flies buzzed around, seeking the moisture that beaded along her brow, and she brushed them away as she wished for a cool breeze. There were not enough legumes ready for picking, but she plucked several, chewing them thoughtfully as she returned to the cabin.

Wilson was busy cutting wood in the bush, and Jazzy was stamping and snorting, flapping her tail and flinching to drive off the biting insects. Judith felt restless and uneasy. She decided to go into the cabin to make some clothes for the baby. She was so glad Wil had bought the soft flannelette material. It was suitable for either boy or girl. Judith grinned to herself, thinking how little it mattered how the child would be dressed. No one besides his or her parents would even see. She wished there was a way they could take pictures to keep a record of the child's early years and growth for the grandparents to see. She remembered when they were preparing for this enterprise they both agreed a camera was not necessary. Regrets helped no one, so she wouldn't dwell on it. She decided to get to work. The baby would need layette blankets, lots of diapers and some little nighties.

Once inside, Judith moved the table over by the window for light and began to measure and cut off pieces of the soft fabric. It would take many stitches to hem each piece and would keep her busy for some time. Absorbed in her work, she didn't notice the darkening skies.

Wilson returned. "I think we are in for some weather. Did you notice that cloudbank in the west? The air is suddenly chilly, too."

Laying aside her work, Judith rose awkwardly and moved to the doorway. "What do you think it's going to do?"

"Oh, I guess we'll get some wind and rain for sure. Listen to that thunder rumble. There is some bad lightning in there. I hope it doesn't start a fire. There was a bad one through here in '45, I think. It's a wonder this cabin was spared. You could see the new growth and the burn pattern from the air when we flew over this winter."

"Yes, I remember you saying something about that. What will we do if there's a fire? We could lose everything."

"We would take the canoe, some supplies, the mare and hit for the river. As long as we're safe and have each other, we'll be OK."

"Do you think we should pack up some survival stuff, just in case? I've been making some things for the baby with the flannelette you brought, see?"

"They're very nice, darlin' and I guess it would be smart to have some stuff ready. I'll help."

Together they packed some food, some rifle shells and several knives into a sleeping bag and tied it securely. Judith could not stop herself from adding the few blankets she had hemmed. "I don't think we'll need this, but it's better to be safe than sorry," Wilson reasoned.

A sudden gust of arctic cold wrenched the door ajar. Wilson rushed to secure it, just before the first freezing downpour. The rain suddenly changed to hailstones that fell faster and harder. The noise was deafening against the cabin roof and walls. The pane in the window smashed, sending shards of glass, leaves and debris spinning into the cabin along with hailstones and rain. "Get back!" he shouted, but Judith could not hear his voice over the pounding ice. Wilson took her by the shoulders, propelling her out of the way and over to the bed. He hurried to the table, swept her material and sewing paraphernalia onto the cupboard and raised the table to block the window. The pounding hail and wind tore the table from his hands, and he had to take shelter with Judith until the worst was over.

"That was some storm, wasn't it, darlin'?" Wilson had his arms around Judith, holding her as she trembled within his grasp. "Are you OK?"

She nodded wordlessly, completely stunned with the havoc inside the cabin. She dreaded going outside to see the destruction there, but insisted on accompanying Wil as he rose to check.

"I think you should stay inside," Wilson suggested, but he knew that once she had her mind made up there was little he could do change it. He offered his hand to help her to her feet. "Come on, then. Let's go see the damage."

He pushed open the cabin door, shoving a pile of hailstones away with the heavy wooden barrier. The clearing was littered with broken branches, trees were felled all around and the garden looked freshly plowed. Wilson Junior was broken into two parts. Not a leaf was showing where their promise of a plentiful harvest had stood. A big jack pine had been broken off and covered the larger meat cache. It would have to be moved. The grass had been beaten and was covered with a coating of hailstones and water.

They stood silently, gazing with dismay at a changed world. Water dripped disconsolately from the trees left standing. They looked more like winter trees; most of their leaves were shredded, and the bark hung in tatters. "It looks like a battlefield after a bombing," Wilson said in a hushed and shocked voice.

Suddenly they looked at each other as the thought occurred simultaneously. "Jazzy!"

Wilson took Judith's hand in his large palm and led her to the meadow, slipping and sliding through the hailstones littering the ground, both fearing what they would find. To their relief they found Jazzy standing, her back to them, head lowered, breathing heavily.

"Jazzy!" Wilson called. He whistled to her, and the mare raised her head and slowly approached the humans. She nickered softly. "Poor old Jazzy," he said. "Did you get a beating, old girl?" She had welts on her withers and across her haunch.

Judith put her hand out and gently rubbed along the mare's jaw line, crooning softly. "Poor Jazzy. Poor girl." The horse pushed her muzzle against Judith's shoulder, nudging Judith several times. Wilson ran his hand along Jazzy's neck, being careful not to touch the welts along the mare's shoulder. He traced the scars where the bear had clawed her.

"What's she going to eat now? The grasses and mosses have been pounded into the ground." Judith looked to her husband.

"The grass will grow from the roots, and we'll give her some oats until it has time to recover. I'm more concerned with what we're going to eat."

"We'll have to be careful with the store-bought stuff to make it last through this summer and winter, Wil. Do you think we can try again next year? Are we going to be able to make it?"

"It'll take some work and planning, but we'll make it. We have to. You're eating for two now. You can't cut back on your rations. We're taking no chances with this little one."

The hailstones melted quickly in the sun's heat, and a rainbow arched its luminescent beam across the sky to the east. Wilson and Judith returned to the cabin to begin the process of mopping up. "I guess we're back to a piece of material and the leather for a window," Judith said as they picked up shards of glass from the floor. Her flannelette was wet and full of glass splinters. She lifted it and raised her eyes to Wilson, tears prickling her eyelids.

The cabin floor was a mire with mud and pine needles, forcing them to leave the door open most days to allow it to dry after scraping out the mushiest parts. More duff from the forest floor with pine needles and branches was carried in, and unfortunately, many insects along with it. Judith forced herself to squelch her aversion to the crawly creatures and either usher them outside or toast them in the fire. Eventually, Wilson and Judith returned their abode to a livable area in which they both felt comfortable. Judith could again, envisage a new baby joining them within the four walls.

They passed the balance of May and all of June clearing away debris from the storm and hunting for food from the forest. They replanted the garden, hoping to harvest some of it before the first frosts, though there wouldn't be the bountiful produce they'd been counting on. There'd be no berries and little meat, as animals fared poorly as well. Wilson kept an eye out for the moose calf, but without luck. Moose were likely to fare well, as water vegetation had not been badly damaged, but the populations of smaller creatures thinned as carnivores were forced to rely on them for food.

Wilson and Judith ate a lot of fish, and stored a fair amount, but grew tired of the same diet. The few things that managed to grow in the garden were welcome additions, but they tried to save some as preserves for later.

When the migratory birds went into the annual moult, Wilson was able to shoot and retrieve ducks and geese, and that added variety to their diet and to their food stores. Judith cut strips of breast meat from the waterfowl and dried them to make pemmican, creating soups with the remainder. Wilson had constructed a smoker, and some of the fish and meat was smoked as another means of preservation, and also for a change of flavour.

By the end of July, Judith knew her time was getting close. She was awkward, heavy and slow, but content. She had taken a pair of Wilson's pants, cut off the excess from the bottom of the legs and used it to expand the waist. By using a strip of material inserted within the waistband she was able to expand them as her girth increased. She had spent many hours stitching tiny garments for the baby, and Wilson had made a darling cradle from some of the crates. Judith lined the bottom with rabbit skins and fashioned a comfortable bed with the flannelette.

Wilson refused to leave her alone for more than a few hours each day now, and on the morning of August 5, as she was preparing breakfast, Judith suddenly gasped. "Wil, I think my water broke!"

"Back to bed, darlin'. I'll take care of this."

"I'm not going back to bed, Wilson Daniels. I feel fine. I've not even had a pain yet. I will change, though. I'm soaked."

Wilson kept watching her, not knowing what to expect.

Judith began to feel minor cramps, and she continued to lose small amounts of fluids. She kept reassuring Wil that all was fine, and it was only late in the evening the cramps became severe enough that it was obvious she was in labour. Wilson insisted she go to bed, but she was more insistent on remaining up until she became sleepy, whereupon she did go to bed and fell into a restless sleep.

He watched her throughout the night, and before morning she was too uncomfortable to stay sleeping. She found by rubbing the lower part of her abdomen she was able to work through each contraction without unbearable discomfort. She made him go to get some food, saying she was hungry and he must be as well. But when he brought her something to eat, she refused.

As the sun began to paint the eastern sky in warm, bright colours, heralding the birth of a new day, Judith felt the need to push. It wasn't long before Wilson saw the top of the baby's head appearing. The entire head emerged soon after. There was a brief pause, and then the shoulders came in a rotation, followed in a rush by the child's blood-streaked body.

"It's a boy. We have a son," Wilson said in a voice of wonder as the baby gasped, wailed and began to wave its tiny arms. Once it was delivered, he tied and severed the cord and placed the squirming boy in Judith's embrace.

"Oh, look at you. Look at all the black hair. Just like your daddy." Judith cooed to the son she had waited for so long and worked so hard to deliver. Then she noticed Wilson turning over the afterbirth. "What are you going to do with that?"

"I don't rightly know, darlin'. Most animals I know, the mother eats it after the baby is born."

"Well, I'm certainly not going to eat that. What did you do to the one from Aileen's birth?"

"I buried it."

"Well, bury that, too." She felt fairly disgusted with the look of it. It resembled a big, dark, red-brown liver. She immediately turned her attention to her new son. He was perfect, looking around with large dark eyes. He had stopped fussing and seemed absorbed with his surroundings. "Wil, look at his scrotum and penis. They're so huge and blue. Is that normal?"

"Yes, my love. All boys are born that way. Later, they change, and each is blessed with appendages in lighter colour and varying size."

Wilson wasn't sure of his facts, but he wanted to reassure his wife. And, he thought, in all other aspects, his son was normal, so this likely was as well.

Judith smiled her relief. "Welcome to the world, my son. Welcome . . . Adam Wilson Daniels."

"Adam?" He paused "Yes, I like that." He smiled at the two of them together on the bed. His family. His heart swelled with pride. Taking the placenta and the wet and bloodied materials from under Judith, he made his way outside to greet the new day.

He could not wipe the smile from his face as he made his way toward the stream. He dug in the soft earth and buried the afterbirth. Then he went to the water, where he washed the cloths. Wilson inspected them to ensure the blood had all been rinsed away, and then he took them back to hang on the rope suspended from the cabin to a tree.

He entered his home quietly and found Judith and Adam both asleep. He stood gazing down at them, a smile showing his pride. Let them sleep, he thought. Time enough to clean them both later. He took the Bible, and opened it to where he found in his own handwriting:

Wilson Andrew Daniels wed Judith Aileen McClosky
April 15, 1946 Calgary, Alta.

Aileen Maigrette Daniels
Stillborn August 10, 1949

And he added:

Adam Wilson Daniels
Born August 6, 1950

23
A Bird of Metal

The lone white wolf patrolled a territory that included the Daniels' cabin, watching their movements with avid curiosity. He learned that often food was left at the edge of the clearing – food he devoured if others hadn't found it first. When the hailstorm hit he was hunting a fair distance away. By sheltering under the branches of a spruce, he managed to escape the worst of it.

With the resulting shortage of food in the forest, hunting became more difficult and he began to frequent the cabin area. The stream and marsh close to the cabin provided a few unwary muskrats, but the beaver seemed to be on their guard these days and he wasn't able to kill one. There were a few deer and moose, but a lone wolf had no hope of getting one, unless he chanced upon a baby unprotected by the mother, which was a rare occurrence. Eagles, owls, hawks, coyotes and foxes competed for the few mice, rabbits and land-nesting birds. Skunks, raccoons, weasels, badgers, wolverines and mink took their share as well. He ate some of the tender grass shoots, but the berry bushes were so badly beaten they did not produce any fruit at all. The odd bullfrog and grasshopper made nice light snacks, but food was very scarce and getting more so as summer wore on. His entire existence centred on food.

✵

One day in early autumn the scent of wolf was carried to him on a stray breeze and he followed it warily, unsure of what he would find. If it were a healthy male, he would be forced to move on, since losing so much weight and being hungry all the time put him at a real disadvantage in a fight.

He came upon the other wolf. She was a young, light grey female, small and thin. She was hunting – trespassing in his territory – but he was glad to see her, nonetheless. He had been missing his own kind for so long, and this could be his chance to start another pack. By approaching her with his head and the front of his body lowered, with his rear raised, his tail wagging slightly and his head held to one side with a silly grin on his face, he showed friendly interest. A short "Woof" got her attention.

She stopped abruptly at the sight of him. When she noticed his playful demeanour, she relaxed. She stood still, allowing him to approach and sniff around her, and then she jumped away and stood still again, flirtatiously. She circled him, sniffing as he watched. Then, at a silent signal, they ran in circles, tumbling over and jumping up, taking turns putting front paws on the shoulders of the other. Their mouths were open and grinning. Both wolves were too lean and both were hungry, but they knew their chances of survival increased by joining forces.

With a hunting pair, it would be possible to ambush larger prey, and if their luck held out they would be able to get enough food come fall, breed and then start a family pack in the spring. By hunting together this winter they would be able to endure the cold season and provide for growing offspring as well.

The grey female followed his lead willingly everywhere except when he neared the cabin. Even when there happened to be food at the edge of the clearing, she refused to have any part of it. She had experience with humans and it was not happy, for she had witnessed their cruelty to her previous pack members. In her aversion she tried to warn him of the great danger lurking in that cabin, but he was obstinate and would not be convinced of her wisdom in this matter.

Hunting together in an orchestrated manner, they managed to take down an old cow caribou that could not longer keep up with the herd. Her tough meat was no problem for their 42 teeth. The six incisors located at the front of the jaw cut the flesh neatly from the cow, and the 12 premolars and molars sliced and ground it without difficulty. Their fangs had gripped her tightly until they brought her down. By eating their fill and remaining close to the carcass, the wolves soon left very little for other scavengers. Caribou were roaming farther south than usual since their sustenance was likewise hurt by the spring hail, and the two wolves took to following the herd, looking for a feeble animal or a youngster too foolish to remain with the rest.

The ruminants paid them slight heed, as two wolves constituted no danger to the strong or wary, but the wolves remained with the herd, watching and waiting, picking off the odd gopher, marmot or weasel as well as any mouse other hunters had missed.

One day while trailing the caribou, they heard the sound of an engine, and the grey female spotted a mechanical bird in the sky, coming toward their prey.

The caribou became nervous and began milling around, and then started to run. The white male wanted to give chase, hoping to nab a straggler, but the grey female broke away and ran off in an easterly direction. Confused, he watched her go, and then noticed the huge bird machine swing off after her. She raced, zigzagging across the land until she reached a north-south running esker. She leapt, but in mid-air she flipped over and landed on her side. She never moved again.

The male turned and ran toward the bush. The strange creature followed him, tracing circles in the sky, but the wolf remembered sheltering beneath the boughs of a spruce when danger from the sky in the form of hail had threatened. He scooted beneath an old spruce, flattened himself to the ground and did not move as the bird patrolled the air. It was not until the sound of the engine faded from his hearing that he eased out from under the spruce and, cautiously, approached the body of his fallen mate.

He remembered his other family lying dead, nothing but the scent of their fear and blood to show for what had happened. Now he knew. Death came from the sky, from a large noisy metal bird. He was not able to connect humans to the metal monster, but the noise of an engine would haunt him forever, spelling a threat of senseless death. The bird had not eaten what it had killed, but had merely killed and gone on. This made no sense to the wolf.

Alone again, and lonely, the wolf began once again to haunt the human family. It was now past the time when wolves mate; there would be no possibility of a partner for him until next year.

The leg that had been injured in the cruel trap so long ago was growing stiff and sore; one day it gave out as he pounced on an unsuspecting muskrat. The rodent managed to inflict damage as it bit him several times before he was able to dispatch it, thus adding to his troubles for the coming winter. The rat was fat and made a good meal, but cost him several days' recuperation. Times were getting tougher and winter had not yet begun.

24
Tough Decisions

Wilson watched Judith with Adam. She was such a good mom. His heart swelled with pride, and now, more than ever before in his life, he wondered how his own father could have abandoned him. He would hold his infant son in his arms, marvelling at the perfection of the tiny ears, the little button of a nose and those perfect tiny lips. His dark hair, baby fine, was beginning to curl. "I will never leave you, my son. You will grow up knowing I love you and I will try to teach you everything I know." Looking at Judith he added, "I guess I know now how very lucky I was that Granddad was there for me. He's the one who taught me what it was to be a man. When I look at my son I can't for the life of me understand how my father could just take off and leave me like he did."

"Perhaps you never will, my love. I know your own son won't ever have those kinds of questions in his mind. He has the best daddy." Judith's eyes were glowing with unshed tears of pride and joy in her 'men.'

"You know, Tommy said something to me the last time they stopped by. He said that spirits talk, but I need to listen. All I hear right now is an impossibility to comprehend how a father could leave a little guy like this."

"Is that all Tommy said?" Judith asked, wondering why Wilson had not told her of this before.

"He said I shouldn't judge, because I don't walk the path my father walked."

"Well, the Bible would agree with Tommy, I think. But when you hold your son like this, I can see where you might find it very hard not to judge the man who fathered you."

Although he was no closer to solving the mystery of his father, Wil felt better for sharing these moments with his wife and son. His bitterness toward Joe Daniels, however, remained as strong as ever, perhaps a little more than before, now it was coloured with a complete inability to understand the man who had sired him.

Wilson harvested as much of the native hay as he was able, but the natural vegetation was rather skimpy, and wild creatures consumed so much of it that there was little food left for any of them. Wil shot a deer, which he dressed, and together he and Judith preserved the meat. The liver and heart were eaten right away, and the parts they didn't eat were left at the clearing's edge. The deer was lean as most ruminants were this season, but the young moose he got later was in much better shape.

They thought of Tommy and Sue, and tried to remember what they had learned from their friends as they travelled. Deciding to try the native way of living off the bounty of the land, they began harvesting cattails. Although they had missed the early spring shoots, the later ones were above water and could be eaten raw or cooked in soups and stews. Later they found spikes in the centre of the cattail by peeling back the outer leaves. As Tommy said, they were delicious, whether boiled and eaten like corn on the cob or eaten raw as a salad vegetable. Judith advised Wilson to collect pollen from the cattails a bit later, as they could use it like flour, allowing them to stretch their supplies of baking products and add a rich yellow colour and nutty taste to the bannock. This was one of the many facts Judith had learned from Sue, and the many varied uses of cattails that Sue had taught her certainly came in handy this year. Wilson gathered the tubers for Judith to chop and soak, allowing flour to leach out. By draining the water and removing the fibres, she got a thick paste that could be dried for flour or mixed as is with additional flour, lard and baking powder. In the fall they collected the cattail fluff from the thick brown seed tails; when pressed between two layers of flannelette, this provided absorbent material for Adam's diapers and if the seeds hadn't burst, they could be soaked in fat and used as efficient fire starters, as they quickly burst into flame.

Sue had also shared her knowledge about rosehips. The berries of the wild roses were boiled for tea, a very healthful drink, and could be used for jams, while the hair inside was good for quelling itching. The bright scarlet rosehips were dry, pithy and full of seeds, but usually plentiful and widespread. "They're very healthy for you," Tommy noted. The hail had greatly reduced the number of flowers on the rose bushes, so there would be few rose berries this year.

The newest tender greens of a dandelion could be added to stews and soups. Wilson gathered some as well, but they found these a little too bitter for their taste. Surprisingly, the freshest green stinging nettles could be boiled and eaten or added to other mixtures, and they were quite good, though you had to wear gloves and long sleeves gathering them as they stung before being cooked. Earlier, Judith had refused to try them as it seemed too strange, but now she could not afford to be choosey. They wanted to get cranberries, blueberries, pin and choke-cherries, hoping the hail had not caused havoc with them as well.

One day as Wilson and Judith went through their meagre supply of food stocks, he asked, "What do you miss most out here, darlin'?"

"You mean, besides the people? Or just food?"

"Anything, except people, because I know we both miss our families back home."

"Hmm, I'll have to think about that for a minute. What do you miss, my love?"

"I guess I miss listening to sports. Like Granddad, I was always interested in sports, and we followed the Alberta teams closely. Of course we always pulled for Calgary rather than Edmonton. They were the Bronks, and just recently they changed their name to the Stampeders, and Granddad said they beat the Regina Roughriders 12-0 when I talked to him from Sherridon. He was so proud. What do you miss most?"

"Potatoes. Big white piles of creamy mashed potatoes with a dab of butter melting on top, and scalloped potatoes and potatoes fried with onions and oh . . . baked potatoes with sour cream and green onions. Oh, I do miss potatoes."

"Potatoes?" Wilson burst out laughing. "Shops, and flowers and car rides, and theatres and dresses and high heels, and you miss potatoes?"

"Oh I miss those other things as well, but oh, I miss potatoes."

"Oh, darlin', you are something."

"It's been tough hasn't it? This place is such a contrast to where we were raised, and we've had to learn a lot on our own. I think we've done pretty well, all things considered, don't you?"

"We have. We are that much closer to being rich. I couldn't have done it without your love and support, though. You've made it all worthwhile. You and this little fellow we have now."

The baby, Adam, was strong and healthy, as Judith produced a good supply of milk for him. "He's completely dependent on you, you know." Wilson told his wife. "We both are, as far as that goes. I don't know what I'd do without you."

"That goes both ways, my love. Adam and I depend on you."

At the end of October, Wilson came in from a hunting expedition without a single creature, and only about a cup of cranberries. He hung up the rifle, removed his hat, coat and boots, put the berries on the table and went to stand by the cradle where Adam was sleeping.

Judith turned toward him, laying aside the diapers she was folding. "Welcome home, my love. Isn't he precious? He's such a good baby." She walked toward her husband, who only put his arm around her but continued to stare at his son. "What is it, Wilson? What has you upset?"

"We can't do it, darlin'." Wilson's voice was low and discouraged. "It's the end of October, we have hardly any hay, the oats aren't going to last since we've had to use them to get through this summer, and we've used most of our provisions already. The meat I have isn't going to last us, and there's precious little game left around here."

Judith's forehead wrinkled in concern. "Dad always said the Lord never gives us more than we can handle with His support."

Wilson sank wearily onto a chair, shoulders sagging in defeat. "I think the Lord has an idea I can handle more than I really can. I've been praying. This whole past month I've been praying. Today, I'm afraid I have my answer. I have to go to town and get some work so we can get supplies to last through winter."

"Adam is too little to travel so far," Judith protested. "I think if we cut back on what we use, we should be OK. We still have kerosene for the lantern." Judith felt as though she had stepped in quicksand. "We could set Jazzy loose. She could probably forage enough to get through the winter with the bit we have left."

"Jazzy would be a decent meal for any number of hungry critters. It would be kinder to just shoot her. And we can't eat kerosene."

"But we can't go now! We've almost lasted the time we need to stay here. We're over the halfway mark now. By early May the three years will be done. If we go now, we'll have to start over!"

"Listen to me, Judith, May is nearly seven months away. I've been mulling it over for some time now and this is what I have to do. I've looked at this seven ways to Sunday, and there's no other answer. I'm going to go, just me, but I'll take Jazzy." As Judith tried to pull her hands away, Wilson held on tightly. "Darlin', listen. If I leave now, work for two months, I can be back before winter gets a real grip on the land, with enough to take us through 'til spring. That way we won't lose the time we've spent here. There's enough food here for one person – you – and you won't be alone, because you have the baby. I'll be back as soon as I can. It's the only way."

"I don't like it, Wilson. I don't like it." Judith searched his face, but she saw he'd made up his mind. She knew this was a very tough decision he had come to; she could see it was breaking his heart to leave them. Judith drew in a deep breath, closed her eyes, and said a quick, silent prayer. Then she rose and wrapped his head in her arms, and held him against her body. Blinking rapidly, she forced the tears back. "If this is the only way, Wil, my love. If this is truly the only way, promise me you will be very careful and come back to us. Promise me."

"I promise, darlin', I'll get back here as soon as I can with food and seeds and a new glass window if I can. I don't like this solution either, but there's just no other way." He chuckled mirthlessly. "I had been hoping Tommy and his crew would be coming through this way, but it's late already and there's been no sign of them. They must have had to change their regular route. Probably the hail messed them up as well. I wish there was another way, but I'm afraid there just isn't. Are you going to be able to do this? Will you be all right until I get back?"

"The Lord will be with me. And He will be with you. I've learned a lot about surviving out here. I'll be OK, and I'll make sure Adam is OK as well. But, oh, we're going to miss you."

The young couple clung together, drawing strength from each other and from their love.

The balance of the day was spent packing up enough supplies to get Wilson and Jazzy to Lynn Lake, since that would be closer and the chance of finding work there was better. That night was spent in a desperate urge to hold onto each other, to capture the love and closeness they would need while they were separated.

October 28 dawned bright and clear. Though it was cold, there was no wind and Wilson and Jazzy were able to get an early start on what looked to be a promising day. Judith watched until they were out of sight and hearing, and then went back into the cabin, where Adam was fussing.

She picked him up, loving the weight of his little body, wrapped a blanket around him and sat on a chair to feed him. As he eagerly grasped her nipple, nuzzling into her warmth, Judith smiled. She tried to ignore her worry and concentrate on remaining hopeful. "You are so perfect, my son. I thank God for you. Daddy had to go, but he'll be back. Daddy will come home to Adam and Mommy. You wait and see, my darling."

25
Trials and Tribulations

For the first week after Wilson left, Judith was able to keep busy, only going out twice to bring in water from the stream where the spring flowed. As the winter temperatures dropped, it too would stop flowing and she would be forced to chisel a hole in the stream and later in the river for fresh water or else rely on melted ice and snow.

After the first week, however, her stock of wood inside the cabin was used up and she had to venture outside often to get more. She would go out after nursing Adam, when he was sleeping. She didn't like leaving him alone, but had no choice. Once when she went for water she had a feeling of being watched, but when she spun around there was nothing there. She laughed at herself and decided her imagination was working overtime. Alone now, with Adam relying on her, she could not afford to take foolish chances, but she couldn't let herself become frightened for nothing either.

The white wolf, in the meantime, had seen the man leave with the large animal they had. He did not return. The wolf found it strange that the man would leave his female alone, especially when they had a young one. He had heard it crying several times. He watched from the shelter of the forest while the female came out of their den and went for water or carried logs back. She sometimes went to the place where they stored food and brought some into the cabin. There was little if any left out for him these days, but he continued to watch in his loneliness.

Somehow, being near other living creatures was a comfort to him in his solitary existence. Being alone and vulnerable to attack from neighbouring packs, he refrained from joining in the howling choruses that often split the night, though the pulsating rhythms stirred a chord deep within and he ached to vocalize his loneliness and sorrow. But no, it was best if he stayed undetected as long as he remained this weak and alone.

He was watching one afternoon as she made a trip for water. She slipped in her haste as they both heard the child crying inside the cabin. As she regained her balance, she twisted around and the wolf didn't have time to disappear. She saw him. He glided back into the depths of the forest, but from a distance heard her struggles as she got the water back into the cabin where the young one was wailing.

Judith had felt watchful eyes as she slipped on her last trip for water, and as she strove to regain her balance and get back to the cabin where Adam had begun wailing she saw a huge white wolf slide back into the bush. It gave her a chill to realize she had been under surveillance. She supposed the creature was starving and knew she made an easy target. The rifle was missing because Wilson needed to take it with him, but she could make sure she had a knife close at hand whenever she had to forego the safety of the cabin.

Once she had attended to the baby's needs, Judith made a holster for the hunting knife that she could wear strapped to her side, within easy reach. She felt more confident on her forays outside with the knife tied securely to her, though a rifle would have made a much better defensive weapon. Both the shotgun and the .22 were out of ammunition.

She coped well, rationing her food but ensuring she ate enough to be able to care for Adam. Judith felt confident for managing so well without Wilson, whom she missed dreadfully. He would be so proud of her, she knew. Her husband had been gone now for nearly a month, and she could cope for another until his return.

Then a week later, on one of her trips to get water, she fell badly on the way back, and this time she twisted her ankle. The pain was so intense she passed out briefly. Snow drifting across her face wakened her to the sound of Adam's wailing as it filtered through the cabin walls. She tried to get up, but her ankle refused to support her and she fell again. Tears of frustration and pain began to freeze on her lashes. Then a calm came over her. She had to think this through rationally to get back to her son with the water. She had been coping so competently. Her son depended on her and she would not let him down. She would manage. She had to. Judith took a deep breath to calm herself and decide what to do. As she battled with her fears, again she felt watching eyes. There it was – a huge, thin white wolf, sitting at the edge of the forest, watching her.

Her first reaction was panic, and she reached for the knife. She sat up, gripping the knife in nerveless fingers, and stared at the creature. He sat on his haunches, tipped his head to one side and regarded her. Her panic slowly subsided. If he were going to attack her, she reasoned, he would have done so already while she lay helpless on the frozen ground. There was nothing threatening in his stance. He was relaxed, only watching. How strange, she thought. What happens now?

"Hey, wolf!" she called. He rose on all fours. She swallowed, her throat convulsing. She stared at him. He still made no move in her direction. "What are you doing, wolf?" He moved back a few paces, still watching her warily. "Come help me, don't just watch. Hey, wolf!" she called as he disappeared like a wraith into the bush.

Judith pondered the event. "You are like a spirit. Maybe you are the spirit of my baby girl." Strangely comforted, Judith decided her only option was to crawl back to the cabin, moving the pail along beside and in front of her as she went. There was no way she was going to be able to make this quick, although the wails of her infant tore at her heart.

Adam was accustomed to immediate care from his mother at his tiniest whimpers. Judith wondered how long he had been crying. She called to Adam. "I'm coming, my darling! Mommy hears you. I'm coming, sweetheart." She made her way slowly but carefully to the cabin, with the eerie feeling all the way of unseen eyes upon her. Even knowing it was the wolf she now thought of as Spirit, she kept turning her head, half expecting at any moment to be attacked, but she saw nothing.

Judith smiled as her baby gulped down her milk. It was worth it. "You are worth any and all the suffering I may have to go through, my little darling. Anything for you. You are Mommy's precious little angel. Your daddy will be so proud of you. You're our little man, our precious little man." Adam stopped his greedy suckling, pulled back, smiled at her and then returned to the business of satisfying his hunger.

Judith was astounded at how important it had made her feel. It was as though Adam had really seen her as his mother, not just a feeding station. Her heart felt ready to burst with adoration for this little child she held.

Now, however, her difficulties began in earnest. Wilson would not be back for more than a month. The food was so low that Judith was forced to ration herself. Her biggest fear was that her milk would stop. Then she considered what would happen if the wolf attacked and killed her while she lay helpless on the ground. She shuddered. What would become of the baby? How long would it take for him to starve to death or die of cold as the fire went out and the cabin got colder and colder? She held him tighter and he squirmed in protest. Nothing, nothing in the world was more important than his safety.

Through her tears she prayed for guidance and strength.

After crafting a support for her swollen ankle, she spent the next two days fashioning a holster to strap him to her body. For guidance, she remembered how she had created the holster for her knife. The new one needed to be stronger and fit across both shoulders to support Adam's weight. It had to hold him in front so she could protect him, yet leave her arms free. The ones used by the women in Tommy's band were carried on the back, but Judith felt Adam would be too exposed that way. She would carry him under her outer clothing, against her body for warmth. This way, she could take him with her whenever she had to go for water.

There was no meat left in either of the storage places outside and only two small packages of dried meat inside. She drank rosehip tea, and boiled the rosehips over and over until the bland tea was reduced presently to mere hot water. Because the cattail flour was used up she was forced to pound Jazzy's oats to thicken her soups, skimming off the husks as they rose to the top. Not every husk was cleared, which made the resulting oatmeal mixture unpleasant. She kept reminding herself this was food – food she needed to remain alive and be able to feed her son. The cattail products were gone. The only grains they had left were marked for Jazzy's feed, and those were being exhausted quickly. Ice and snow covered the reeds so deeply they were inaccessible. Adam demanded to be nursed more often. She wasn't sure if his needs had increased or the milk was less nourishing, but there wasn't much she could do about it. As she continued nursing more often, with less to eat, Judith began to lose weight, and had to tie a rope around her waist to keep her pants from falling off.

She decided she had to try to snare some rabbits or they would both surely starve. She did not have experience in setting snares, but Wilson had explained how he did it. This was not anything Judith had ever anticipated doing, but necessity forced people to do extraordinary things. She didn't know if she was becoming stronger or simply more desperate. Not knowing she would ever have to do it herself, she nonetheless had listened carefully as Wilson explained the process to her. Therefore, by following his instructions as well as she was able to remember, Judith set a half-dozen snares in likely places. With her ankle bound securely she managed to hobble, the child tied in front, and her now-diminished weight supported in part by a padded, Y-shaped pole cut for that purpose, which she tucked under her armpit.

The next day she checked her snares. There was nothing in the first five, but in the last there was one skinny rabbit. She killed the struggling rodent, and was ashamed of herself for not setting the snare high enough to strangle it. Wilson had told her about that, but not exactly how high it would need to be. She skinned out the rabbit and gutted it there, as it would be frozen stiff before she reached the warmth of the cabin, and once again she felt eyes watching her. She realized there would be nourishment in the hide, head, and the guts, and that she should really stretch the skin out and dry it, but something impelled her to leave those for the wolf. She hoped it was Spirit she felt watching. The weight of Adam was across her shoulders; she was thankful the baby was sleeping. She feared that if he began to cry then the wolf might decide to take him from her, though realistically he likely did not mean to harm them, for he could have killed her on her way back from the stream while she was unconscious. Still, with her baby, she couldn't afford to take any chances. By leaving the entrails, head and the hide, whatever was watching her would have something to eat and be less likely to go after her and the baby.

Once she returned to the cabin she cooked the rabbit, adding a bit of the horse's grains along with some of the few remaining rosehips. After boiling what was possible from the bones, she tossed them out at the edge of the clearing. As she waited there, she thought she saw a white form drift between the trees, but then she supposed it was only mist.

26
Wilson Starts Out

Before the weak sun brightened the southern horizon on October 28, Wilson Daniels left his family. His only companion for the journey was the mare, Jazzy, loaded with the canoe and supplies. The late fall moon cast a cold light against the frozen ground, bright enough to throw shadows from the trees by the creek. He had the bearskin so he could make a windproof shelter, the rifle and ammunition for hunting and protection, two packs of pemmican, a pail for water, the axe for wood and matches to make fire, the canoe, feed for the mare and a small quantity of ground coffee. He figured he would reach Lynn Lake in four or five days if the weather co-operated.

The first day consisted of uneventful travel, the mare plodding along behind him, as he picked out trails beside the rivers and streams. He had the canoe with which to cross when he had to, but only if necessary. The water was freezing and would be too hard on the horse, and ice might damage his canoe.

Just before complete darkness he struck camp, setting up the bearskin around a lean-to he made with deadfall. It was quite cozy with the blazing fire in front, the heat filling his shelter, and making a comforting crackling sound. He collected water from the river and chopped off some of his pemmican to make a nourishing stew for supper. He sat before his fire, watching the sparks shooting and twirling skyward, the spicy scented smoke swirling upward, while the moon laid a silver swath on the flowing water of the river, a path that danced along the ripples.

The forest was silent except for the snapping and crackling of the flames, distant echoes of wolf song and the owl calling from the top of a scruffy old jack pine, answered moments later by another several miles north. He curled up and fell asleep almost as soon as he lay down, tired from the exertion of the day.

The following morning, before daybreak, he was awakened by Jazzy snorting and pawing the ground. Wilson got stiffly to his feet and threw another log on the fire to brew some coffee to wash down a feed of pemmican. He didn't want to take time to cook anything over the fire, as he kept thinking of Judith and Adam at the cabin waiting and watching for his return. Although he'd be gone for two months, every day spent travelling added time to his absence at the cabin. He made two trips to the river to get water. It was miserable to dip into the freezing liquid once he broke the ice sheet at the edge, but he needed to douse the fire and extinguish the glowing embers. It would be unthinkable for a wildfire to start because of any carelessness on his part.

Checking to make sure he had left nothing behind but ashes, Wilson loaded Jazzy and set off, again heading in a northwesterly direction. He wasn't exactly sure where this Lynn Lake base was, but figured the plane traffic would help him pinpoint it.

This second day of travelling was harder than the first, partly because of fatigue and partly because he was fighting doubts that he was doing the smartest thing for his family. He trudged along, his stiff limbs adjusting gradually to a regular pace. Wilson urged the mare to keep going, and stopped her when she would snatch too many mouthfuls along the way. She would have time to graze when they stopped, and while they travelled there was plenty of time to think.

His thoughts were often on Judith. Would she be able to manage alone there with the baby? Caring for a baby was a full-time job, and she had to remember to keep the fire going, make sure there was water in the cabin all the time and be on the lookout for food should she get lucky. He hoped against hope that their native friends would somehow stop by, perhaps thanks to a delay in their plans, though he knew there was little chance of that happening. Still it was possible. If they did, Judith and his son would be safe. He knew Tommy would see to that.

Wilson thought about his father. Why did he make the stipulation that his son remain for three years alone in the north? Was he trying at last to get his son away from the woman he had married and then abandoned? How much money was there to inherit and where did it come from? The man must have saved that money during the war years, when there was precious little money to be had. Through Judith's letters from overseas, Wilson learned about a wartime life of food stamps and rationing – a way of life that seemed hard even compared to his daily experiences overseas. From the letters his mother sent, he feared they were on the edge of starvation. His Granddad's communications made him think life was going on as usual back home. Even so, he didn't know then that Judith and his grandfather were trying to be cheerful and encouraging so he wouldn't know how dire times really were. In the services they were seldom hungry, though their rations became boring, and much of the time they were terrified, living with the constant sound of bombs exploding and the ack ack ack of machine gun fire, but the worst was having to deal with men burned almost beyond recognition. He remembered having the same knife, fork, spoon, tin cup and mess tin the entire four years he served. The utensils fit him and he cared for them himself, never adding them to the greasy dishwater in which some of the others were soaking. Generally, he had found that life in the armed forces was much like life anywhere. You got out of it what you were willing to put in. If you treated others with respect then, nearly to a man, they treated you respectfully in turn. Of course Wilson knew there were always the shysters, the tricksters and cheats, but they were in the minority. This brought to his mind one of the guys who spent his time overseas trying to come out of it a rich man. Wilson chuckled when he thought of the repatriation the fellow would have had to go through to gain his discharge. No one was allowed to take back with them more than what the regulations allowed.

So how did Joe Daniels come to get rich? It sure couldn't be from trapping. And come to think of it, why did they assume he had even spent those years in the north? He had been there at one time – the deed for the land the cabin was on proved that – but the cabin was in such a shambles, that it must have been years ago. So where did Joe Daniels live and how did he get rich? And who were the other beneficiaries? Were there partners in whatever enterprise he had been involved? Was the money gotten by legal means, fair or foul? Did it matter?

Oh, yes, Wilson decided, it mattered. And anyway, how were they going to get answers to these questions? Obviously the lawyer, Mr. Sweeney, knew more than he told them. Around and around the questions went, until Wilson concentrated on more pleasant thoughts of his wife and child.

On the third day Wilson heard the distant sound of an airplane. It was west of where he and the horse were, and though from the ground it was impossible to discern distance, at least he could hear it. The droning sound of the engine faded northward. Wilson was certain he was heading in the right direction, and he was grateful to have had that confirmed by the airborne transport.

On the fourth day, around noon according to the sun, Wilson and Jazzy heard a roaring in the near distance. They continued threading their way toward it, and at length discovered a series of rapids in the river that crossed their route. "Well, Jazzy, I guess we found out where all the noise was coming from, Old Girl," he yelled to his mare. "We have to cross this river, but not here. Let's keep going north and follow it until it calms down."

They came to some cliffs that were gorgeous to look at but challenging to circumnavigate. Once they did, though, the river was not near as daunting. Wilson unloaded the mare, stowed the supplies and gear in the canoe, broke a trail through the ice with his paddle and climbed in, holding tightly to Jazzy's bridle. The mare did not take kindly to being towed into the icy water and pulled against the rope, nearly upsetting him.

Deciding caution was the better part of valour in this case, Wilson clambered back out of the canoe, pulled it out of the water and took Jazzy to a tree, where he tethered her. Then he rowed the canoe across the river, fighting the current, and ended downstream, where he beached the canoe and emptied the supplies. The ice along the shore made for a treacherous landing, and had to be broken before he could get to the bank. He carried the canoe upriver from the tethered mare so that he would end up close to her. Then, again, he broke open a trail, resettled the boat into the river, got back in and returned for Jazzy. If she were going to fight him and tip the canoe, he figured he would have a better chance if the conveyance were empty; moreover, the supplies would not get soaked, or worse, lost entirely.

The mare balked again at the water, but after a few reluctant starts she fairly bolted across, the canoe in tow. As soon as she reached shore on the other side, she shook the water out of her coat, rolled on the sandy beach, and then stood to shake again. It was pretty clever of her, as she managed to get fairly dry that way and shower Wilson so he got to feel what it was like to be wet and cold in November.

He hastened to erect a shelter and get a fire going to dry off and warm up. Jazzy came fairly close to the heat. Wilson was exhausted by the time he had eaten hot pemmican soup and banked his fire for the night. He was asleep before he stretched his body out fully.

✳

He dreamed that night of his wife and Adam. The baby was crying and crying, and Judith was not with him. In his dream, Wilson kept looking for her and couldn't find her anywhere and the baby kept crying. A loud shot woke him, and he yelled, "Judith!" The snapping flames and lapping water were the only sounds in the night. The shot must have been one of the pine logs bursting, he supposed. He lay down again, but he was unable to sleep because the dream left him shaken. His heart was pounding and he was heavy with dread.

Then he heard the long wavering call of a wolf – a sound that was picked up by another and then another, until the woods were ringing with the chorus of wolf song. It was strange and beautiful. Wilson chuckled, guessing that had been the wailing baby of his dream. He threw a couple more logs on the fire and fell back to sleep, to a lullaby sung by wolves.

27

A Long Trek

Wilson was awakened by Jazzy snorting and pawing the ground, shaking her head and causing the bridle to rattle. She was cold and anxious to get moving. It was still dark, so Wilson had to take a blazing stick from the fire to light his way across the loose rocks that covered the grey clay. He made his way safely down to the river, and then broke enough ice away from the shore to get water for breakfast. He wasn't sure how clean the water was, but decided to not think about that as he put the water close to the fire to heat and threw in his last piece of pemmican. His stew had been getting thinner as the days passed, and now this was the end of it. With luck he would manage to get some kind of meat today, or he would be starving before he reached the mining settlement.

As he waited for the stew to cook, Wilson thought about the map he and Fred, the pilot, had pored over when he was in Sherridon last spring. The cabin was on the west side of Rat Lake, and between Rat Lake and Lynn Lake there was a large body of water, but he hadn't caught the name of it, if it was named at all. No, wait, he thought. Pickerel Narrows was somewhere there, and the lake was. . . Gran something, Granville, yes that's what it was. Maybe those rapids he and the mare had encountered were on one of the narrow junctures of Granville Lake. If that were the case, he still had a long way to go before he got to Lynn Lake. He really had counted on covering a greater distance each day. He would be lucky indeed if he made it at this rate.

He figured he was somewhere between a third and a half of the way there. The going had been slow near the cabin as the forest was thick, and tangled underbrush made travelling tough and sometimes impossible, so he'd had to stick close to the meandering water routes, where there was little if any tree growth. Following animal trails was easier, but they seldom seemed to go the direction he wished.

As the cold dawn arrived, Wilson devoured his thin stew, not knowing when he would eat meat again. He licked up every trace of breakfast, packed up everything, loaded Jazzy and extinguished his campfire. Trees were few and far between here, and were little more than ragged caricatures of real trees, so he decided he had better collect any deadwood he found for his fire that night as they travelled cross-country over the muskeg-covered rocks. The small puddles in the muskeg would be frozen now, so they could travel more in a straight direction instead of following waterways and animal trails.

Jazzy was able to graze on reindeer moss as they trekked, and the breakfast of pemmican stew kept the man's hunger at bay until the sun was in the southwestern part of the sky. Wilson listened for plane engine sounds as they trudged along, but heard nothing. It was a strange and silent land.

Suddenly an explosion of wings startled mare and man alike, as a flock of ptarmigan rose in a flurry almost at their feet and sailed away across the barren land. Wilson cursed himself for not having the gun ready. A shotgun would be much more effective for getting a ptarmigan, but he had shot several back at the cabin with the rifle. He got it out and ready. With the gun in his right hand and the mare's lead in his left, he trudged along, forcing his tired limbs to carry him though his muscles trembled and cramped in the cold.

As the sun set, he decided it would be smarter to stop than keep going in the dark. He set up camp on the open tundra, where there was no shelter.

Wilson cursed himself for not getting a bird when the ptarmigan flock burst skyward at their feet earlier. He was going to starve slowly at this rate. Picturing the feast, he could almost taste the rich juices of the plump bird he didn't get. At that, he decided to stop torturing himself with such visions and get some sleep. He rolled up into the sleeping bag and pulled the bearskin around him over that. It was bitterly cold, and he had to put his head inside the covers. Before he fell asleep he said a prayer for help for himself and for Judith and the baby who were relying on him. All the while he tried to ignore the hunger gnawing at his insides and the cramps knotting the muscles in his legs.

He woke a few times in the night, hearing wolves howling and the mare's nervous movement. Wilson added a bit more of his precious wood to keep the fire going. It felt so good to crawl back into the warmth of his bedroll that each time he fell asleep quickly.

✳

The next morning was cold, clear and cloudless, which portended a chance for the sun's heat to reach him during the day's travels. He collected some ice, melted it and drank hot water that was flavoured only barely from the last few grains of coffee he'd shaken from his pack. Then he loaded up the mare, extinguished the fire and headed northwest. It was his eighth day of travel.

Toward noon he saw more trees ahead of him and was glad, for while it was slower going through forest he had more protection, not only against the elements but also against prowling carnivores. The wind was light. His left side was warm from the sun. Jazzy was beginning to show fatigue, and the prospect of an unending journey without water or decent feed made her snort in protest. Reindeer moss was edible, but it didn't compare to the succulent oats she remembered.

Dinner once again was ice heated for water. By now his hunger was such a constant that it hardly registered anymore. He constructed a lean-to with the bearskin, crawled into his bedroll and was too exhausted to do anything but fall into a deep sleep.

His dreams were strange and disturbing, causing him to thrash in his sleep. At one point he dreamed he was facing a German officer wielding a flamethrower. His screams woke him in time to realize the bedroll was beginning to smoulder. He pulled it away from the fire and set it to cool against the frozen earth.

Then Wilson sat up by the fire, feeling overwhelmed with despair. "Are you seeing me, father?" he called. "Are you happy now? I don't intend to join you. I don't want to abandon my wife and child like you did. I don't want Adam to wonder why I left them and never came back. Why? Why did you leave me? Why in God's name would you sentence us to live out here, to struggle like this, maybe to die? What were you thinking? What kind of man are you, father? Did you take me for a sissy? A sissy who would never be able to survive out in this miserable north country? I don't understand. I don't . . . Oh God. Damn you, father, damn you! Damn you!" Wilson's harsh screams died down into whispers and he put his head against his knees and sobbed his desolation. "What am I supposed to do? I had to leave her. This is the only way I could see. Did I make a mistake? Was I wrong? No, we'd all have starved this winter. I have to get work. We need food." He sobbed at his helplessness. "Let me get to Lynn Lake. I have to get back to Judith and the baby. Please."

Feeling not quite so alone, Wilson lay down again and fell asleep once more.

28
The Long Trek Continues

The next morning Wilson awoke, weak and sore, hunger now a constant companion. He saved some of his hot water from breakfast to drink along the trail. Once the reluctant Jazzy was loaded and the embers were smothered with stones and moss he set off once again. The rifle was at his side, and though he doubted he had the strength to aim well enough to shoot a ptarmigan on the wing—a difficult shot at best —he still held out hope for meat along the trail.

He trudged along, sometimes leading the mare, sometimes following her. Before the sun was midway across the sky a snowshoe rabbit sprang up in front of them. He dropped quickly to his knees, behind a deadfall. The hare stopped, not afraid of a horse, and looked back, standing high on its back legs. The hare's error in judgment was to Wilson's advantage and he shot it in the head.

He built a fire with fumbling hands, and baked the rabbit, hair and all. There was a terrible stench as the hair burned, but he held firm. He was too hungry to wait, so he pulled the rabbit off the fire, cut off a front leg and began gnawing on rare meat while the carcass continued to cook over the flames. No meal in memory tasted so good, but Wilson stopped after eating only a small amount. He knew enough about starvation to realize he was on the edge of it and needed to eat slowly and prudently until his body adjusted.

He packed up the rest of his meal and loaded the mare again, as they could still travel for a couple of hours before it got too dark. He hadn't gone very far, however, when they came upon another fast-moving stream that hadn't yet frozen solid. Jazzy almost ran to it, and he let her quench her thirst first before he went upstream to fill his pail and drink deeply of the icy water. Too deeply – he was getting so cold that he began to stumble. His hands were shaking and shivers wracked his body, so he stopped to build another fire. In his clumsiness he wasted two matches before he managed to start a blaze. He held his trembling hands over the flame, flinching as the heat stung his numb fingers.

He boiled his pail of water and drank some. He scraped his rabbit to remove the blackened hair and skin, propped it close to the fire to heat and then began devouring parts as he tore them off. The day had cost him time, but at least he was not going to starve or die of thirst. He decided to unload Jazzy and bed down for an early night.

Each time he woke, Wilson ate a couple of bites of meat and drank a bit of the hot water he kept in the pail by the fire. Then he added more wood to the embers and stretched out for more sleep. The wind blowing across the bearskin from the back kept the smoke away, but heat still reached him.

By the time the first rays of sun touched the tops of the jack pines, Wilson was up, had emptied his swollen bladder and eaten more rabbit, and was ready to load Jazzy for the continued journey. He felt rejuvenated and more hopeful as they resumed their trek over virgin territory, where no paths were laid, no milestones erected, guided only by desperation and instinct.

The bush grew thicker in some areas that huddled in dips within the rocky surface as they moved ever north and west. Wilson followed Jazzy's lead. As they continued, the mare browsed on whatever she found edible along the way, while he chewed on cold meat that was kept from freezing by being stored inside his bedroll against the horse's back. They surprised a moose along one frozen creek, but Wilson refrained from shooting at it, knowing it would be senseless to kill an animal so large he would be unable to use it properly. The young moose began to move away. Wilson shouted to it. "Keep going, fella! Next time I see you, you won't be so lucky!" The moose strode through the bush on long, gangly legs, his head held high, and soon disappeared in the bush.

By the time it was getting too dark to keep going, Wilson and Jazzy were ready to call it a day. He set up camp, built a fire and set upon the rabbit again. It was starting to smell spoiled, so, once he'd eaten a fair amount, he decided to throw the rest – precious little more than bones – away.

He wished he had thought to chop some of the cattails out of the reeds by the creek where the moose had been. There would have been some food there, and the fuzzy seeds on the cattails would have made good fire starters. He realized he wasn't thinking rationally, and that worried him. He knew he had to reach Lynn Lake soon or he wouldn't make it. Again he said a prayer for his family before he slept.

The next day he was up before the sun. In his hunger he sought the rabbit carcass, couldn't find it and then began a frantic search for it, until he finally remembered throwing it away as it was starting to stink. He decided it was better than nothing, and spent a long time hunting for it without luck before giving up and chopping ice to melt and drink.

He sat by the fire, nursing his hot water, until the mare came up to him and butted him in the shoulder. He shrugged her away, but when she again pushed against him, nearly knocking him over, he looked at her, puzzled, and then shook his head as he got to his feet.

Wilson loaded his things onto the mare, this time forgetting to put out his fire as he left. It was pure luck that he headed the right way. He no longer had any idea how long it had been since he had left Judith and his son. Nor did he have a clue how far he had gone or how far he had yet to go; he knew only that he had to keep moving. He forgot to tie the canoe on top of the horse's load, and walked away, leaving it behind.

He staggered along, tripping over stones and stumps, falling on his face when he had to cross a deadfall, but he got up and kept on going, forcing his feet to follow one after the other, onward, ever onward. Before nightfall he stumbled upon a wide opening, stretching as far as he could see in each direction. He stood looking along the open stretch, wondering what it was. It looked like a wilderness highway. That was silly, he thought; there's no such thing as a wilderness highway. He started to laugh at the absurdity of the idea. Jazzy nickered, tossing her head up and down. She snorted again and began to move along the opening, dragging Wilson along with her. He followed her lead stupidly, not knowing what else to do, and staggered along with one hand holding the mare's bridle.

The little mare continued, dragging Wilson along and stopping to wait while he regained his footing after each fall. Jazzy heard sounds coming from the bush ahead and smelled humans. Being raised by people who cut wood all winter, she found the sounds so familiar that she headed straight for them. Before long she scented her first master. Her current master was now being dragged along, barely helping himself as she approached Jimmy. She whinnied a greeting to the other horses and to Jimmy. The young man looked up, shocked to see the mare he'd parted with several years previously. He spoke to her in his native language and Jazzy bobbed her head. Jimmy walked up to the mare, talking quietly, but he stopped abruptly when he saw Wilson Daniels. The man's hand was tied tightly in the reins, and he was nearly unconscious.

"What happened?" Jimmy asked, moving to help the other man to his feet.

The sounds from the man were incoherent. Wilson mumbled and weaved, his eyes unfocussed.

"Nokum. Ashtum." Jimmy called to his grandfather. "It's Wilson, and he's nearly dead. We have to get him to the mining camp."

The first thing Wilson was aware of was being in a building; other people were talking to him and trying to force some kind of liquid into him. He choked, and tried to push someone's hands away and sit up, but other hands held him down by his shoulders. "What? What?" he muttered.

"Take it easy, my man," someone said. "Just rest. You're OK now. You need some sleep first, and then we'll talk. You just lay here and get some rest. Everything is OK. There's nothing to worry about now. Just rest."

Wilson took the advice and shut his eyes. For several hours he knew nothing. When he woke again, someone gave him some hot, rich broth. He grabbed it and tried to gulp it down, but the cup was pulled away and someone said, "Now take it easy, my man. You can have it all and more, but just a bit at a time, OK? Just a sip now. There you go. See, it's OK now. Have another sip. OK, just take it easy now." He slept again.

When he woke up it was hot. He lay still, looking all around, wondering where he was and why he was there. He tried to think. He was supposed to be moving. Moving, walking somewhere. Leading Jazzy. Jazzy. Judith. Where was Judith? He sat up, got dizzy and put his head into his hands as he tried to regain his balance.

At once a man came and stood beside him. "Feel like talking now, my man?"

"Judith," Wilson croaked. He didn't recognize his own voice. "Where is Judith? Where is my horse?"

"Your horse is here, outside. Some Indians brought the horse and you into the settlement. You were more dead than alive. You're lucky they found you when they did, or you'd be a goner."

"Where am I?" Wilson rasped. "What is this place?"

"This is called Lynn Lake. You're in the office of Sherritt Gordon, the company running this mine. Where were you headed?"

Wilson tried to think. Slowly, things began to come back to him. Lynn Lake. Lynn Lake. That sounded familiar. Judith. "Where, where's Judith?" he asked.

"She's here. The Indians have her. They're taking care of her. It's a good thing you had her with you."

Wilson thought about that for a few moments. That wasn't right. "No. No, I left Judith and Adam at the cabin. She never came with me. Nobody is taking care of her. I have to get back to her."

"It's OK, don't panic. I thought Judith was the name of your horse."

"My horse? My horse . . . she's Jazzy. My wife. Judith is my wife, not the horse."

"All right, take it easy. Judith is your wife. She's not here. Where were you going?"

Wilson forced his brain to concentrate. These were important questions. He had to know where he'd been going. Suddenly he knew. "I was going to Lynn Lake." Wilson spoke in jerky sentences as his thoughts cleared. "I need work. My family is running out of supplies. I need supplies. We won't make it through the winter if I don't bring back supplies."

"OK. You'll get work here. We'll make sure you and your family will be OK this winter. You need to get more rest and get your strength back first. We can't have a half-dead man on the payroll, you understand? Your horse, what's her name? She's OK. The Indians are taking care of her. They seemed to know her."

"Jazzy. The horse is Jazzy. I'm OK. I . . . I can do this. Show me what I can do to earn some money."

The other man frowned. "Oh, no. You're not getting up and falling flat on your face on the floor, 'cause I'm not picking you up to put you back on that cot, you hear? You stay right there and I'll get you something more to eat."

Wilson tried to get up, but he couldn't. He couldn't even push himself off the cot to stand up. He sat, slumped over, his head hanging, hands on his knees.

The other man brought him a steaming cup of hot broth again, this time with a bit of biscuit. Wilson accepted both gratefully, not realizing he'd been fed broth several times already. "Thanks. Thanks a lot. I do appreciate this, and I'm sorry to trouble you." He looked at the man as he bit the biscuit and sipped the broth. The man appeared to be in his mid-50s, was short and on the thin side, with a balding head that he attempted to hide by combing a few long strands across the top. His ears seemed too small for his head and his nose too big. His eyes, though, were kindly, and he smiled easily. He wore round, wire-rimmed glasses that sat midway on the bridge of his nose.

"Oh, it's no trouble. You just take it easy and you'll soon be fit as a fiddle again, you'll see. Now get that into you and get back into that cot. We'll have you on your feet and heading back to the little woman sooner than you think."

Wilson did as he was told. Before he fell asleep he asked, "What's the date?"

"It's November the 9th today, or at least it was. The 10th tomorrow."

"I left the cabin on October 28," Wilson muttered.

"Where's the cabin?"

"By Rat Lake."

The other man's eyes widened. "You've been travelling for 11 days without proper supplies and gear for the climate and season. You must have a powerful reason or a guardian angel that works overtime, maybe both." He looked at his patient. The man had drifted off to sleep again, the empty cup resting on his chest. The thin, balding man moved over to the huge map on the wall of the 12-by-28 and studied the map, finding Rat Lake. From Lynn Lake, judging by the scale it was more than 70 miles – tough, cross-country miles. This fellow had walked that far in winter temperatures without proper supplies. The man shook his head in awe at what this young fellow had accomplished. He was lucky to be alive.

After a few days of rest and food Wilson regained enough strength to demand work. "I need a job. I have to earn enough money to buy supplies for the winter and to hire a plane to fly me back. Can I get work here?" He beseeched the man who had been caring for him.

"Well, you're talking to the right man. My name is John Farqueson and I'm the person in charge here. Any hiring and firing is my department."

"Will you hire me?" Wilson asked.

"Ever done any mining work, my man?" asked Farqueson.

"Nope, but I can learn."

"Can you fly a bush plane? Fix engines? Do carpentry? Teach?" At each suggestion Wilson was forced to shake his head, negative. "Are you a mining engineer? A diamond driller? A geologist?"

John Farqueson took a deep breath. "Can you cut firewood?"

"Yes, that I can do. What does it pay?" Wilson asked, brightening somewhat.

"We pay the Indians here four dollars to $4.50 per bush cord, and if you are really good and you make the quota you get an extra 50 cents to a dollar for all the cords you cut. You would get the same pay, but at the top end of the scale."

Wilson knew it would take quite a few hours for one man to cut a bush cord of wood, thus it would take him a long time to raise the money he needed. He thought it over, frowning. It seemed as though

Farqueson was testing him to see how willing he was to do manual work at the lowest jobs available.

Then the man added, "By the looks of you, my man, you aren't going to be cutting wood for a few weeks yet, and you're in no shape to be a labourer in the mine, but you could work here in the office."

Wilson looked around the office. It was a simple building, 12 by 28 feet, with bare studs and exposed rafters. Frost was thick on all the walls, and almost every nail wore a long frost hat. There was a tin Airtight stove, its stovepipes stretching across the building, suspended by wires strung from the rafters. Those pipes exited through the opposite wall via a metal-lined opening. A wood box sat beside the stove, and strips of bark and wood ash littered the floor around it. There were open shelves along one wall with papers piled in each cubby, and a desk with a chair on wheels in front of it where the other man often sat to work on paper. A telephone hung on the wall close to the desk, its receiver hooked at the side.

"OK. Sure. What would my job be?" Wilson asked, eager to get at it.

"For this week, you take care of the stove. Keep it full because it sure cools off in here fast when the stove runs low. And you can empty the ashes when it gets too full. If you can manage that this week, we'll see what else we can find for you around here."

"Well, I want to thank you for the job, but mostly for taking care of me and feeding me and all. I'll do my best. You won't be sorry you took me in."

"First thing you're going to do is get yourself another set of clothes from the commissary and have yourself a shower at the wash house. You can wash those duds you are wearing or throw them away. I bet they could stand up by themselves." Farqueson gave Wilson a despairing glance. "And you had better introduce yourself if you are going to be on the payroll."

"My name is Daniels, Wilson Daniels. Here's a card with all my particulars." Wilson dug through his filthy overalls and handed him the documentation. "Now, if you can point me the way to the commissary I'll get some decent clothes and clean up a bit. It'll sure feel good."

As soon as Wilson returned to the building where Farqueson worked he asked a question that had been haunting him ever since he regained his senses. "How did I get here? The last thing I remember is walking with my mare, stopping overnight, and travelling as soon as it was light enough to continue."

"A young half-breed named Jimmy brought you in on a wood sleigh. He's the grandson of the chief we hire to haul wood here."

"Tommy? Tommy Lightfoot?"

Farqueson nodded. "You know him?" At Wilson's nod the other man continued. "Well, Jimmy was very insistent that we take good care of you. Said you had a wife waiting for you in the bush. We weren't sure you were going to make it, you know. You're darned lucky you never lost your fingers or ears to frostbite."

"Did Jimmy say how he found me?"

"Nope. You'll have to ask him. They bring in a few loads every day or so. You'll see them when they come, as they check in here to report to make sure they get paid."

Sure enough, later the next day, Tommy came to the door, stomping his feet to knock off the snow and wood debris. As he entered, Wilson rushed over to greet him. Tommy was blinking, trying to adjust his eyes to the dark interior of the building after the brilliance of the sunlit snow outside. "Well, well. Young Wilson. You look much better than the last time I saw you."

"Tommy, it's good to see you. Mr. Farqueson here tells me Jimmy saved my life. How did he find me?"

"The little mare he sold you brought you right to him. You were being dragged along, barely stumbling beside the horse. As soon as she stopped, you fell. Jimmy carried you to the sleigh while we were putting the wood on. He tied you on. Covered you with his heavy hide blanket and raced to the mine here. He came back later and said he brought you to the boss and told him to make you live. He'll be glad to hear you are all right."

"Tell Jimmy . . . no, I have to tell him myself. I owe him my life. How is Jazzy, my mare? She OK?"

"Oh yeah, she's fine. Back to work with Jimmy like she never left. You might have to pay for her again though. Jimmy was glad to see her." Tommy laughed as he teased his young friend. After checking with Farqueson about the amount of wood they'd brought in, Tommy left again.

With his right wrist weakened, and also cut by rope burn, Wilson found the effort of stoking the stove and cleaning the ashes was almost more than he could handle at first. The burn cut deeply; he knew now how he'd tied himself to Jazzy. As the days wore on, his confidence grew along with the strength, and in addition to those tasks he cleaned around the wood box and the stove. Soon he was filling the wood box with logs from outside that were cut to fit the stove. He split larger logs to start fires or get one burning quickly.

Before long he felt ready to do more, to be able to earn real money so he could get back to Judith and Adam as soon as he could. He was soon to get his wish.

One afternoon, he had just done his chores and was looking around to see what more he could do when there was a huge commotion outside and the door burst open. A group of men rushed in, supporting a man who was bleeding profusely from the forearm. The injured man was screaming in pain as the blood ran freely. It covered his outer clothing and soaked the ripped sleeve of his coveralls.

Without thought, Wilson jumped to his feet. "What happened to this man?"

One of the others answered. "He fell into one of the machines. I don't know, but I think he cut off his arm."

"Get him onto the cot!" Wilson ordered. As the other men lowered the injured man, Wilson took charge. He grabbed a pair of scissors and cut the sleeve away to expose the injury. It was hard to evaluate the severity because of the copious amount of blood spurting. Wilson hollered for towels and hot water. The kettle on top of the stove was full of hot water and was brought immediately, but someone had to run to the commissary for towels. Wilson asked Farqueson for his belt. The man looked puzzled, but took off his belt and handed it over. Wilson fashioned a tourniquet with it as the towels arrived. He grabbed one and wiped the blood away so he could see the injury. The arm was cut deeply, but the cut mostly followed the contours of the muscles. Once it was stitched it would heal quite nicely.

"It's going to be all right. We can fix this." Wilson kept talking to the man, knowing those screams were caused by fear as much as by incredible pain.

Blood continued to leak out, soaking the surroundings, and Wilson knew the man was in danger of bleeding to death. The tourniquet couldn't be too tight, as cutting off the blood completely would cause damage as well. While applying direct pressure to the gash that opened the vein he barked orders for antiseptic solutions, clean cloths, sterile solutions, bandages, tape, needles and catgut, and lacking that, thread, and the others hastened to get him the closest they had to what he needed. He called for whiskey, and, after some hesitation, a mickey was produced. Wilson told the man who produced the bottle to make the patient drink some.

"He don't drink," the fellow objected.

Farqueson stepped in. "He does today," he stated grimly. He poured the whiskey into the man's open mouth, and when the fellow coughed and sputtered, the boss told him to swallow, as it would help lessen the pain.

Wilson reached for the bottle, poured some along the open gash where the bone was exposed, and began to stitch the wound closed.

Every once in a while the man was given another gulp of whiskey, as his groans and breathing showed the pain had become unbearable.

One of the men who had brought the injured miner in went outside to throw up while the other miner, though pale as a snowbank, did his best to assist Wilson.

After the sutures were in place and the bleeding was almost stopped, Wilson bound the arm with care and fashioned a sling to support it. The injured man had passed out, though whether from pain or from the whiskey was not known. The miner who assisted Wilson was shaking and needed to step outside for fresh air.

Now the immediate danger was over and he'd done what he could, Wilson was trembling. He, too, felt like throwing up. He forced himself to take a deep breath, and then he addressed Farqueson.

"I'm not sure how much use he's going to have of this arm once it's healed. He should be sent to hospital. He needs antibiotics, and therapy. How soon can he be flown to Winnipeg?"

"He'll be on the next plane out. Why didn't you tell us you were a doctor? We surely need a doctor here since the town's doctor, the nurses and the hospital are still at Sherridon."

"I am not a doctor," Wilson replied. He shuddered, remembering the young men and boys he'd patched up to send back into battle and those he'd watched die.

"Well you sure act like one, and you did a fine job doctoring up Olaf's arm, so to my way of thinking, that makes you a doctor," Farqueson replied.

"I'm not a qualified doctor," Wilson insisted. "I worked as a medic in the war. I spent some time overseas and patched up quite a few of our boys in the field hospital, but I'm not a doctor." Wilson was adamant.

"Without you Olaf would have lost his arm, and maybe we would have lost a good miner. We need you here. You'll earn far more here as our doctor . . ." He paused as he caught a glimpse of Wilson's face. "Or medic, or whatever you want to be called. You'll earn twice as much than in any other capacity. Will you take the job?"

"I swore once I left the forces that I would not be working with blood and death anymore." Wilson felt trapped.

"I didn't see you hesitating when the men brought Olaf in though, my man."

"Old habits die hard?" Wilson offered. "I guess the training just automatically kicked in. I saw a guy who needed help I could give and I never thought about it."

"So, you'll take the position? We'll make it well worth your while."

Wilson looked at Farqueson. He didn't want the job, but . . .

"It'll get you more money, more for supplies for your wife at the cabin and get you back to her much faster."

Wilson gritted his teeth, took a deep breath and nodded his head reluctantly.

They agreed on a rate of pay far surpassing any that Wilson had thought he would be able to make, and Farqueson told him when he wasn't patching up injured men he could still keep the stove going. Wilson's job extended to answering the phone, handling some of the correspondence, running errands, and sending out supply orders. The first one requested medical supplies for the camp. Several times he was able to patch up minor injuries the men suffered on the job – setting a broken arm, wrapping a sprained foot, removing a steel splinter from a man's face and attending to various cuts and scrapes, none life-threatening.

He ached to get back to Judith and Adam. He had been away for nearly two months now. He had earned enough to get all the supplies he needed, but it cost 13 cents a pound for freight and his load would be heavy, plus he had to hire a pilot and plane. He prayed his family was coping well in his absence. How he ached to hold his sweet Judith and his darling son tightly in his arms again; he prayed they were coping well in his absence. Slowly, he bought supplies that were badly needed at the cabin, and was thankful when the company allowed him to store them in the extra space at the commissary.

Then, on December 15, a Norseman crashed as it came in for a landing on the airstrip at Lynn Lake, injuring the pilot as well as his passenger, the pilot's teenaged son. Wilson patched up both of them, and did such a fine job that Andy, the pilot, offered to fly "Doc" Wilson anywhere as soon as he was fit to pilot a plane again.

Wilson went through his supplies, bought more, and thanked John Farqueson enthusiastically for all the help. He was prepared to be ready to leave as soon as the pilot was fit. Farqueson reminded Wilson of his promise that they would not regret hiring him as their medic and jack of all trades. "And, you know, I certainly do not regret hiring you. You have a job here waiting for you if you ever decide to come back."

A week and few days later, Wilson was glad to pronounce Andy fit to fly, and they prepared to take off the morning of December 22. "You'll be home for Christmas, Doc Wilson," Andy said. "What a present that'll be for your wife."

"What a present that will be for me, you mean," Wilson replied. "I've been going crazy here thinking about Judith and our baby alone back there. I got to get home soon. I just hope they're all right."

Mother Nature had other ideas, however, as the planes were grounded by a blizzard on the morning of their planned departure. The weather continued to be bad, and no sooner would they manage to get dug out from one then another would hit. The old year ended, but Wilson was unable to join in the celebrations that marked the occasion. With Judith and Adam so far away and in need, he didn't feel the least bit festive.

30
Strange Alliance

Hunting was poor, but the huge white wolf managed to survive. He watched the woman now toting her child. That was not a good idea to his way of thinking. She was less able to fend for herself, and the two made an easy target for a hungry hunter. He followed her, and ate any food she left behind. Winter was going to threaten their very existence, as he was forced to spend almost all his time looking for food, while continuing to watch the human and her young. He felt a strong sense of curiosity and strange protectiveness toward her.

As for Judith, she seldom saw him but felt his presence, not as a threat, but almost as a silent, invisible companion. Once in a while she did catch a glimpse of him, but never for long.

In spite of the hardships Judith was enjoying her role as a mother, and was pleased with her ingenuity in inventing the harness with which she toted her baby on longer ventures outside. She changed Adam's diaper and mentally thanked Sue for the idea of stuffing them with cattail fluff to absorb moisture. She had made a pocket in each diaper and filled it with the soft seed fuzz. Once the soiled diaper was removed, she turned the pocket inside out and shook out the soaked seed fluff. It worked surprisingly well, making one job easier. Other tasks were more daunting, and she missed her husband's help. She counted now on seeing Wilson soon. The two months were almost up. He should be back any day now.

Then, on December 22, a three-day blizzard covered the entire forest around her cabin. Her first instinct upon arising the first day to hear the shrieking wind was to cry in rage, frustration and fear. Adam's grinning little face looked up at her and stopped her. She set about to heat water for his thin gruel. "Good morning, my sweetheart. Your grin just makes my day, and I know I can endure anything for you. Daddy will be home soon, my baby."

She had to supplement her milk as Adam was growing. He was four months old now, and she was having difficulty supplying his nutritional needs with her milk. She felt it was best for them both if he slept in his own cradle, but with the wind howling like that she would need to take him into bed with her tonight.

When he slept in his cradle and woke up during the night she would nurse him and build up the fire so that the cabin stayed warm through the dark hours. But now that he seemed to be ready to sleep through the night, she would need to make alternate arrangements, or he would be waking up cold.

Once she had fed him the gruel, Adam wanted more, but the dish was empty and she dared not give him more yet. He settled for nursing the bit she had for him and finished with a small drink of water. She busied herself with cleaning and polishing the cabin to make it ready for her husband's return. Wilson should have left the minute he heard of the blizzard. If that were the case he would have been with them already. No, he must be at Lynn Lake. She would not even consider the possibility he didn't make it there. He would arrive as soon as he was able. Judith had to believe that. Anything else was unthinkable.

She was able to get wood and keep the cabin warm, and thankfully the temperature was not that cold, though the relentless wind and blowing wet snow made it seem so. The lack of nourishing food was a concern, and she didn't know how they could keep their strength without meat. Once the blizzard let up, she set her snares. Each time she ventured far outdoors she brought Adam with her, but the cold was hard on him as well. She carried him inside her clothes, in the holster she'd designed to leave her arms free. This worked fine when he slept, but when he became restless Judith found walking was difficult. Her ankle still hurt and it was weak. She was so afraid of falling again, especially if she took him down with her.

She feared that they would not be alive when Wilson returned, because it was getting harder and harder for her to carry the little fellow. He was not growing much anymore. Diminished nutrition caused Adam's growth to slow, and her strength was ebbing by the day. She decided Adam must stay back at the cabin when she made her forays, as it was simply too difficult for her to carry him any longer. She left him utensils to play with when she went outside. He didn't cry when she left, but Judith did, and she would stand outside the cabin, listening for his wailing that never came.

During the blizzard the wolf sheltered, curled up with his face buried in his thick tail brush as wolves do. Covered with snow, he kept warm through the three days that wind and snow had dominion over the world in which he lived.

After the storm, he found it easier to hunt rabbits by following their tracks as well as their scent. He caught a hare that was in good condition and devoured it with gusto, then happened upon another, which he also dispatched. He figured he would save it until he was hungry again.

As he carried it along, he came across tracks made by the human female and followed them. Suddenly there she was, sitting alone making strange sounds as though she were in pain. He noticed she did not carry her young with her. She seemed in distress and he decided to leave her the hare. He felt as though she were replacing his family for the time being. Wolves are not usually solitary creatures, and like mankind, they need a social network to survive.

Once again Judith had found nothing in the snares, and this time she did cry, feeling hopeless and helpless. What were they going to do? How could she care for Adam? What would be left when Wilson returned?

Feeling eyes upon her, she raised her head to see the ghost-like shape of a wolf before her, with a freshly killed snowshoe rabbit hanging limply from its jaws. It whined, and then it placed the lifeless body of the rodent down in the snow. After another whine it disappeared into the undergrowth of the forest. She scrambled on all fours and grasped the little body. Thanking the wolf, and crying with gratitude, she skinned and gutted it, leaving hide, entrails and the head for Spirit.

She made her way back to the cabin to find Adam playing quietly. He whimpered, and then he grinned at her as she began stewing the rabbit. They ate fully but carefully, saving some for the rest of the week. The stew was thickened with ground grains and powdered oats that had been meant for Jazzy. She skimmed off the hulls of the grain before mixing the gooey thickening agent into her pot. She saved the bones for Spirit.

The weather continued to be stormy, with only a couple of clear days between bouts of blowing snow. Judith built up a pile of snow to act as a deterrent to the windblown accumulations of snow that threatened to block her door. It certainly helped, but the storms continued.

Judith checked the calendar and learned that they had ended another year and were on the eve of 1951. And no Wilson yet. She said a special prayer for his safe return before she went to bed on New Year's Eve. She asked that this be the last one they would ever spend apart.

On the first day of 1951, another blizzard raged out of the west. Was there to be no end? Fortunately, they had a bit of the rabbit still, thanks to Spirit. By giving most to Adam to supplement her scant milk supply, Judith hoped to make the food last until the current blizzard was over.

She dressed, gave Adam some things with which to amuse himself and went to push the door open. With her full strength against the door she was unable to force it open wide enough even to scrape a little snow to melt for water. There was only one thing she could do: remove the hide covering the window and climb out that way. Once she opened it part way, Judith brought in snow to melt while she cleared the door.

Before she could do that, she had to bundle Adam up against the cold that would come in until she could replace the hide. She would have to build up the fire, though most of the heat would go out the window and the cabin would likely fill with smoke again. Judith sat on the chair beside the table, sobbing. Adam watched her, his eyes huge and troubled. It wasn't long before his lower lip turned and began to quiver. Judith noticed he was going to begin crying as well, so she stopped.

"It's OK, sweetheart. Mommy's OK. She has to think things through, that's all."

Judith looked at the window. The hide had been nailed on with narrow strips of wood Wilson had fashioned like laths. An idea came to her, and she took a hammer and carefully loosened the laths, leaving the nails in the thin wood. If she took the hammer outside with her she could nail the hide on the outside of the window. Then the cabin would remain warm and free of smoke. Judith got to work. Once the hide was removed, indeed, the heat swirled out, creating a mist, and smoke began to filter in from the fireplace to replace the heat that escaped. Judith climbed onto a chair and scrambled out after tossing out the hide. She clutched the hammer and the laths, making sure to keep the nails in place. Once outside, she nailed the hide back onto the window. That done, she needed to rest. She was so weak. She studied the snow-blocked doorway. Fighting back tears of frustration and fatigue, she made her way to the door. The snow was packed so hard she was able to walk on the top of it. That made for easy travel, but hard work digging it out.

In her weakened condition it took her the rest of that day to move enough to be able to squeeze through the slim opening, and most of the next to dig out the door properly. By then the rabbit stew, thinned more every time they had some, was gone. Adam was whining with hunger that the thin gruel and her scant milk and water did not satisfy.

Had she been alone, Judith would have given up at that point, but she had to keep going for Adam's sake. First, she needed to set some snares. She knew she did not have the strength to dig down to the ice, chop a hole and try to catch fish. To do so would take more strength than she had; it would entail leaving Adam for a long period of time, or bringing him outside with her, and though he wasn't gaining weight now he was too heavy to haul around with her on such a strenuous undertaking.

31

Survival

The wolf ate what the human left behind and continued to hunt, sometimes having success and sometimes not. For two days the wolf bedded down while the blizzard raged. After the storm he arose, shook off the insulating snow blanket and stretched. It was time to satisfy his mounting hunger.

He found the tracks of a deer that had made a trail as it foraged. Deciding to investigate, he flowed along the trail and caught up to an old stag. The ancient animal was fairly exhausted from travelling through the snow and chewing off the branches and bark of deciduous trees. It snorted and backed into a bush so its back end was protected, and eyed the carnivore. If the wolf came too close, a sharp kick from a front hoof should make him look elsewhere for his next meal. Unfortunately for the deer the bush it chose wasn't very thick, and the huge white predator was able to get behind it and bite at its hind legs. Fearing the wolf would hamstring it, the deer floundered through the snow in search of a better position.

The wolf knew he had a good chance of a kill with a feeble old stag in deep snow, so he stayed behind, nipping and retreating, finally harrying the deer into snow so deep it was unable to run. The wolf seized his chance, leaping onto the deer's back, grasping its neck and hanging on as it bawled its rage. Soon it could fight no more. The white wolf slipped around to the stag's throat and sliced through the jugular vein. As it bled, he began to eat from the body. He lapped up the blood, opened the wound to expose muscle tissue, and then worked his way up through the front right shoulder.

Replete, he kicked snow over his bounty, and then urinated all around to mark his territory. He rested beside his kill for a time until he felt a sudden curiosity in the human female. He set out for the cabin, trotting easily across the hardest patches of snow and managing to avoid most soft banks. Before he got to the cabin, he scented her. By following it and the noise she was making he found her again wailing in the snow.

Judith had placed Adam in a safe area away from the fireplace, and provided things with which he could amuse himself. She dressed to go out, feeling desperate to be forced to abandon him to his own resources while she went in search of food. This time, he made a bit of a fuss when she left, but after a few minutes she heard him settle down and become interested in banging the cup and bowl together, while making sounds that imitated speech.

Judith felt pulled in two directions. It was unthinkable to leave her child unattended, but if she didn't hunt for food then neither of them would survive. Taking a deep and desperate breath, she turned away from the cabin, forcing her feet to wade through deep snowdrifts to where she had set snares in the past. She drove thoughts of her son from her mind. She had no choice but to get food. After warming her freezing fingers inside the sleeves of her coat, she worked on trails rabbits had made though the deep snow, or across the frozen banks. It was tricky suspending a thin wire at just the right height and forcing broken branches around it to make a kind of fence. Judith found it hard enough without trying to set up the kind Wilson favoured – the type with a flexible willow tied so that the rabbit snapped up into the air and was killed quickly. He explained the fast kill made the meat taste better. Rabbits that struggled tended to have stronger-tasting flesh. She did make the attempt however, because the thought of having to kill a struggling creature was hard to face, harder than eating strong-tasting rabbit flesh.

She plunged through deep soft drifts of snow, sometimes skirting on top in places where the glacial winds had blown hard enough to pack the banks solid, only to suddenly sink up to her knees in places where the snow was fluffy. She trudged as far as she was able, searching out rabbit trails, placing snares and fences.

Once the last snare was set, she retraced her steps. Every one was empty, suspended just as she had left it. She sank onto the snow and sobbed her frustration and despair. Her baby was hungry, and she had nothing to show for her labours of the day. Tears of rage clouded her vision as she pounded her fists in the snow sobbing, not knowing what else to do. Sitting there, rocking in misery, she became chilled and noticed a fine snow falling gently. It melted and froze on her face. As she drew a breath of icy air, she thought she heard something. She gulped back her sobs and listened. Hearing a familiar whine, Judith raised her head to stare with a brief moment of shock and fear into the yellow eyes of the white wolf. He had nothing in his mouth to offer her this time.

She empathized with him, keeping her voice very low. "It's tough for you too, isn't it, boy? Did you get the rabbit bones I put out for you?" He whined again, but instead of leaving, he turned slowly and looked back at her.

She watched, silently, and he whined again. Finally understanding that he wanted her to follow, she rose slowly to her feet and trailed him. He led her for nearly a mile through the forest, sometimes walking securely on top but often plowing through deep drifts. She nearly turned back several times, thinking of her little son waiting in the cabin, but something compelled her to continue to follow Spirit.

Suddenly, and without warning, Spirit was gone. She called, but only the sound of her own voice echoed in the surrounding forest. Then all was still. Was this all for nothing? She pounded a scraggly spruce, bruising her numb fists. She could not believe she had thought the wolf had something to show her. How stupid could she be? The wolf was a wild creature, not a pet dog. This had been an act of foolish desperation. It would be dark soon, and she was far from the cabin. If she didn't hurry back soon it might be too dark to find her trail.

Judith collapsed on the snow, beginning to cry in despair. The fine snow continued to float down and freeze on her exposed skin. She shivered and sighed, knowing if she didn't get up and get moving, she'd freeze to death where she huddled. Then what would become of Adam? Maybe there'll be a rabbit in one of my snares by now, she encouraged herself as she struggled to her feet.

She took a deep breath, wiped her hand across her face and prepared to retrace her footsteps. Rising to her feet, holding onto the spruce she had beaten, she became aware of raucous calls of quarrelling ravens and whiskey jacks. Knowing they must be fighting over some type of meat, she set out to investigate.

By following the sounds she soon came upon the carcass of a deer. It had been killed recently, for the flesh had not yet frozen solid and the blood appeared fresh. It was obvious that a wolf had been the instrument of death. She could see his huge paw tracks and the hole in the shoulder of the deer where he had fed. Birds were feeding from that cavity, and as she approached they rose in an angry cloud, settling in the surrounding spruce trees, squawking their displeasure at the loss of their feast.

Taking her knife from the sheath, she cut a piece of stiff meat and ate it raw. It was tough, but she convinced herself she was eating very rare steak, and it was good. As she gnawed she began to think of ways she could get some of it back to the cabin. If she cut some of the hide from the carcass, she could fashion a kind of sled with which to pull the heavy meat back with her.

She set to work. The carcass was freezing already, so cutting was hard work. It would not have been possible had she arrived much later. She started where the wolf had opened the throat, and sliced up around the neck and down the left shoulder as far down the leg as she was able, digging out the trampled snow as she went. The skin on the foreleg would make the strap. Knowing she would be unable to get the hide from the deer's belly, she cut around the shank and then along the side, over the tail and up the right side to where the wolf had eaten at the right shoulder. She struggled to peel the hide from the carcass, as the freezing cold made her movements as stiff as the hide and meat. By the time she had succeeded in skinning the deer. Judith was panting and sweating. She flipped the hide over and cut a slit in the right shoulder. Then she tugged the part that had covered the left leg through the slit and tied a knot in it, forming a loop she would use as a harness that she could wear to tote the meat back. It should slide easily, since she would be pulling with the grain of the animal's hair.

There would be food now for both of them, but she had work ahead of her yet. She cut chunks of flesh off the left shoulder and both rear haunches, piled them onto her sled, and then cut into the body along the ribcage. She found the liver and took it, leaving the spleen and gall bladder intact to be removed later in the cabin. If she broke the gall bladder it would spoil the liver. She pushed lung tissue out of the way to grasp the heart, and was amazed to see a faint trace of steam as she lifted it into the cold air. The heart and liver would not be as tough as the muscle. The tongue would cook up nicely, and she could mash it for her baby's toothless mouth, so she took that as well.

With the last parts loaded onto her hide sled, she rubbed her bloodied mittens and sleeves in the snow to clean off some of the gore. "Thanks, Spirit. Thank you, Lord," she whispered, and looked upward towards the restless ravens and magpies before she set off for the cabin. It was dusk already, and the birds would soon be roosting for the night. They had settled down to await her departure. Judith prayed she would find her way back to the cabin without getting lost.

The return trip should have been next to impossible after her Herculean efforts of the day, especially when she was laden with a heavy and awkward load skidding along behind her staggering footsteps, but in her triumph the trail seemed shorter, the walking easier.

The white wolf watched her eat from the carcass and make a means of hauling some of it back to her den. This was good. There would be food for him and for her for a few weeks to come. He watched her work, and then he followed her back to her den, staying well back out of sight. Several times it looked as though she might not make it, but she did. After she went inside, he settled there briefly to watch. He heard her moving around inside then saw her come out and place meat in another den underground. He watched for a while longer, but then it was time to ensure no other creatures were after his kill. He went back and buried what was left of the carcass, marked it and the snow around it with urine, and then kicked the tainted snow over the skinless deer to warn would-be scavengers they were at great risk.

It took Judith a long time to get back to the cabin, and she blessed the heavens for being cloudless and bright with moonlight to show her the way back. That made the night so cold, but her body stayed warm from exertion. Many times she stumbled and nearly fell, but elation kept her going. As she entered the cabin, she strained her ears for sounds from Adam, but heard nothing. She felt her heart tighten. "Oh please, he must be all right. Please," she begged, whimpering in fright.

"Adam, baby?" she called, and heard him cry out in his sleep. "Oh, thank you, God, thank you." The poor little fellow had cried himself to sleep, and he was cold. She wanted to scoop him up her arms and rejoice, but knew the first thing needed was to get a fire going, and warm up the cabin.

She stirred the ashes, found a few hot embers and blew on them, gradually adding twigs and bark until she had a good flame. By carefully adding split logs until they caught fire she was able to put on two large chunks of wood that would burn for a long time. Adam cried out several times while she worked, and she hushed him. Then she set to work making something for the two of them to eat. While their supper was boiling, she filled the interior cache with meat before hurrying out to store the balance of the venison in the outdoor cache.

The next time Adam stirred she woke him and offered him some cooked and mashed venison tongue she'd cooled. He ate ravenously at first, and then grinned at her as he grew full. He played for a short time, but soon fell into a contented sleep. After eating, she was finally able to get some rest herself. Before she allowed sleep to overcome her, she offered up a prayer of thanks for the help sent to her in the presence of Spirit, and an earnest request for the safe deliverance to her of her husband.

32
Invasion

Before Judith could check her snares, another blizzard engulfed the cabin, and she knew once it was over she would again have to go out the window to dig out. She had dressed hurriedly and fetched extra wood for the fireplace and a sizeable piece of venison as soon as she noticed the wind picking up. Once she stepped out into it the wind snatched at her breath and her clothing. Visibility was bad, but she managed to retrieve the meat first, since it was farthest from the cabin. The wood was stacked right against and in the lee of the building, so she dug out as much as she was able to carry, and returned twice to be sure they wouldn't run out while the storm raged.

Judith hated to leave the snares set without checking them, in case some creature was caught and left to die that way, but there was nothing she could do but wait out the storm. All day and night and part of the next day the wind wailed around the cabin, sucking the heat up the chimney. Wood burned rapidly, sparks flying as the pine resin boiled and popped. As she waited for the blizzard to blow itself out, she kept busy feeding the fire, tending her child and making him larger clothes.

Adam was cheerful these days with his tummy full of rich broth and meat that was pounded soft and tender. He was filling out again. His face took on the chubby appearance babies are supposed to have; gone was the pinched, pale-faced, fretful little fellow who had tried to be good through the tough times.

She spoke to him, telling him of his father, of the things of her childhood, of towns where many people lived close together. "There is a huge wolf named Spirit, Adam. He saved our lives again. He's our guardian spirit. No one would believe how he has helped us, and no one would think a wild timber wolf would get a human to follow him to where his kill was and share his food. Even I have a hard time believing it. But you do, don't you my baby? Hmm? You believe Mommy." Adam laughed and cooed at her, making her smile. She loved to hear his baby laugh, but oh, how she longed to hear the beloved voice of his father.

That evening she sat by the fireplace for light and did her best to make Adam's nighties longer, knowing that soon additional cloth added to the bottom hem wouldn't be sufficient as he was getting bigger, and not only in length. She glanced up from her stitching and saw the baby was sleeping snugly in his cradle. That was when she heard snuffling and snorting at the window.

She held her breath, panic seizing her, her blood pounding in her ears as her mind ran through the possibilities of what it could be, not realizing her visitor was the most vicious animal in the northern country – a wolverine. This one was a mature female with a den containing a litter of two kits depending on her. Carrion and small creatures on which she usually fed were scarce, but she could smell food behind the hide.

Terrified, Judith seized the hunting knife and stepped to the side of the window. She held her breath, her arm raised above her head ready to slash whatever it was. Long, curved black claws rent the hide into shreds, and a thick front leg with a broad foot reached inside, claws slashing toward Judith. She screamed and brought the knife down with all her force, almost severing the forepaw. A horrid odour filled the air as the animal screamed and growled. An evil mask of hatred thrust itself through, snarling and spitting, as Judith slashed again and again at the bear-like face. Over its snout and around its small eyes it had a black mask that narrowed to a stripe over its round head. Its ears were short and rounded, with a silvery stripe that curved from the under jaw and climbed over the black mask on each side. The knife sliced open the side of its face. Blood was spurting as the creature tried to scramble through the window. The running blood had to blind it, but still it came on, snorting, hissing and growling. Its long, pointed teeth snapped as it attempted to grasp the hand that held the knife. Judith wasn't even aware that she was screaming and Adam was shrieking and crying. She was aware only of the danger she was battling. Whatever the animal was, she thought, it was capable of killing her and her baby. She began jabbing the knife toward its face, hoping to puncture an eye or the snout. Snarling and spitting, the creature slipped back from the window. Judith continued screaming and shaking until she became aware of her son.

Adam's screams of terror and the cold air rushing in the shredded hide stirred her to life. Blood splattered the hide, the walls and the floor of the cabin. She was caught between reassuring her child and readying for another attack from the wolverine. The knife fell from her nerveless fingers as she trembled. She tried to calm Adam, but her voice came out as a croak, and he couldn't hear her above his frightened screams.

She bent to retrieve the knife, seeing blood all over it and herself. She didn't know whether she'd been injured or not. Holding the knife and keeping a chair between her and the riddled hide window covering, Judith moved toward her terrified child. Her heart had not slowed its furious pumping. She decided she had to close up the window. That was the only way that horrid creature could get in, and smoke from the fireplace was filling the cabin's interior. She forced herself to ignore her panicked child for the amount of time needed to block the opening.

She grasped an empty part of the kitchen cabinets and reached for the hammer. The nails – she needed nails. The can spilled, but a few nails stayed within her grip. Somehow she used those to nail the cupboard against the window. She then got more nails to fasten it securely. Whatever the animal was, it would not be able to get in again.

She was trembling and Adam still was crying. She picked him up, rocking and jiggling him to quiet and reassure him that all was well, pacing back and forth to get herself calmed down also. "It's OK, my love, it's OK."

Once she'd calmed down and got Adam settled she set about cleaning the blood off herself and her kitchen, as well as collecting the scattered nails. Judith knew she had wounded the animal badly. It might be lurking around to continue the fight, however, and she would have to go out again sometime for meat and wood. As long as she stayed inside, she felt safe with the window securely boarded up. But what would happen when she went back outside, as she must tomorrow? The storm seemed to have subsided, but they were almost out of wood. Judith was sorely tempted to remain secluded in the cabin, burning their furniture and cupboards if she had to. Once she put the last two logs on the fire, she looked at the cupboards, the table, the chairs, and the bench. Wilson had worked so hard to make them, and she couldn't just burn them. Besides, that would only delay the inevitable trip she'd soon have to make to collect more wood anyway.

She dressed to go out, shaking inside as she forced herself to leave her sanctuary. She held the knife at the ready as she forced open the door. There was a snowdrift across it, but she was able to squeeze out and set to work cutting enough snow blocks out from the door so that it opened wide again. She was on the alert constantly as she worked. Each snow block was used to build up a wall to act as a windbreak to protect the door. When the doorway was cleared, she looked around, and, seeing no tracks beyond the blood-splattered wall by the window, she moved around to the woodpile. The entire way, she kept her eyes open and her senses alert for danger. After the first armload of wood was inside, Judith sat to rest and recuperate. She congratulated herself on her bravery.

As she went out to fetch meat from the cache and bring in more wood, her hand never left the hilt of the knife. She was extremely cautious, and listened for any movements. The crunching snow ought to divulge the presence of any creature outside with her. It was several days before Judith felt a bit safer outside her cabin, but eventually the terror faded.

On his prowls, the wolf scented the wolverine. Blood splattered along the foul-smelling one's trail guided the wolf. He tracked the wolverine for some distance, before overtaking and killing it. True to its stink, the wolverine's flesh made an unpleasant repast. The insides, heart and liver were edible and fresh, however.

He returned to the deer carcass and dug it out of the deep snow-bank that had formed over it. Though others had visited it there was plenty left. He chased off the ravens and whisky-jacks that tried to get close enough for the odd beakful, and threatened a pair of coyotes by exposing his canines and keeping his ears erect and pointed forward, head lowered and eyes glaring. His hair rose, and as it bristled along his neck he was formidable. It didn't deter the coyotes. One would feint a charge to lure him away from the food to allow the other to dash in for a bite, but this only worked once, and earned the baiting coyote a ripped shoulder.

The frozen stag venison, though tough and stringy, helped take the taste and smell of the wolverine from his mouth and delicate nose. He ate as much as he was able. The coyotes would return; he waited there all night, more to thwart their efforts than anything. After a few last delicate bites, he urinated near the carcass and kicked the yellow snow onto it before leaving.

Several days later the wolf successfully killed and devoured a fat snow-shoe hare. The last time he had visited the site of his deer kill a wolverine had been there previously, crushing the bones between its powerful jaws for the marrow inside, and what little was left stank.

The hare satisfied his hunger and put him in a very good mood. It was such a glorious morning, and he was full and filled with energy. He decided to pass the human den on his way back to his own resting place. On hearing a terrible scream from the woman, he leapt to investigate.

33
The Battle

Judith opened the door on a Christmas card scene. The early morning was bright and sunny. Frost sparkled on the trees and snow as though diamond dust had been sprinkled lavishly about, and no wind disturbed the silence. The world looked innocent and fresh as she went out to bring in wood for the day and get more meat from their cache. This was an awful yet awe-inspiring country. Today was glorious, and she breathed deeply in the cold clean air. It was great to be alive on such a day.

As she bent to pick up the first piece of wood from the woodpile, a snarling, spitting fury smashed upon her back, driving her face-first into the woodpile. Teeth sank into her scalp through the back of her hood. She felt them puncture her head, but shock numbed the pain. She screamed in fear, fighting to regain her feet so she could get the knife that was strapped to her waist. As she twisted, the weight of the creature on her back slipped sideways and teeth sank into her elbow, rendering her right arm useless. She screamed again as she desperately tried for the knife with her left hand. She was aware of the same fetid odour as when her hide window had been ripped apart. A second blow to her back sent her flying face-first into the snow at the edge of the pile of wood.

She could hear sounds of a ferocious battle. Turning painfully, blood blurring her vision, Judith watched as Spirit and the wolverine battled for supremacy. Spirit was bigger, but the wolverine was stronger, and swift and vicious as well. Snarls, growls and roars tore the air. She got her knife into her left hand, struggled to her feet and watched for her chance. The battling animals knocked her to the ground again, stomping over her legs in their fury as each tried to kill the other. The knife she was holding gashed her parka open along her side, poking into her thigh. Staggering upright, she tried to stay away from the writhing animals but remain close enough to help if she could. She saw the wolverine was on top, with its teeth fastened into the throat of the pale wolf. Without thinking, she rushed forward and thrust the knife into the back of the furred demon. She yanked the knife out and raised it to stab again.

Dropping its hold on Spirit the wolverine turned to grab her, and Spirit grasped the throat of his enemy. Spirit flung his head from side to side, causing the wolverine's body to thrash wildly while Judith swung the knife again and again at the writhing body, often connecting and ripping the snarling beast open, until finally all three were still. Judith sat upright first. Wiping blood from her face, she placed a hand against the body of the wolf. She felt its heart, beating steadily. The eyes of the wolverine, most likely the mate to the previous intruder, were open but glazed. It was dead. The snow all around was trampled and stained with the blood of all three. Again Spirit had saved her, but at what cost?

She held her wounded elbow to slow the bleeding, wiped dripping gore from her forehead and eyes and groped her way around the cabin to the door. She pulled open the heavy door with her left hand, wondering briefly where her knife had gone, then staggered inside and pulled the door shut. Adam stopped his crying when he saw her. He looked all right; she would attend to him later.

She made her way to the cupboards, opened Wilson's medical bag and bound her worst gashes with strips of gauze. There was nothing she could do about her head punctures at the moment, beyond pressing a clean towel against them to staunch the blood flow. She found his needle threaded with sinew ready for use, a bottle of hydrogen peroxide, a smaller one of iodine and a pair of scissors. Taking all three, she retraced her steps outside to the wolf that had saved her life. Thinking back to the time she'd had stitches in a cut on her arm as a teen, and the time Wil had stitched the four gashes on Jazzy's shoulder, she tried to remember how it had been done. Each stitch had been tied off separately, not like sewing clothing. She had no idea how to form a proper knot, but she'd do the best she could. Any attempt would be better than leaving the wolf to bleed to death.

Opening the hydrogen peroxide, she poured a liberal amount on the gaping wound in the neck and watched it fizz and bubble. Thankfully, the huge jugular vein in the throat was pulsating and uncut, though blood leaking from the torn skin and bubbling in the peroxide made it hard to see. She forced the needle through his bloodstained white coat and closed the gap using the sinew, making knots as she stitched. She carefully closed the deepest tears in the wolf's body, without really knowing the proper method of stitching wounds. The huge white form shuddered once and she paused in her work, but when he didn't open his eyes she continued, pouring the antiseptic and then closing the gaps. Just as she finished stitching up his right front leg, the huge wolf regained consciousness, raising his huge head to look at her. They stared at each other eye to eye. Each was wary, yet both were so exhausted they could only watch the other. Gently, she removed the needle, leaving a rather long piece of sinew hanging. Speaking in murmurs, she backed slowly toward the cabin door. Spirit lay still, his sides heaving, his eyes following her retreating figure.

She entered the cabin, offered a prayer of gratitude that Adam had fallen asleep, and then stumbled to her bed and fell into a troubled sleep.

His whole body throbbed with pain. He was alive. She had helped him. He got stiffly to his feet, stood trembling for a few moments, and then limped with great difficulty back to his den to recuperate. Maybe this winter would be his last.

34
Recuperation

Adam's fussing and crying finally pulled Judith back to awareness, and the cold in the cabin reminded her of her intention to replenish their wood supply. Thankfully, there were still embers in the fireplace, and the last two logs were soon burning brightly and cheerfully.

She went outside to get more wood and was astounded to see the condition of the snow around the cabin. It had been so pristine in the early morning light, sparkling with frost diamonds pure and virginal. Now it was trampled; blood splattered the uneven surfaces, and the torn body of a shaggy, brown and black wolverine lay slumped across one drift. The silvery white strip along his side was torn and bloodstained. There was no sign of Spirit except for tracks weaving into the forest.

Judith stood for several long moments thinking of the battle, the horrible sounds the three of them had made as each fought, her efforts at repairing the damage to the wolf. She was astounded at the size of the wolverine. He was about three-quarters the size of the wolf, and built somewhat like a compact bear. She gazed into his small eyes, open in death, and marvelled at the strength of the creature. It was obviously a larger edition of the previous attacker. "I killed you. I had help, but

I killed you," she spoke aloud to the carcass as she reached down and jerked the knife from its side and bent to collect the bottle of iodine she hadn't used, and the almost empty hydrogen peroxide bottle. They would need to be cleaned up and placed back in Wilson's medicine kit. Judith shuddered and wrinkled her nose at the stench surrounding the cabin on this side.

She stumbled to what remained of the woodpile. Every muscle in her body ached. Her head was still pounding and it would be days before she would feel like herself again. It took her twice as long this time to fill her wood box, as her right arm was aching and sore. She had to lift each log with her left hand, place it carefully onto her bent right arm until it could hold no more, and then, grasping another in her left, make her way around the cabin to the door. She had to drop the log from her left hand to open the door, and then bend to retrieve the log before she entered the building. The logs were placed into the wood box one by one. She groaned in pain with the effort, but had no choice. Five times she repeated this, having to pass the fetid body of the wolverine each trip.

When the box was half full, she remembered they needed meat as well, so she hobbled to the cache. She felt like crying when she saw the deep snowdrift covering it. Sighing, she made her way back to the cabin, took the knife and cut snow blocks to build a protective wall as she cleared the way. Once there was enough snow removed, Judith struggled to move the rock from the wooden door and raised it. She saw snow had filtered in and the venison was covered with it. The pieces were not frozen together, however, being frozen before they were placed inside. She grasped a front shoulder of deer meat, pulled it out and up and placed it beside the cache on the hard-packed snow. Then she had to close the door and replace the heavy rock. Once it all was completed, Judith stopped to catch her breath.

Just for a moment, through her exhaustion, she felt victorious. She'd killed a wolverine, stitched up a wild timber wolf, hauled wolf-killed meat in the darkness of night through the forest and packed it away, and kept the cabin warm through the many snowstorms, and though she was battered and sore, she was still alive and would remain so.

Slightly rested, she shook her head, thinking, you're not done yet, girl. This venison had to be cooked and the wood box was still only half full. With some difficulty, she dragged the shoulder of meat through the snow to the cabin and lifted it inside. She paused long enough to put the stew pot with the frozen chunk of meat in it on to boil, while she continued to bring in wood. At one point she had to stop, undress and feed her son. She felt no hunger herself, but because she was feeling dizzy she forced some of his pap into her own body, washing it down with hot water. Once Adam was satisfied, she put him in his cradle to play and hopefully to sleep again. Once more she dressed in outdoor clothes to finish filling her wood box. It took all morning and part of the afternoon to accomplish what should have been a half-hour job.

She knew the next day she would have to heat enough water to wash the blood from her hair. Thankfully, its length likely protected her as much as the heavy hood on her parka, and she was glad she had let it grow. Her parka also needed mending, as she had felt cold stealing through the tears. Her arm was going to be all right. Fortunately, her elbow had not been broken. She changed the dressings after applying more carbolic salve. Vile-smelling stuff though it was, it sure helped guard against infection. She hoped her husband brought more of it, as there was not much left. The shallow cut on her thigh from the knife was healing already. Her warm outer pants and parka needed to be stitched back together as well. It had been a horrendous ordeal, but she had come through it. She was going to be OK and Adam was fine. Her body would heal, the clothing could be mended and the mess inside the cabin could be cleaned.

After a brief rest, she tackled the chaos in the cabin. Then she fed Adam, ate a bit of the rich venison broth and fell into bed.

Alone in his den, the wolf heard another of his kind howling, but he was too sore and tired to even think of answering. He licked at his many wounds, speeding the healing. The hare he had eaten sustained him for many days, days in which his strong body healed.

The wolf knew from past experience a wolverine is the most vicious animal his kind had to face. A wolverine the size of the one attacking the female in the wooden den was capable of stealing a kill from a wolf pack or a full-grown bear. Their strength and tenacity were out of proportion to their size. Usually it was wiser to back away and let the beast eat its fill. If it didn't urinate all over the carcass, the wolves could return later to finish off whatever was left. This time he'd gone into the fight to protect that two-legged female. Now, however, he would just concentrate on recuperating.

The next morning her scalp wounds were still leaking blood, so Judith decided against washing her hair just yet. There was no way she would be able to stop the bleeding, and washing it now would loosen any scab that may be forming, causing profuse bleeding anew. Besides that, her right arm ached so badly she could not move it, and her left one was stiff and sore, likely from the repeated stabs she dealt the wolverine combined with hauling in the wood nearly one-handed. How she would manage to wash her hair with her arms aching so was beyond her.

She wasn't able to lift Adam, and the awkwardness of feeding him with her left hand didn't help his spirits. Nursing him was going to be difficult, she knew, but presently she saw a way. With care, she tipped his cradle over onto the floor beside her, snuggled up to him, and fed him that way. From the floor she was able to lift him with her left arm and put him onto their bed, and then get his cradle back in order.

It would be easier for both of them if Adam played on the floor. The impromptu carpet of pine needles was no place for a curious infant, however, and so, with much effort, Judith pulled the down-filled sleeping bag from the bed, and spread it on the floor. Soon, Adam was rolling happily. With more time to practise that, Judith knew he would soon be able to start sitting up.

Her son was growing every day, and his father wasn't here to see it. Tears filled her eyes at the thought. How she missed her man. When would he be back? She watched the little boy, thinking of how he was getting more and more like his father every day. The dark baby hair was getting longer, and it had a definite curl any little girl would cherish. She snickered, remembering Wil's frustration with the curl that insisted on flopping down onto his forehead. He'd developed a habit of pushing it back. Judith bit her lip to keep her sobs at bay. She was strong. She would be strong until he returned, but Lord, please send him back soon, she thought.

She heard the howling of a wolf just before she drifted off to sleep that night and hoped it was Spirit. Dear Spirit. She prayed he was all right.

35
Wilson at Lynn

The new year had come, and life at the mine went on. Wilson was working as the camp medic, a position he agreed to accept once he learned how much the job paid. It wasn't long before he'd saved enough to purchase the supplies he needed to carry back to the cabin, with sufficient funds besides to hire a plane to take him there. He'd been living with John Farqueson, a 55-year-old bachelor, in a non-insulated building called a 12-by-28. Wilson had not seen Judith or Adam for over three months and a baby changes a lot in that length of time. He knew precious little food remained when he'd left. How had his wife and infant son survived alone? What would he find upon his return to the lonely cabin? He forced his thoughts away, unable to contemplate disaster, forcing himself to remain optimistic. They had to be OK. They just had to be.

The radio provided his sole contact with the outside world. The telephone system at Lynn Lake was connected only to the one at Sherridon for mining business. He yearned for news that a plane was available so the pilot he had patched up could fly him back to Judith and Adam. There was no doubt Judith had become much more resilient since working as a schoolteacher, but she was alone, short of supplies, and caring for a baby out in the wilderness with no other people around for miles.

The weather had finally turned fair enough for flight, but now the planes were desperately needed by the mining camp to fly in supplies and people. Being frustrated with the delay didn't prevent Wilson's fascination with the tractor swings that were just starting up for the first time. It was SGM's unique idea to move the entire town of Sherridon 150 miles north to the new mine location. The first loads hauled were mining equipment, but soon buildings arrived as well.

At any hour of the day or at night, under the starry black velvet sky, the winter stillness would be disrupted by the ungodly roar of the open-throated muscle of a sled train of four Caterpillar tractors. There was a mighty screeching and groaning as the 12-by-28s, loaded on the sleds, were dragged across the frozen wasteland. Each of the identical buildings was constructed of non-insulated board walls covered by shiplap siding and owned by SGM. Mine families paid a small rental fee for their usage. Bringing up the rear of each tractor train was a caboose containing four bunk beds, cooking and eating facilities, plus the crew. The tractor swings would arrive, unload, repair the engines and leave right away. The Caterpillar tractors offered little protection except a windshield for the drivers, who seemed to prefer exposure to the elements rather than work in enclosed cabs that offered little chance of rapid exit, ever since one plunged into the Churchill River, taking the tractor and driver with it. Sherrit Gordon owned the mine and most of the town, and the mine's needs were felt to be more important than those of one lone man whose only connection to the mine was as a temporary first aid provider. The first plane from Sherridon brought in a doctor, which greatly eased Wilson's mind as he felt a responsibility to the miners and the company who had rescued him. He fairly ached to get going, but he was totally at the mercy of SGM.

At one point Wilson turned to John Farqueson, wondering aloud, "What about the hotel? Will they be moving it here as well?"

"Oh, no. Have you seen it?"

Wil nodded. "It's a huge building, four storeys high."

Farqueson shook his head. "They won't be able to move it at all. Some of the larger buildings will have to stay, and from what I hear, some of the people plan to stay behind as well."

When he wasn't on duty, Wilson spent many hours visiting with his friends in the native tent town: Tommy Lightfoot's people, who were hired by SGM to provide cordwood for heating the mine buildings and the houses. Wilson spent a lot of his time talking with Tommy and his daughter Sue, learning more about the country and how to survive in it. He had a much keener appreciation for their skills, having learned first hand just how hard living in this beautiful but unforgiving land could be. He seemed to need less time for talking with Tommy's ex-soldier sons, Bruce and Nelson, who appeared more at ease with their memories of the war, though all three doubted they would ever be completely free of the horror of it all. Wilson renewed acquaintance with Charlie and Libby Bighawk and their little boy, Denis. Seeing this small child reminded him of his own son so far away, and stirred the fear that his own baby would not know him once he returned home. He got to know some of the other Indians better as well, enjoyed their easy camaraderie and felt at home with them.

Each time Wilson visited Tommy's camp Jimmy would make himself scarce by slipping away. The third time this happened, Wilson excused himself and followed Jimmy outside. "Jimmy. Could you wait a minute or two, please? I would like to talk to you." Jimmy stopped, but did not turn to face him, so Wilson walked around to confront the younger man. "I just need to tell you how much it means to me that you saved me. I owe you my life, Jimmy. I want to thank you. If ever there is anything I can do for you, all you need to do is mention it. I'll never forget what you did." The younger man accepted his thanks with an unsmiling nod. He did take Wilson's outstretched hand, though reluctantly, and shook with him. Otherwise, he still maintained his distance.

The day finally did come, however, when, with a little help from Farqueson, Wilson's pilot friend Andy was allowed to use a Fairchild Husky – a new bush plane model with a large freighting-type body that was ample to haul the load of supplies Wilson had accumulated. With assistance from several off-duty miners Wilson and Andy loaded the Husky, and the entire town came out to wish "Doc" Wilson good luck on his return home.

Falling into a deep and much-needed sleep, Judith dreamed that Spirit came to her. He entered the cabin to see if she was recovering from their ordeal. She felt his cold, wet nose against her cheek and reached up to touch him. Her hands met the thick fur on his neck, cold and damp. Struggling upright in the faint, flickering light from the fireplace, she was astounded to see the face of her beloved husband, her hand in the fur on his parka hood.

The two held each other in silent joy until he noticed her gorgeous light brown hair was matted and sticky at the back of her head. Her right arm was bandaged.

"What happened, darlin'? You're hurt. Is Adam OK? What happened?"

"Adam is fine and so am I. Can you just hold me? Never stop holding me, Wil. I'll tell you all about it, I'll tell you everything, but later, OK? Later."

They had many stories to share after so long apart, but they knew they had the rest of their lives for that. For now it was enough to vow they would never again face the world alone, but only as a united couple.

36
Connections

Wilson woke the next morning, his wife snuggled against his side, and from his position in bed he looked around the cabin. After all he had been through he felt like a king in a palace. He recalled huddling in a bear hide with a crackling fire in front, and come to think of it, where was that hide now? He must have left it as well as his canoe, since he'd arrived at Lynn Lake with nothing but the mare, not even memories of the last part of the journey. But he was home now. Home in his father's cabin. No frost coated the walls. The rustic cabin was much warmer than the 12-by-28s with their thin board walls and shiplap siding. And best of all, his family was here – his beloved wife, in pain with an injured arm, her head soaked with dried blood, and his darling son. His loved ones. He slipped out of bed and went over to his son.

Adam woke up, rolled over in his cradle and stared up at the strange man standing over him. His little face began to pucker up in readiness to cry, so Wilson spoke gently. "Adam? Hello, my son. You don't remember your daddy? Daddy's home now, honey. You want to come to Daddy?"

Adam's lip quivered and turned down and outward.

"Come, my sweetheart. Come. Daddy will pick you up and we'll go see Mommy, OK, my son?" Wilson stretched his arms out toward the little fellow.

Adam continued to stare at his father almost in tears. Judith got up and walked over to Wilson, leaned into him and kissed him. Then she turned to Adam with a smile.

"Look, sweetheart. Daddy's home. Daddy came back to us, just like Mommy said he would." Adam then allowed Wil to pick him up, but he held his small body stiffly in his father's arms. "Don't worry, he'll get used to you," Judith said. "He's not accustomed to seeing anyone but me, you know. Give the little man time."

Sausages and pancakes, canned orange juice and freshly brewed coffee, made a complete contrast to the thin gruel she was accustomed to having, and Judith said it was a breakfast fit for royalty. "I'm so glad you thought to bring this particular package with you last night, husband. I can't remember ever enjoying a breakfast more."

"There's a lot more on the river where Andy and I unloaded the plane, but more about that later. I want to know what happened to you. You haven't said anything and I can see you're still in pain."

Judith explained how the wolverine had attacked her by the woodpile and the wolf had saved her life. Wilson's face paled as she told him of the attack and the fight between the two carnivores. "My God, Judith. You could so easily have been killed."

"But for that wolf, I might have been. I owe my life to him. You can doctor me up after we finish eating, Wil. And I need to know all about your trip and why it took so long for you to get back to us."

By the time breakfast was done, Adam had accepted his father.

"I can't believe how big he's gotten, darlin'. And I can't believe how you've managed to survive with nothing to eat except venison. And how the blazes did you get deer meat with no rifle?"

Judith told him about the wolf and how its efforts had saved her and Adam from starving. She explained the boarded-up window because of the first wolverine.

"There were two wolverines?" Wilson did not attempt to hide his shock.

"Not at the same time." She explained how she'd injured the first and that the second one had been bigger and it had almost killed Spirit. "I tried to sew up the wolf's skin where the wolverine ripped it, the way you sewed up Jazzy after the bear attack. I'm afraid I used up a lot of your medical supplies from the kit."

"You stitched up a timber wolf? My God, Judith, it could have turned on you, especially if it was injured and in pain."

"He was more dead than alive, and while I worked on him, he was unconscious. As soon as he came to I backed away and got back into the cabin. That wasn't the first time I was close to him. He saved my life more than once, twice giving me rabbits he'd killed, when he brought me to the deer kill and when he attacked the wolverine. If I hadn't stabbed it to death it would have killed him."

Wilson stared at her. He could not believe this was the little girl he'd known, the delicate school teacher he'd married, and the broken woman who'd lost her first-born child. "I'm sorry, darlin'. I'm so sorry that you had go through all that alone. I can't believe you managed."

"Well I did, with the help of the wolf, and with God's help, I made it and now God has answered my prayers and brought you back to us."

"Well, let me patch you up." As he opened the kit, he noticed that indeed there wasn't much left, but he set to work removing the stained binding from her elbow. He examined the wound, cleaned it and treated the infection that was starting. As he rewrapped her arm, he marvelled that she had done all she claimed. Next, her matted hair was washed and dried. He attended to the infection that was beginning in her scalp. "Puncture wounds are difficult to treat and horrible to endure, and head wounds tend to bleed profusely," he said.

"Tell me, Wil about the trip you made. I need to know what you did and how you bought supplies. Did you work in the mine?" Judith questioned her husband as he worked his magic on her.

As he tended her needs, Wilson told her of reaching Tommy's band where they were cutting timber. "Jimmy brought me to Lynn Lake and once I was fit, I got work there in the office and as a medic, treating the miners, until they got a doctor flown in."

"That must have been difficult. You never wanted to work like that again after the war. I'm sorry you had to do that."

"It wasn't so bad, you know. In fact when that injured miner came in I just acted by instinct and got him patched up. It wasn't like in the field hospital during the war, not really. It actually felt kind of good being able to help. One thing though was worse than the field hospital. They didn't have anything in the way of medical supplies and I had to improvise like crazy."

"Oh, my goodness. What did you use for antiseptic?"

"Scotch whisky. Used it to kill his pain, too."

"I used hydrogen peroxide on Spirit, but I had nothing for him for pain."

"Spirit?"

"Yes, that's what I call the wolf. He has been our guardian spirit while you were gone. Without his help I don't think Adam and I would be alive."

"So you were saying before breakfast. And I owe my life to Jazzy and Jimmy. We're tough, darlin', but even tough people need help now and then, hey?"

"Yes, and I need you. I'm so glad you are back with us. Don't ever leave again like that."

"Well we have sufficient supplies to see us through winter easily now, and soon we'll be rich enough to be able to live anywhere and do anything. But right now, we have to get the supplies back here to the cabin, and we don't have Jazzy to help now."

Once they had eaten, Judith proceeded to attach Adam to her body with the harness and dress herself. Wilson was amazed at her ingenuity in creating a device to carry the baby warmly and securely with her. All three set off to haul their supplies in from the river, though she and Adam accompanied him only on the first trek. When they got outside, Wilson stopped her and said, "You know, the best way to do this is for me to make a travois and pull it myself. I'm sure I'll be able to haul a big load that way, much more than trying to carry it."

"Wil. That's a great idea. I will lead you."

Wilson threw back his head and laughed. "Oh no, you won't, woman. I may end up hauling like a pony, but I'm no horse. I know the way quite well without being led."

As they made the trek they talked. There was so much to catch up on since being apart for so long. "This is just like old times, hey?" Wilson remarked happily, looking over at Judith's beaming face, rosy in the fresh cold air. "Are you sure you are OK carrying Adam like that? I could carry him to the supplies and you can carry him back."

Judith laughed. "I love to hold him and he's fine right now. If he gets restless I may take you up on your offer, but this harness won't fit your broad shoulders, and the air is too cold for him to be exposed." They held hands as they walked, the snow crunching cheerfully under their feet.

"I'm sure glad Andy was able to land and turn on the river, or we'd have had to go all the way to the lake."

"I could walk forever, Wil, as long as you're walking with me."

Wilson kissed her on the mouth in full stride, nearly upsetting all three. After a brief hug and another kiss they set off once again and soon reached the pile of crates where Wil arranged the travois, piled as many supplies on as possible and tied the load. "Ready to go home, wife?"

Judith laughed. "Isn't this where I get to lead you, husband?"

"OK, darlin'. I'd follow you anywhere," Wil agreed and sent her on ahead where he could watch her progress. Judith carried a light crate on her back and Adam on her chest.

Once they reached the cabin and unloaded the travois, Judith had to stop to feed Adam. His parents also had a quick lunch before Wilson set off again to fetch the remainder of the supplies while Judith started unpacking. It took Wilson four trips and the rest of the day to haul the entire load to the cabin. Judith remained inside after the first trip, going through the supplies, overwhelmed with the amount and variety. They would not go hungry again.

Once everything was inside and unpacked, they ate canned ham and vegetables for the evening meal. When Judith suggested they place the bags of oats, flour and garden seeds under the bed to raise it, Wilson insisted on leaving it for the following day. Judith realized how tired he must be and agreed.

The next morning they put the new window into the wall, real glass once again, and Judith cleaned and repaired the beautiful leather from Jimmy. Wilson was busy digging through the bags of oats. Finally Judith turned to him. "Whatever are you doing? Just put them under the bedding." Wilson grinned. Reaching behind, he pulled out a small bag of brown oblong tubers.

Judith leaped to her feet and flung her arms around his neck. "Potatoes. You brought potatoes? Oh, Wil," she cried as tears streamed down her cheeks.

"I packed them inside the oats to keep them from freezing, but they are a bit frosted. If you cook them up right away, they should be OK. Now stop crying and get them peeled, woman."

As she peeled the precious potatoes, Wilson hung the soft leather for a curtain, and thus they were quite comfortable through the winter months that were left. Although the window frosted up as badly as before, it did bring a cheerful note of brightness into the cabin. Judith loved having newly constructed doors on most of the cupboards, and the wooden floor around the table was great since Adam was beginning to eat food he could hold in his little fists and tended to drop a lot. The crates had greatly improved their cabin's interior.

As spring approached, their thoughts turned toward the future. Their three years were coming to an end, and they pondered what they would do with the money they would be inheriting. "What do you think, Judith? Should we not bother planting a garden or planning for the summer and the next winter? What do you want to do? We should be hearing from the lawyer sometime this spring."

"I don't know. Do we have to decide now?"

"Well, darlin', if we're staying here we need a garden, and that needs to be started now. We should be hauling Jazzy's used feed to fertilize the soil."

"Jazzy's used feed?"

"Yes, all the crap she didn't dump on you when you had a ride on the travois, and all her other piles scattered around here."

"I would like a garden whether or not we stay. It won't go completely to waste if we leave it. Remember how you said we were feeding the livestock? The animals here will eat it if we don't. We'll be here long enough to eat some of it anyway, and if we go, we'll be able to bring some with us. But before we do anything, can we go and visit the grave and see how it is after that winter we went through?"

Wilson glanced at her, and he wondered how tied she was still to the baby they'd lost.

As the little family made their way to the hill behind the house where the roses grew, Wilson wondered if Judith would be able to leave this place where her first-born remained. The little fence was weathered, but mostly still standing. Wilson stood up the few poles that were leaning haphazardly.

"I can't believe the hailstorm last summer didn't damage it more than that," Judith remarked, and Wilson never let on that the greater part of one hunting trip was spent repairing the burial place of their daughter. He knew it would break his wife's heart to see the damage that had been done. Judith knelt beside the little cross Wil had made. She touched it gently. Wilson watched. He was willing to give her time. But their son was not. Adam was getting fussy. Judith rose smiling through her tears. "Yes, my son." She placed the palm of her hand against his soft cheek, and with a glance toward the resting place of her daughter, accepted her husband's hand as they walked back to the house to feed their son and themselves. At eight months of age, Adam still had his nap twice a day, so they would have some time to talk more about their plans for the future.

Gradually, they readied the garden. Wilson made a new scarecrow, and this time, true to his promise, it was a female named Jude. He made a larger, stronger version of the harness Judith invented, and rigged a place in a sturdy tree to suspend the child. From there, Adam could sleep or watch them work, and he would be safe within their sight and hearing.

✳

They were outside one morning, admiring their garden and enjoying a wonderful early summer day, when they heard a familiar cry: "Hallo the cabin!"

Wilson and Judith rushed to the landing at the edge of the stream, with Adam securely in his father's strong arms. Wilson handed the baby to Judith as he helped their friends land the canoes. He hugged Tommy and pounded his friend on the back, though not as hard as before, for Tommy was showing the years.

Sue rushed to Judith. "Jimmy. Jimmy, come and see the baby."

To Wilson's surprise, Jimmy went right to Judith and reached for Adam, who, more surprisingly, went willingly to Jimmy. Sue's smile split her face and lit up her eyes. Everyone congratulated the couple on the beauty of their little boy.

Libby's son, Denis, was a few weeks older than Adam and a bit bigger. Judith admired him as well, while Libby smiled with pride. Charlie and Wilson crowed proudly about the boys they had fathered. Sue and Judith exchanged glances and grinned, eyes dancing at the way the fathers were claiming bragging rights, when mostly the mothers had done the work.

Nelson brought Jazzy along and handed the lead rope to Wilson. "You had better hide this horse, or Jimmy will keep her. Hurry, 'cause that nephew of ours just might want you to buy her again." Wilson accepted the rope and patted his mare.

"If Jimmy wants me to buy her again, I will. I owe the both of them my life," he said, glancing toward Jimmy, who still held Adam. Jimmy appeared not to hear, though he was close enough.

Tommy said his band no longer had to travel south for work and back north for the caribou hunt, so they had made the trek to the cabin before the caribou migration. Caribou used to come as far south as Lynn Lake, the first year even wandering through the beginning town, but with the mine's expansion and the noise and confusion of human population they would not do that again. Because the intrusion of humans disturbed the migration, caribou would avoid the Lynn Lake area, either remaining farther north or going eastward. Mining to the west would keep them from heading that direction. Since SGM had relocated to Lynn from Sherridon, the caribou hunt would not be as long a trek. His people would need to go north again, but the trip would not be nearly as far, and that left time this spring for them to travel along the waterways to visit with Wilson and his family.

Through the racket of greetings and exchange of news, they heard the roar of a plane landing on the river. Everyone exchanged questioning looks, then it dawned on Wilson that it could be someone from the lawyer's office coming to ensure they were at the cabin, since they had completed the three years' residency the will had stipulated. "That could be the lawyer, Judith. I suppose I'll have to go meet the plane at the river, 'cause he won't be able to taxi up this creek."

"I will bring you, Wilson," Charlie offered. "You don't have a canoe anymore."

Wilson thanked the other man and they moved together to the landing, followed by the rest of the people. Jimmy still held young Adam, who seemed perfectly content in his arms.

Judith watched as the two men paddled until the canoe moved out of sight around the bend in the creek and was hidden by the tall brown reeds. She wondered who had brought the package from Calgary and if the person would be returning with Charlie and Wilson, if indeed it were the lawyer. What would the message contain? She knew the lawyer had said there would be the deed for the cabin and the land it was on, the balance of the inheritance, which would be double the $5,000, and a letter from Wil's father. What would the letter say? How would it affect her husband, who yearned to learn more of the man who'd sired him and abandoned him so early in his young life? Would it answer some of the many questions that ate at Wilson? What was taking them so long?

As the pilot caught sight of the canoe, he taxied in the direction of the creek, where the paddlers were working hard to move their conveyance closer to the plane. The stiff breeze on the river made their task difficult, although the current helped somewhat. The plane stopped as the canoe approached. Charlie drew up to the pontoon and Wilson climbed precariously onto the cigar-shaped floating device. He made his way to the door of the cockpit, where a young man dressed in a business suit with an overcoat and scarf asked for some identification.

"What do you mean, identification? I didn't bring any. Charlie, tell this guy who I am."

Charlie responded, "He's Wilson Daniels, Joe's son. His wife and baby are back by the cabin."

The young passenger in the plane agreed that Wilson did match the description he was given, except for the long hair and bearded face.

"It's not very easy to remain clean-shaven out here," Wilson told him. "I did manage for the first few months, but when my razor got too worn I gave it up as a lost cause. I don't know what else to tell you. If you insist, I guess we could row back and get my ID or, better yet, you can accompany us back to the cabin."

Wilson forced back a grin as he saw the look that crossed the young man's face. "No, no," the fellow hastened to reply. "That's quite all right. I believe you are the man I was to meet. This is for you. You need to sign for it showing you have received the package, and then we'll be heading back to civilization."

That accomplished, Wilson accepted the package and scrambled carefully back into the canoe. As soon as he and Charlie had moved a few yards away, the plane began to taxi along the surface of the river until it became airborne again.

The package sat at his feet, and Wilson felt as though it were a grenade. What would be in it? There was bound to be the fortune, but what was coming with it? What would he learn about the man who had been his father? How would this change his life – his life, Judith's and now Adam's? The canoe seemed to be moving so slowly, but as they rounded the final bend they saw the other boats, bobbing along the bank while the people lined up along the edge. His eyes sought Judith, and seeing her, began to search for his son. He was surprised to see Jimmy still holding the baby. He and Charlie drew up alongside the last canoe, and while Nelson and Bruce assisted them, both men stepped onto land. Wilson carried the parcel, and as he approached his wife he saw her eyes move from it to him. He watched the emotions play across her expressive face, the green eyes questioning.

"You and Judith go open your package while we set up camp here," Tommy told them. "We will stay for a few days, but then we have to go. The caribou won't wait for us."

Wilson, Judith and Adam returned to the cabin, where they eagerly opened the parcel. Enclosed was a cheque for $20,000. They both looked at it incredulously. That was enough money to buy a big new house, furnish it, purchase a car and set them up in business. Once they overcame their shock, they turned to the remaining contents, which included a deed to the cabin and land, and an envelope addressed to Wilson. He held it briefly, turning it over and over, and Judith was reminded of the day in Calgary that Wil received a letter from the lawyer. She smiled, encouraging him to open it. He slit the envelope, removed two sheets of ruled paper and began to read aloud.

The letter was written to Wilson Andrew Daniels. It read:

> To my son, Wilson,
>
> Sometimes the hardest thing to do is to walk away. I did the hardest thing because I loved you. I hope to God what I did was the right thing.
>
> The letters I sent to you and your mother were all returned to me, unopened, so I finally quit sending them. I went back to Calgary once, but your mother didn't want me to see you. You would have been about five years old then. I think she was afraid. She said seeing me would upset you, and I didn't want to cause you grief. I am sorry I had to leave without setting my eyes on you one more time. I sent another letter again when you turned 18, and it was returned as well. I am hoping that it was your mother, and not you, who returned it.
>
> Wilson, I could not live the life your mother wanted me to live, and I guess she could not live the life I needed to live. I came to realize that if we had stayed together, we would have eventually destroyed each other and maybe you, too. That is why I left Alberta and came to northern Manitoba. I worked for a while in the mine, but I hated it. I couldn't stand being underground like a prairie gopher. It was here I earned the nickname Tex for my wild ride on an Indian pony one time. I left the mines, bought up some land farther north and met my second wife, Sue Lightfoot.

✳

At this point, Wilson handed the letter to Judith. Tears were running unchecked down his face and his voice became too husky to continue. Judith took the letter and continued to read to Wilson from where he had left off.

We were truly happy together, and by the time you read this, you will most likely have met your half-brother, Jimmy. My son, I left you physically, but never mentally. I kept you in my heart and I have prayed for you every day since I left. I made a life for myself, but I never forgot you. Like I said at the beginning, it was the hardest thing I ever did, leaving you behind.

I leave you in the care and under the watchful eye of my friend and father-in-law Tommy Lightfoot. I leave you the freshness of the air, the wide-open skies, the clear water and the bountiful trees. I leave you the property I bought when I first went north, and the cabin I built with my own hands. I leave you a brother and a stepmother. I leave you the life I loved. I hope you have learned to love it too. If not, my son, I leave you the money.

The rest I leave to my other son, Jimmy Lightfoot Daniels. I made the money by selling my interests in property, where there was a deposit of nickel and copper. The mining companies are hungry for minerals here and they paid me well. I hope you use your share of the money to build a good life for yourself.

Tommy has assured me that I will able to watch over you and protect you once I have become spirit again. I believe Tommy. He has never steered me wrong. Therefore, whatever your decision, my son, I accept it. I will watch over you and protect you in any way the Lord sees fit to let me. I do not know the day or the year in which I will leave this life, but I have been in contact with lawyers in Calgary who agreed to follow my wishes whenever my time shall come. I gave them this letter to be given to you three years after you have lived my life in the wilderness. The other letters I left are different, in case you decided my life was not a life you could understand and live. If so, you are more like your mother than like your father.

I have provided for Sue and Jimmy in a similar manner, so I am not sure of how they will be living at the time you receive this. Whatever they decide to do is OK by me. I enjoyed their way of life too much to change, so the money meant nothing much to me. But everyone has to decide for himself the kind of life that is right for him. I found that out when I married your mother. It is not up to me to decide that for Tommy's people or for you. I needed to force you to live my way for three years, though, so you would get to know who I am. This was the only way I could see to do that.

I hope you understand. I wish things could have been different between you and me. I wanted to raise you or at least help to raise you, but it wasn't in the cards, son. Please forgive me if what I did has been hard for you. I love you; I have always loved you.

Your father,
Tex Joe Daniels

As Judith completed the letter, she looked at Wilson. He smiled through his tears, and in a voice filled with awe, said, "I have a brother."